Grizzly Dance

Grizzly Dance

A NOVEL

ANN LOVE

KEY PORTER BOOKS

For David and Jane

Canadian Cataloguing in Publication Data
Love, Ann
   Grizzly dance

ISBN 1-55013-565-1

I. Title.

PS8573.084G7 1994   C813'.54   C94-931238-X
PR9199.3.L68G7 1994

Key Porter Books Limited
70 The Esplanade
Toronto, Ontario
Canada M5E 1R2

The publisher gratefully acknowledges the assistance of the
Canada Council and the Ontario Arts Council.

Design: Tania Craan
Typesetting: MacTrix DTP
Printed and bound in Canada

94 95 96 97 98 99 6 5 4 3 2 1

Warren Tasker stretched his long legs into the cramped space under the steering wheel, shifted his knees and hips stiffly to the left and shivered to find a more comfortable position. The car seat vinyl, brittle with cold, pinched out a squeak so thin it set his back teeth on edge.

Tasker bit down hard and rubbed his hands roughly together. It wasn't easy to stay ahead of the mercury – the temperature must have dropped twenty degrees since he'd taken up this stakeout.

Last evening he'd parked his beige pickup on the pad outside "Receiving," tight between two semis, at the South Gate Shopping Mall. Crowded in for hours, he had to work hard to keep his thoughts steady on the grey, cement-block carwash he'd been watching all night.

Tasker opened his window a crack, inhaled the chill, mineral air and let his eyes circle the swath of asphalt around the carwash. Dawn was coming, he thought, but with it no relief at all – only pavement, smothered grassland.

He smiled at himself. He sure had a way of digging in deeper. There wasn't going to be any payoff for this unrelenting wait – why not leave it at that?

Tasker's eyes strained past the carwash, searching for his partner in the other unmarked vehicle. He made out her profile reflected in the plate glass of a storefront awash with the blue light of a "Laundromat" sign. Tonight had been a waste of time for the young corporal too.

The staff sergeant had hinted Tasker was overworking and should delegate more, but Tasker had logged on tonight anyway. In the thirteen years since he'd left the Yukon, he'd built up a name for himself on the Regina drug squad, devoting most of his waking life to it. When he'd first heard of this drop, he'd had a hunch it was going to be big – and he liked to credit all his hunches.

Tasker had kept alert most of the night figuring out the "Chess Game of the Week" in his head. An old trick. Memorize the diagram in the newspaper, and when only the street lights cut the darkness, figure how "black mates white in five moves." So far, he had white in eight.

Tasker wasn't much at chess. As a kid, he'd thought the strategizing in the game would help him prepare for work as a detective. A little naïve, he realized now, but this memory of his past was amusing, even pleasing, to look back on. Jim Weatherby, a mentor and his chess teacher, often warned Tasker against taking any game seriously, especially if its universe was reduced to stereotypes and time didn't count. Tasker's first big murder up north proved Jim right. When you're dealing with crime, he learned stumbling through that rookie case, you can see some of the moves and some of the players, but there may not be a pattern to their game and you can't know all the moves the players are capable of making.

"Enough," Tasker said out loud, bringing himself to the present. Chess was fine for keeping alert on a stakeout. Better than letting his mind circle around and around, dwelling on past failures. Better than longing for a shot from that bottle of single malt in the cupboard at home.

Tasker shivered again. He'd focus on the present, review the case at hand. A pickup camper carrying a shipment of heroin supposedly unloaded in this carwash every month. Inside, among the rotating brushes and nozzles, the stuff was divided and delivered to drivers who pushed it on kids throughout the Midwest. Clean cars, filthy plastic zip-lock packages.

A nifty idea, but probably bullshit. He poured the last of the chicken noodle soup from his Thermos and decided to call it off in ten minutes. He set the timer on his watch.

Tasker sensed it was already getting light. He lifted his right hand to tilt the rear-view mirror and caught himself staring into his own eyes. For a moment he wondered if they really reflected what the corporal last night had called his "trademark" intensity. But all he saw were brown eyes staring back with curiosity, then self-consciously, finally in foolish humour. He blinked, pleased his eyes were still his own. After forty-two years they'd better be. He grinned.

Tasker looked down from the mirror to the newspaper lying on the passenger seat. He could see now to check the chess diagram again. But this time he caught a short piece at the top of the page – only a clip. An old Yukon doctor killed south of Whitehorse by a grizzly. He hadn't been mauled, just hit once with such force that he was found with his torso facing backwards to the lower part of his body. Split in half and spun around on his vertebral column.

Tasker shuddered. But there had to be a reason, there always was: the man must have come from upwind, surprising the bear. That's what happened with bear attacks: someone always came up with a logical explanation – afterwards. What a way to go.

He glanced up to check the carwash again and noticed something fluttering by the exit. A piece of litter, he thought as he sipped his soup, and looked back down at the newspaper – "Retired Doctor Killed By Bear."

Tasker knew what finding that corpse would be like – the

body grotesquely twisted, blood ringing the waist and soaked black into the earth, the tangy smell of bear, and fear pulsing into the dark bush . . .

Funny, he thought, that it was a doctor. Bear attacks usually involved prospectors, old trappers. There'd been a recent incident with a field biologist, one of those radio-collar trackers. He'd got out, but left his face behind. Maybe this one was Dr. Straun. No, he smiled to himself, that was too much. A crazy head-spin after remembering his first big murder case, the tragic one that sent him transferring to saner, southern territory and to a unit where he could count on the good guys being good and the bad guys being bad, or lazy – at least most of the time. Tasker shook his head and smiled broadly. Crazy coincidences were fun to toy with.

He read the clip again. It was an odd attack by a grizzly, and he couldn't get rid of an image of Dr. Straun in that twisted body, eyes probably open, glazed, skin a heavy grey-blue. Grizzly, he knew, usually maul at the throat and face with their long, razor claws, and it's the slicing that does the harm, not a brute assault powered by those massive shoulder muscles. In fact, a true mauling is an odd, mincing dance, like the bear wants to stay some distance back, disgusted by the smell of its victim.

Tasker focused his eyes on the carwash again. He thought he could see the grey of the cement block actually lightening. It seemed to be sucking in light, not even offering the interest of shadows.

His mind drifted back to the news story. He'd observed lots of grizzly in his time – stumping through old-growth forests, browsing along broad gravel bars at the curves of swift rivers, on sandy gopher flats, up sub-alpine slopes rubbery green with crowberry bushes. There was something about grizzly and humans, and he wasn't the only one to notice. Grizzly are said to have bad eyesight, but in fact see well, ignoring what they don't want – like people. And grizzly can be remarkably adept with those clumsy-looking front legs, delicately picking berry bushes as clean as any homesteader does. Tasker had found a grizzly skinned once, face down, and it looked like a naked man, narrow hips, the way the elbow bent out, not like an animal. And he'd seen the victim of a mauling too . . . Grizzly were unpredictable and he knew enough to leave them room.

Growing up on a Yukon homestead, Tasker had soaked in plenty of wilderness common sense – where to look for food, how to prepare it in the bush, how to make do, how to hide, how to sense danger. Survival skills his father taught him – anticipating grizzly behaviour was just one of them. Tasker worked on those skills after his dad died, building for himself a detailed knowledge of all the life around his isolated home. He didn't realize how much he actually knew until he went outside to school and could draw comparisons.

At first he downplayed those interests, keeping them to himself and avoiding the scorn of a handful of recruits who called him "Birdwatcher." But he wasn't so retiring any more – he knew the value of his knowledge lay in the collecting. His ability to spot seemingly insignificant details, odd angles and connections, what some young corporal had tagged his "legendary" observation skills. Whatever they were, they all came from those happy hours as a kid. Given a little time, he still liked to sit and sketch animals and plants to illustrate their adaptations – more scientific field sketches than artistic ones, with different views on the same page and short notes in the margins. The one pastime he knew where he could get totally lost, absorbed in the doing. Years ago, he had sketched a grizzly picking crowberries – front view, side view – using that backwards human elbow, and as he drew he had in mind the skinned bear and what he remembered about the muscle sheaths under the fur. Those straps of muscle and that elbow would have a lot to do with how the retired doctor had been killed with one brutal swat.

Odd, he thought, that he should remember that old Yukon murder and then read about a doctor fatally attacked out of Whitehorse. He opened the newspaper wide, shook it closed at the front page and folded it, running his thumb and forefinger along the crease. Last night he'd read the headline stories about the land claims stuff – barricades, river diversions, bridge closings. Thirteen years ago, they were in the background of the Yukon case as well, but no one had had the sense to take Native people seriously then.

A tooth-grinding squeal sliced into his thoughts – tires, near the carwash. Then the smash of breaking glass and the shriek of a burglar alarm. "Shit." Tasker strained his eyes, trying to focus into the flat light. Across the mall from the carwash, a kid was dragging something huge along the pavement into the blue glare of the "Laundromat" sign. A safe, maybe. The kid was hunched and twisted around and jerking his prize, like a big weasel, a wolverine, hauling a deer thigh with impossible strength, right there across the asphalt.

Tasker grabbed the radio to stop his partner – but not soon enough. The corporal wheeled out from her hideout and careened over to corner the boy.

The kid started to run, but stopped short when the headlights caught him. He shuffled back to the safe – loose body, arms flung wide, fingers apart, facing the carwash. He wasn't gritty like any weasel. He wasn't desperate at all – he was a diversion.

Tasker started his engine, tense, watching. He followed the boy's stare to the canvas curtains of the carwash exit fluttering in the soft breeze.

Tasker realized the damn exit door was open and had been for some time. His mind raced trying to grasp how he'd let his thoughts wander, failed to notice, to observe . . .

He swung his pickup out from between the semis and accelerated headlong towards the carwash exit. Too late. A white camper broke through the canvas straps in a spray of gunfire. Tasker's windshield flashed opaque and he felt a vicious shove, then hot pain in his right shoulder.

There was nothing he could do now. Nothing. It was up to that young corporal . . .

Although it was crazy, the carwash didn't matter any more. It meant nothing. Instead, Tasker thought about phoning his old girlfriend. Thought about phoning Ida to find out if it was Dr. Straun who'd got it from the grizzly. Head swimming, gunfire outside, his fault, and he thinks about Dr. Straun and Ida and that old murder case in the northern bush.

And with thoughts of Ida, even through his pain, Tasker's head filled with the husk of her voice, the warmth of her hair. It was dizzying, insane; he felt drunk.

Tasker panted, his cheek pressed to the steering wheel. His long legs had gone slack, but he didn't pass out. He kept alert, driven by an urgent need to relive that chapter of his life. Savour the story, deliciously, knowing that despite his past inexperienced efforts, maybe the girl had finally been avenged.

It had all started out so innocently, so easily. He was young, a kid who hardly knew anything but thought he did, who carried more responsibility than he ever should have. And it had taken him so long to finally see the storyline developing ahead and behind him.

2. YUKON. June 1978 – thirteen years earlier

Warren Tasker leaned into the turn, smiling with the sensation of no grip. The rear end of the cruiser shuddered, fishtailed, but this corporal had her under control. He accelerated, just like he'd practised over and again, and let the tires grab the gravel as he straightened her out. Something rattled in the trunk – the jack must have shaken loose.

He kept the cherry spinning, just for something crazy to do, and watched the light cut a red circle round the black, predawn forest. No siren – didn't feel like it now. Tasker preferred travelling before dawn, before the ore trucks pounded the Tsehki Junction Road, churning up clouds of dust that scummed up everything, his cruiser in particular.

Tasker sank back into the headrest, his shoulders relaxed. There would be time to visit his old mentor, Jim, before reporting in. Good – Jim had never even seen the beard he'd grown for the Rendezvous contest. His Whitehorse friends had said Tasker didn't have it to grow a full beard with only seven weeks between a clean shave and the judging of the bushiest – but he'd done it. Mind you, he hadn't won the prize. But he'd kept the moustache, and not because he was too lazy to shave, as Ida teased. It took as long each morning to trim it to regulation width and length (no more than an eighth of an inch beside or below the mouthline) as it did to shave. No, he'd kept the moustache because it made him feel good. Tasker pinched the thumb and middle finger of his right hand into the soft spot under his nose and then spread his finger and thumb apart along his upper lip, feeling the wiry fullness of the hairs. He knew his old friend Jim would be impressed.

Jim let Tasker know he believed in him . . . if Ida didn't. His ex-girl now. Last night she'd really let Tasker have it. She'd said he had a hangup with authority and she couldn't stand the way he was judgmental. He never saw the grey between right and wrong, she'd told him, and it was time he hit the road. And just exactly who had that authority hangup, Ida? Funny, he wasn't feeling hurt any more. He was feeling kind of loose. Like, so what?

Tasker gave it more gas. He liked the stretch of road coming up. The forest shrinking to scrub, and once over the pass, closer to the border with B.C., the highway crossing that stretch of tundra before it plunged into the black spruce again. On that patch of tundra at the top, there would lie the whole Tsehki valley, rounded into a dipper shape by glaciers, gouged by boulders and sand grains, by rock grinding on rock, under incredible pressures for centuries. Now, with all that ice and grinding gone, the expansive view always made him feel free. And he knew that as he drove down the road where it dropped back into the bush again, into the shadowy bowl of the dipper, Tasker would see himself in that landscape as if he were still watching from the top – powerful, as though part god, separate and above his own body, watching Tasker the man break into his future.

Tasker could slip so deep into that kind of thinking it was hard to pull back out. This time he let himself play at the edges, and then, to keep from falling in too far, he switched on the radio, rolled the dial with his forefinger till he caught the twang of Johnny Cash, and turned it up. A great sound to take over the pass.

It was still dark when he got to the top – except for a touch of light, dawn perhaps, that glinted off the chain of lakes way down the valley, their surfaces glowing silver, their ragged shapes outlined by the blackness of the hemming forest. Tasker caught a reflection off the Henderson River too, as it ran from a glacier far to the west, curving down into the valley where it poured its ribbon of churning, milky water into Natasahin Lake near the village of Tsehki Junction.

His boyhood home. Yesterday's dispatcher forgot he was local and assigned him his home town for the weekend – an extra body to cover the fishing derby, watch the drinking, keep a lid on things. He'd find out who the dispatcher was and take him back a big one. There would be time off to fish for sure. Tasker smiled again and gave it more gas. He longed to feel the tug of that big one on his line.

Dust. "Damn!" he said out loud. Who else would be kicking dust at this hour?

He'd better watch the speed. Still, he didn't like chewing road grit.

Ahead, tail lights glowed through the dust. It was a Ford van going slow, just at the limit. Tasker rocked forward impatiently.

The van slowed down and pulled over. "Good thing!" Tasker muttered. Holding his speed even so as not to spray gravel, he flashed his high beams in a quick salute.

The driver of the van looked across – pale eyes in a large, startled face. Tasker had never seen that face before – blond, almost white hair in a long brushcut. About thirty. The van was shiny clean – painted with queer figures that made Tasker uneasy. He pulled past quickly, listening for the moment when the loud crunch of gravel muted and he could slip back into his lane again.

The road drew Tasker back down into the bush. In this light, the forest held no detail. It felt like one immense soft-bellied organism breathing, pulsing, watching, even subduing.

Tasker thought of his memories of Tsehki. Ones that had left him pretty much on his own since grade school. He flicked off the cherry and coasted to within ten kilometres of the limit. Well, he'd reach town by 6:00 a.m. At least he'd have an hour for coffee with Jim to catch up on the news. Jim would reminisce too – stories about the old times when he and Tasker's dad first came to the valley.

He turned his radio up louder, and the yearning, nasal wail of a ballad singer muffled the relentless rumble of the tires, pounding down the gravel.

Tasker called the Tsehki station as he swung up the mine road. "Corporal Tasker checking in. I'm early. Thought I'd take a spin up to the mine. Over."

An older man's voice, cut with static and crackle, replied, "OK. Report here by 7:00." Tasker recognized that voice – Sergeant Reg Flint, a man known to be marking time to retirement in less than a year. One-cop towns usually got a corporal or constable, not a sergeant, unless maybe he was bushed. Tasker accelerated up the incline – a great stretch for a Corvette – and, feeling it bank with the curve, leaned into the first switchback.

Right ahead, parked, pickups were strung across the road. "Damn!" Tasker said and braked hard.

The morning sun, just over the ridge now, highlighted the gathering: sleepy men and women lounging against hoods, all dressed in worn blue jeans and bush jackets, all talking, kids darting – all Natives. A few onlookers stood twenty metres back, non-Natives, sipping coffee. Probably mine workers, Tasker figured, who couldn't get up the road.

Tasker radioed again, "A party on the main mine road. At tree-line, the road's blocked. I'll check it out. Over."

Flint snapped back, "I'll be up. Hold tight until I get there, if you can."

Tasker turned off the ignition and looked to size up the road-block. The people seemed so insignificant compared with the shoulders of Crag Mountain rising on either side. Huge shoulders, massive in an emptiness of crusty green lichen, rock and buckbrush.

"Warren! Great to see you!" His friend Jim, an older Jim, emerged from among the onlookers and opened the cruiser door, his outdoor face creasing into a warm grin around his deep brown eyes, and one thin, blue-veined hand running along his own upper lip, mimicking Tasker's moustache. They both laughed.

Tasker made a show of inspecting Jim up and down as he took off his field cap and climbed out of his car. Jim was looking pretty good with his wiry body, though he must be pushing sixty-five.

"Great to see you," Tasker started off eagerly, but when he looked past Jim, mid-sentence, he sensed the roadblock was going to drag on his day, and the energy in his voice felt hollow. Part of him wanted to let this small-time demonstration peter out. He wasn't in the mood for more wrangling after what happened last night. But he had to check it out, get ready to break it up. He pulled his field cap back on, tugged and straightened the bottom of his issue jacket. Respect for the public, that's what Ida called a crisp and tidy presentation. Tasker called it window-dressing. Her profession was one that manipulated people, treated patients like they didn't know what was best for them. Her starched white uniform was part of it.

"It's a protest, Warren – you know, keep them from ripping apart the countryside."

"You mean the mine? Everyone's talked up expansion for years! I thought you worked for the mine?"

"Yes, I still do part-time carpentry repairs, mostly to outbuildings, fencing, some locksmithing . . ." Jim put a hand on Tasker's shoulder, rocked back on his heels and slipped into his chatty, country drawl. "The mine owners, they don't live here. From back east somewhere, they aim to accelerate the operation, enlarge the plant, get the copper out open-pit. Just remove the whole side of the mountain. All gone in ten years with nothing left but a neutralizing acid lake. The band is saying no way. Good thing, too. Someone had to say it." Jim ran his eyes along the roadblock and then turned to Tasker and asked softly, "How's your mother?"

"The same," Tasker said and Jim nodded. "The doctor keeps reminding me it's an illness, but it gets to you." Tasker stopped and Jim nodded again. Jim understood – everyone who was close to his mother felt guilt in some way. Depression had that effect on people.

Tasker felt removed now. The roadblock looked harmless enough – rusty old Chevys and Fords carelessly angled across the road and into boggy ditches, families milling around, kids stuffing their hands into bags of potato chips, music thumping somewhere. Mostly young people, except a group of older men and women, the elders, stood to one side by a patch of fireweed.

"Want some tea? In the truck. It'll keep a spoon standing." Jim laughed.

Jim had the rusty, green pickup with a couple of Second World War rifles mounted in the back window and a thumbed birders' field guide on the passenger seat. He made a habit of owning nothing new.

Tasker warmed his fingers round the tin cup hot with tea, noticing for the first time that the air had a real chill. He smiled to himself, feeling better, remembering this was a Tsehki morning, where the dawn cut raw with wind fresh off the glaciers. Tasker looked over the roadblock for faces from the past. There was Howard Daniel, not tall, but stocky across the chest, about twenty years old and standing among the elders, elbows out and fingertips stuck into the front pockets of his jeans, talking and kicking gravel with the toe of his cowboy boot. He was wearing his hair long and tied back in a braid – that was new. Howard was a carver, with a sense of humour – he'd probably move to a big town soon. There was something about the way he was kicking the gravel today, though, that made Tasker think he was listening to what he didn't want to hear.

Howard's older brother was the reason Tasker had chosen law enforcement. He'd considered wildlife management – that homesteader, Blake, had encouraged him – but after what happened to Gary. . . Tasker remembered he'd never told Ida his part in that story. It was down her line, too.

"Where's Blake McIntyre?" Tasker asked Jim. "Why isn't Blake here? Last time the town got riled up – that concentrating operation – didn't he take on the mine, spearhead the cleanup?"

"He'll be there someplace. I haven't set eyes on him though." Jim scanned the protesters for Blake. "Actually he's kind of going it alone this time, promoting a wilderness park. The band has a different idea."

Suddenly everyone turned, tracking a sound up the zigzag of the road above the roadblock. Tasker felt the rumble of the rig before its cab parted the dust. He realized he was too late, he should have broken up this party long ago. The driver obviously saw the roadblock and was able to gear down hard. Hissing air brakes. A big load of ore.

Then, from the other direction, the van appeared, with those figures painted on its side – skinny children tumbling and diving, no thighs, in red and yellow and blue, kiddie's crayon colours.

The van driver blasted his horn and jumped out beside Tasker, shouting, "What's all this?" He had a boy's voice, but his body, as he raged, was a man's, with tight folds of flesh at the back of his neck and contracting, powerful forearms planted on the hips of his navy blue coveralls.

An attractive young woman in a beaded moosehide jacket stepped forward from the roadblock to speak, but the van driver jumped away from her and back into his seat, spun his tires in reverse, and then jerked forward again, steering wildly to get around the roadblock through the ditch. His bumper bashed against the end of an old pickup, crumpling his own fender and denting one of the painted figures.

Tasker bolted to his cruiser, angry at himself for just drinking tea and watching this all unfold. Now he had an illegal roadblock and a guy wilfully damaging his own vehicle – he'd have to block the van's escape, disperse the crowd.

But the van was too quick and swung back down the hill, swerving round the passenger side of a wagon that was just drawing up.

It was the RCMP wagon, and Sergeant Flint leaned out his window, shouting, "Time to break this up, Tasker!" Then, he called, "Hey you, Larissa, come here. We're going after your boyfriend."

Larissa, the young woman who'd approached the van, walked across to the sergeant. As she bent her hands over his partly raised window, Tasker noticed how big they were. A fleeting image – Tasker was striding to the centre of the road – but enough for him to think how odd it was a pretty girl had such large, bony knuckles. And it didn't take anything away from her looks. When Tasker turned to confront the protest, he caught a glimpse of her again, skirting the ditch and heading for the greening tundra.

"Time to break this up," Tasker called as he looked up and down the line of the roadblock. He crossed his arms on his chest and waited.

The sergeant reversed his wagon, turned and sped off downhill alone. Who was that van driver? Tasker thought. Who was Larissa? The sun glared off the pickups, hurting his eyes. A raven croaked overhead, a strangely musical note.

Tasker would rather be in the sergeant's boots, giving the orders and not taking them. He heard, in his mind, the voice of the inspector at police college: "Men, you have what no one else has. Authority. Use it!" Authority, why did that word echo doubt?

Tasker's voice broke harshly, "Clear the road! Move along! Right now."

He felt Jim's eyes on him – proud maybe, but more likely not.

"Move along! Hurry up there!"

A couple of engines started, sullenly. Jim was disappointed, Tasker could tell. A word Ida used.

"Clear the road! Move along!" This was mop-up. It wasn't looking good.

Someone turned a radio on loud. Phil Ochs's "We Are the Cops of the World." That someone must have come prepared.

Tasker looked sideways across the tundra, but the girl, Larissa, had disappeared on foot down the slope. It was like she was never there – just a game trail parting the lichen crusts in a thin strip of quartz-white sand.

"Let's get a move on here!" Tasker found himself calling, stepping forward. It didn't matter what anyone thought. He had a job to do and he'd better get doing it.

Suddenly, Howard was blocking his path, a funny, mocking grin on his face, stone-hard eyes and menace in his voice. "This is no white man's mountain and no white man's park. Kakhteyi belongs to my people."

And then the huge ore rig, grinding through one gear after another, started to roll downhill and Howard was gone on the other side of it.

What a homecoming! This one had not been handled with class, Tasker thought.

3. TSEHKI, YUKON. June 1978. Later the same day

Tasker jogged from the RCMP station over to the ball field. He was finally in civvies, in jeans and the new red Forty-niners sweatshirt he'd bought with Ida.

The day improved once the roadblock cleared up; he wasn't going to let it get any worse. The sergeant said he could "fraternize" tonight, but no beer. Sergeant Flint didn't have to say that. Tasker knew he was always on duty in terms of his conduct: an officer never escapes the scrutiny and evaluation of the community. No one drank beer at Friday-night baseball anyway, just afterwards, and that was personal time. Every now and then Tasker would make a point when the force cramped his civil rights, but not this time, not after the morning's lousy start. He'd drink coffee after the game . . .

Tasker realized he hadn't seen any booze on patrol all day. Even those cartons of empties, Labatt's Blue and Old Style, once stacked so high beside the cabins in the village they looked like siding, were gone. The village looked half-decent, no hardtop or flower gardens, but people cared for what they had. The new Native Cultural Centre being built apparently had the works – studios, meeting rooms, a gift shop and a fancy sign out front saying "Construction by Athapaskan Warriors, Inc."

At the detachment, Sergeant Flint wasn't particularly friendly, never saying it right out but still letting Tasker know he didn't like how he'd handled the roadblock. But Shorty had been OK, for an RCMP cook, and helped Tasker get settled. He'd shown

Tasker the quirks of opening the windows, where the towels were kept and what he was welcome to take from the kitchen. When he'd given Tasker the full tour and was shuffling away down the hall, Shorty had said in a low voice, "The sergeant'll take it easier. Just don't leave anythin' for him to finish up. It's better that way. He's not one for doin' more than he has to."

After dinner Shorty slouched near Tasker with a cup of black coffee, and a cigarette hanging off his grey-stubbled upper lip. He talked about his life, about drifting through jobs all over the north – hospitals, residential schools, mining towns, work camps. Shorty was part Scot, but was the kind of guy who didn't rely on it. Instead he seemed to define himself with his own stories, and the way he told them usually left his listeners spellbound. He knew all about everyone and everything, going back fifty years, and put a kind of "life's like that" sour brush on it all. He even had a way of punctuating his most dramatic points with a smoker's cough. Shorty got started on a story about some new-comers going under trying to start a coffee shop in town.

"They didn't know the rules." Shorty shook his head. "Some people think they can come into a town and do their own thing, but it don't work that way. Not if they want customers and co-operation from local authorities. One time I went in, the hippie owner kept on at me about Rudyard Kipling. Did you know Kipling did readings in Bermuda? Did I care? Another time it was about the American government pourin' aid into Argentina because of the oil there. But the worst, it was the time he was on about the mystery of the Egyptian pyramids. Somethin' about the only possible explanation was levitation. And the reason? – the Great Pyramid contains every natural measurement known on Earth, even the circumference of the planet. That's what he said. Who wants to listen to stuff like that?"

Tasker got hooked for a while, but finally tired of the coffee-shop hippies. Fortunately he remembered baseball.

The game was in full swing when he caught his first glimpse of the ball field. And it was exactly like he remembered it being as a kid: a casual mix of Natives and whites, mostly in jeans and bush shirts, all the fielders dangling their flabby gloves at their sides. Same old dried-out benches and bases with an outfield of prickly brown and purple foxtail grass.

And even with the mining squabble, everyone showed up for ball. Like when he was a kid, the Anglican and Pentecostal preachers tried to steal each other's congregations all week; but on Friday night, baseball was sacred, and they played on the same team, talked about the weather and the game, and never referred to the Gospels at all.

There in the dust behind the chickenwire backstop, kids too little to play clambered over the same rusty, abandoned pickups. The steering wheels were intact – yes, getting a steering wheel mattered most. And piling pebbles to throw at the gophers when they whistled and scolded.

Blake McIntyre was pitching – he'd probably organized the teams. Although he wore overalls, beads threaded on a leather thong around his neck and a short ponytail, Blake was no hippie. He was too smart – called "the Prof" by the guys in the Grizzly Den Bar. Tasker watched as Blake walked over and touched the girl at first base, giving her a few pointers. Same girl, Larissa, with the bony knuckles he'd seen at the roadblock. She looked tired around the eyes this time. Tasker remembered Blake always took time to give players on his team encouragement.

"Stay there, Warren! In centrefield," Blake called. "We need your talent."

Tasker nodded, grinning, and punched his right fist into the stiff pocket of his glove. He knew the home rules: snap up the grounders if it was a guy at bat, fumble a bit for a kid or a girl – but no mercy once they got the hang of it.

Eve, Blake's wife, was one you treated like a guy. She'd been playing ball for years. Struck out today though.

Eve's niece, Jessica, and Howard Daniel showed up for the game at about the third inning. Reggie was with them, Howard's little brother and shadow, clowning and waving at the guys in the batting lineup. Howard and Jessica walked close together – Eve watching from third base. Jessica was young and already good-looking. Held her face in a sort of angry pout. Big dark eyes, lots of red-brown hair, and long legs in tight jeans. As tall as Howard, but younger, maybe a lot younger. Tasker wondered how much the town had really changed and turned half-decent. When he was a kid, no girl in Tsehki over twelve was a virgin.

Blake had positions ready for Howard, Reggie and Jessica. But Howard didn't want to play, said he had to go, and Jessica held her hands up to turn Blake back. She wanted to sit the game out. Reggie hesitated and then, with a whoop, joined the batters.

Blake surveyed the field from his mound. He seemed pleased. But suddenly he threw his glove on the sand and roared at the kids playing on the pickups, "Stop stoning ground squirrels." His face was contorted and his voice so violent, one of the little kids burst out crying.

Howard turned and strode back to Blake, picked up Blake's glove, and said in a loud voice, "We don't talk to our dogs like that."

"Children should be taught respect for wildlife," Blake retorted.

"No kid ever hit a gopher with a rock." Howard pushed the glove into Blake's stomach. "And every kid who grew up here tried."

Reggie and a tall, thin friend called out, "Yah, lay off!" Then snapped their hands over their mouths, not really stifling their hoots of laughter.

"Hey, guys," Tasker shouted. "Batter up! Play ball!" No way he was going to let a fight start.

Blake put on his glove like nothing had happened. And Howard stomped off, frowning.

The game went on till the sun set and then some. The easy feeling came back. Early summer in the north, with its shadowless twilight that lingers in honey tones for hours – that's what Tasker remembered longing for all winter, cooped up in a dark, smoky cabin.

It was still light when Eve waved her long arms and called, "Tie game! Flies're out!" She'd always said that no matter what the score, Tasker remembered.

The players laughed and gathered at the back of her camper for homemade root beer and oatmeal–raisin cookies.

While they were chatting a van approached, churning up clouds of dust that the light played through along the edge of the field. Tasker recognized the driver from the roadblock and joked, "Look who's coming, hot on the trail of fresh-baked cookies."

Reggie quipped, "Him? Ivan Peders never eats nothing but french fries."

Peders certainly didn't look hungry when he jumped out. His fleshy face quivered as he jeered in his high voice, "The paper shows who the fools are in Tsehki Junction."

Tasker and the other ball players stared blankly back at him, his rage was so out of place. Peders was breathing heavily, with dark smudges on his face and hands and fresh wet stains under the armpits of his navy coveralls. When he twisted to grab the paper from his front seat, Tasker saw the blond hairs along the rolls of his neck spiked out stiffly with dried dirt and sweat. He'd look like a brute, Tasker thought, if there hadn't been an odd grace to his commando movements.

Peders turned and flung a copy of a newspaper on the ground.

Then he jumped back into his van and accelerated off. Reggie and his gangly friend laughed at the retreating van while Blake picked up the paper. "Today's *Whitehorse Star*," he mumbled.

Tasker looked over Blake's shoulder to read the headlines: "Anti-Mine Forces Divided – Local Environmentalist and Band Don't See Eye to Eye – Environment Minister to Visit Tsehki." Underneath was a cartoon of Blake, it was clearly him, holding up one end of a fancy Golden Gate–type bridge so that all the people and pickups on the bridge were sliding into the river. "Wilderness Park Option" was printed on his T-shirt. One of the figures disappearing into the water had the word "Native Sovereignty" on his ballcap. The cartoon caption said, "When the troll and the billy goats can't cooperate, change is suspended." The cartoon had been circled in bold red marker.

Tasker decided the meaning of the cartoon was pretty obscure and patted Blake on the shoulder and laughed. "Great likeness!" But Blake didn't look up. He stared at the cartoon, a hurt expression on his face, his elbows jutting out from his body and his ball glove sagging off his left hand.

The good mood of the game had mostly broken, and Tasker watched as the other players drifted away from the field. The dust from the retreating van hung in the air and caught in the back of his throat, an unpleasant aftertaste to Eve's cookies.

Tasker stayed on until he was all alone, surveying the old ball field. Things had gone kind of sour and he couldn't entirely figure out why. It was like he was missing the thread of the story or something. Tasker had plenty of good memories of the old ball park – he realized how much he wanted to keep them.

Blake showed up at the Grizzly Den Bar in the hotel after the game. He rested his leather boots up on an empty chair at Tasker's and Jim's table and drank beer after beer. A crowd of single men from the mine were throwing darts in the far corner, drinking Old Style and filling the room with cigarette smoke. Shorty, the RCMP cook, joined them. Blake watched their game from a distance and occasionally grunted, acknowledging a good shot.

One of the players called back, "Hey, Prof, no speech about non-smokers' rights tonight?" and everyone laughed, including Blake.

Jim ordered an Old Style and talked about the good work the Athapaskan Warriors were doing on the new Cultural Centre.

Early in the evening Kay Anderson joined their table too. Tasker had known Kay for years. She and Jim had been friends ever since he could remember. It was a discreet, old-fashioned relationship, but Tasker figured there had to be more to it than seeing each other at the bar Friday nights.

Kay's cabin was close to Whitehorse on the Tsehki road. She'd retired there after selling her ranch with its small sawmill operation on Whitney Lake. She'd be as old as Jim, mid-sixties, and stocky, with tinted glasses and short white hair brushed behind her ears. Tasker's mother had a story that Kay was born into Montreal high society, had been a debutante, left after a short marriage with a no-good playboy and sank her inheritance into sub-arctic ranching. But Kay never talked about her family, ever.

Although Kay was quiet in Jim's company, Tasker always thought of her as tough. The kind who could take charge and whip this bar full of men into doing whatever she wanted, if she chose. Tonight she sat close to Jim, simply enjoying the company.

"What's with Kakhteyi?" Tasker asked the group. Howard's comment at the roadblock had got him interested. Besides, he figured the question might be a way to get Jim started on one of his great stories.

"An old legend," Jim answered. "The Natives say it was located at the big spruces. Some university types have found supporting evidence – at least the remains of an old settlement there."

Blake grunted and got up noisily for another beer at the bar.

Jim leaned forward, his brown eyes thinking, the inside of his thin lips shining wet – like Tasker always remembered him, even as a boy, when he started a tale. Kay nodded her head and smiled, crossed her arms and, listening to Jim, idly watched the dartboard.

"It's a wonderful story the way they tell it. Here's one version," Jim began. "The first people to live in Kakhteyi had everything they would ever want – they pleased the animal spirits. The river flowing past the townsite was so rich in salmon and berries that each family could survive without anyone ever having to travel more than a day from his bed. And copper nuggets shone on the river bottom. The women traded them for shells and eulachon fish grease from the coast.

"But the people of Kakhteyi got too used to their wealth; they began to waste it. You know, the usual." Jim put his hand around his beer glass without looking down at it. "Young men poured hot pitch on the backs of salmon mating in the river or killed caribou and goat for fun, leaving whole carcasses to rot on the mountainsides. One day, the men brought a live grizzly cub into town lashed to a pole. They let the children throw it in the fire and the river still tied up. An older boy finally rescued the cub, bandaged its burnt paws with white rabbit fur, and set it free. But the animal spirits were enraged at the arrogance of the villagers."

Jim looked at Kay and took a sip of his beer. They exchanged a smile and then his dark eyes locked with Tasker's again.

"The next day, three burly strangers appeared in Kakhteyi and invited the villagers to a feast up the mountain. The villagers were curious to find they had neighbours. Many young men and women accepted and climbed the steep slope to a plank house above treeline. They sat down at long tables to a feast of blueberries fried in gopher grease while the new neighbours, splendidly dressed as grizzly bears, danced for entertainment." Jim smiled and said, "You know, I'd like to see that, grizzlies dancing."

Tasker, enjoying himself fully, said, "Let's hear it for dancing bears, but without the gopher grease . . ." Kay laughed out loud and Blake turned on his bar stool to listen.

Jim grinned for a moment and then continued with a serious face. "One dancer, wearing white fur moccasins, approached the boy who'd pitied the cub and invited him outside. The dancer told him to stand steady behind the feasthouse no matter what happened, and then disappeared, leaving the boy alone. Suddenly the plank house shook, split apart and tumbled down the hill in a terrible roaring slide. Of all the guests at the feast, only the youth waiting outside survived. Then a huge grizzly bear with white paws appeared and spoke to him, saying the spirits had destroyed his people because of their pride.

"When the boy reported his story back at the village, the elders were full of shame and sorrow. They packed up the few remaining children and abandoned the site, leaving the wealth of Kakhteyi behind."

Blake staggered back to Jim's table, sliding his refill along the surface. He cut into the quiet moment at the end of the story: "Now the Natives claim the big spruce forest along the Henderson River is the site of Kakhteyi and their cultural heritage. Only trouble is" – a real edge to his voice – "the rockslide scar on Crag Mountain above the copper mine is likely older than any known human habitation in the area – no one has been able to date it accurately. And salmon probably never bred this far inland. This would be a far wealthier community if there were salmon to net. If Kakhteyi ever existed, there is no evidence it was there." He slapped the table with the flat of his palm.

Jim shrugged. "The woman who gave me the story, she tells it and folks don't have trouble with it. I think it's a good one."

"Variants of that legend occur all over the northwest. It's not unique here." Blake was lecturing now, his head wagging. "If they were serious about stewardship, they'd accept my plan to preserve the area as a wilderness park! Their sovereignty issue, it's drowning the environmental one." Blake stood up and, with a drunken jerk of his arm, sent three empty beer glasses spinning across the table top. "Anybody give me a ride?" he slurred.

Kay winked at Tasker. "You've stuck to coffee, Warren, maybe you'd drive Blake home . . . take my new truck."

Blake chugged his beer and staggered towards the door. Tasker mocked a salute to Jim and Kay. He thought he could use a little fresh air and was game to drive any new pickup. He planned on getting one for himself when he could afford it. As he lifted the keys off the table, he noticed Jim and Kay were holding hands under it. Tasker smiled broadly, but then a feeling of being the one left out crept under his smile. He thought of Ida – he'd like to be curling his hand around hers under a table right now.

At the door, he inadvertently elbowed Shorty stumping out of the men's room. There was a faint smell of vomit as the door swung shut. Shorty said, "Hey, watch where you're goin'!" more irritably than Tasker would have expected. Tasker started to apologize, but Shorty brushed past, heading for his table. Tasker cut the apology and followed Blake outside.

Blake fell asleep as soon as he got into the truck. It might have frustrated Tasker – no conversation, mosquitoes in the cab and a winding road without power steering – but Blake was just a sour drunk now. He had taken that newspaper cartoon too hard.

Blake and Ida were totally different, Tasker thought as he drove along, but they both sure could prickle, make it clear they were in the right. Tasker usually let on he wasn't interested when company got like that, but not last night with Ida. He should have let it go. It was about some patient she'd seen two years ago – and how Ida knew she'd done the best thing. She'd gone on and on about it – seemed stupid to go over a story so often. Ida was getting the patient ready for some test in the Whitehorse hospital when she noticed purple scars on the girl's stomach, like from whatever instrument they used to sterilize women by cauterizing their insides. Sounded like spaying a dog. Ida asked the girl how long ago she'd had the operation, but the girl knew nothing about it. Didn't seem to understand or care. Ida suggested she ask her doctor what the operation had been for. Tasker told Ida it was her duty to report the surgeon; nobody could do that to a girl without consent. But Ida's idea was that it was up to the girl. She'd planted the seed, now the girl could follow it through if and when she wanted. Maybe she didn't want police and social workers in her life. Then Ida said Tasker had this hangup with authority. That's what started their argument. Seemed so stupid now, such a stupid way to lose what he had with Ida.

Tasker opened his window for the cool night air to keep him awake on the drive. It was a good thing, too, because he had to jam on the brakes partway down Blake's lane. There was something across the road.

Blake, roused by the sudden stop, stumbled out of the truck before Tasker. Ahead, in the gloom was another roadblock. The two men approached cautiously, trying to make out what lay ahead.

The forms on the road were dark and misshapen. Like bodies. Blake whispered, "Moose heads."

Seven animal heads lined up in a row, mostly moose, but there was at least one pig too. Decorated – single fireweed florets pressed into the flesh eaten away around the eye sockets. Pink blossoms forming designs, outlines of eyes within eyes.

It was so weird it was spooky. Tasker called out, "Who did this?" He heard a thumping in the bush, like a sluggish heartbeat. Or was it faraway laughter?

Blake started to cry. A baby blubbering. He was staggering drunk and his tears drained into the foam from the sides of his mouth.

Tasker couldn't tell if Blake was scared or what, but it sure was disgusting. He tried to roll the heads into the bush. As they moved, wobbled, the meat let off a horrible stench and roused clouds of sleepy, gorged flies. Tasker let out a hollow laugh. "Stink!" His voice was muffled and deadened by the thick silence. Blake crawled back into the truck, sobbing.

When he'd cleared the road, Tasker gunned it to the cabin. He wanted to talk to Eve, warn her about the vandalism, but found the homestead in darkness. All he could do was lug Blake onto the sofa behind the kitchen stove and leave.

As he passed the dark moose heads on the way out, a part of Tasker imagined their shadowy forms reaching for the truck, trying to pull it into the bush. He told himself nothing was after him, there was nothing to be afraid of.

Once he got to the main road and was heading south to the village, Tasker forced himself to drive slowly. He remembered Jim's story about the burly strangers who turned out to be bears. Crag Mountain from that legend loomed behind him – he tried not to think about the roaring rock slide.

Howard. He tried to think about Howard. "Maybe Howard did it," Tasker said out loud. Because of the flower designs pressed into the moose flesh. Yes, they were Native designs. And only Natives could hunt moose off season.

By the time he reached the Chevron station at the north end of town, Tasker had Kay's pickup cranked well over the speed limit.

4. TSEHKI JUNCTION. June 1978. The next day – the fishing derby

Tasker paced back and forth across the bridge spanning Tsehki narrows all through the morning of the fishing derby.

The bridge was like a chilled finger, he thought, stretching hopefully from one side to the other, looking for the warmth of human contact. On the south bank, one of Tagish Mountain's shoulders rose sharply above the elbow of flat land and shaded cabins of the Native village. On the north side of the bridge, the land stretched low for several kilometres, some of it bush and some sand dune, along the shore of Natasahin Lake to the mouth of the Henderson River, the big spruces and finally the lower slopes of Crag Mountain and the mine. There was expanse in the broad valley, and sun and wind, but the buildings of the white settlement – the hotel and Grizzly Den Bar, Flo's General Store, the school, the churches, the RCMP detachment, the cabins – were all huddled at the foot of the bridge.

From the height of the bridge, striding back and forth and looking over rooftops to rock outcrops, bush, kilometres of shoreline and ice-cold water, Tasker was struck by how few locals were comfortable to stand alone in the disproportions of wilderness. Jim was, Blake was, his own father had been, but even Tasker, an outsider now, craved the warmth of human connection in this town.

A boy from Whitehorse first saw the form drifting far down the lake towards the mouth of the Henderson River. He hadn't caught a fish yet, so he moved off the bridge and threw in his line where Natasahin Lake curved into the narrows. That's when he saw it.

Then the kid caught a big orange-fleshed lake trout, so several others tried their luck along the gravelly beach too, and they noticed it.

A woman said, "Must be a couple of kilometres down. Big log, maybe, caught in the current."

Ivan Peders went over to try the new spot and he saw it. He trudged back to his van and got a pair of binoculars to take a better look.

The boy from Whitehorse asked, "A raft?"

But Peders shrugged like he didn't understand, so the kid repeated louder, "A raft?"

"Too far away to tell," Peders muttered, breathing quickly. Sweat clung to the fine blond hairs all along his upper lip. Only a fat guy would sweat, Tasker thought, with that coolness off the lake. It was noon on a clear mountain day when any exposed skin that didn't face the sun quickly chilled.

Tasker got his first good look an hour or so later. He decided it was one of the huge spruce trunks drifting in and out of the snowy reflections of the mountain on the blue-green water. Kind of pretty. He noticed how it floated in an odd way, unbalanced for a log, but didn't think it was worth striking out from the shore to investigate.

Watching it took Tasker's mind off the frustrations of today's job. No fishing for him. This kind of police work had to be suffered through before he'd be offered exciting stuff – jobs good enough to tell as a story at the Grizzly Den. At least he had company.

In the late afternoon, a procession of Natives appeared on the bridge, every face charcoal-blackened in traditional mourning, footsteps marching to the beat of a flat skin drum.

Tasker hurried from the beach back to the bridge. The gravel was thick, and it felt like he was running in slow motion. He knew he'd better be on top of this. By now the Natives were filing across, solemn, chanting a repetitive song. Even Reggie took the protest seriously.

The chief, Albert Daniel, told Tasker they had as much right to parade on the bridge as anyone else. The lake had called them to sing its dirge. The mine expansion would soon kill it.

Tasker radioed for advice, but Sergeant Flint said as long as they were orderly and kept moving, they weren't committing an offence.

The fishermen wouldn't stop complaining though. The biggest one may still be out there waiting to be caught. The noise would scare it away.

And the organizers of the derby – the new hotel proprietor and the mine manager – told Tasker he had no guts. Told him if he had any, he'd break up the demonstration. A plodding, no-win situation.

Then Howard arrived and led the procession off the bridge and down to the shore of Natasahin Lake. Tasker followed, keeping an eye on them, more frustrated than ever.

He saw the log again; it seemed suddenly much closer now. It bothered him till he decided it was two logs locked together somehow. The woman said there must be a big branch underwater because of the funny way it dragged.

The kid from Whitehorse asked Peders, this time loudly, to look again with the binoculars, and Peders said what he saw looked like a boat. He seemed surprised.

Jim, who'd just arrived at the bridge, said, "It couldn't be. Let me see."

When he looked through the binoculars, Jim said later, he had in mind most local boats were freighter canoes with small motors on the back. Even though he couldn't focus the binoculars right, he could tell it wasn't your regular boat.

Jim said he'd stroll up shore a bit to check. He got sidetracked by the Pentecostal minister's wife, who asked him to fillet her grayling for dinner since they were too small for the contest. Her daughters were wearing matching fluffy pink knit capes, and Jim took time to compliment them too.

When he finally got around to looking down the lake again, he thought it couldn't be a boat. But then he thought of Blake's river dinghy, his rubber Zodiac.

Jim stumbled back through the heavy gravel to the narrows, his face flushed, yelling at Tasker to help him launch his freighter canoe. He called for a tow rope, and someone on the bridge tossed a coil down. After several tries, the motor caught and he gunned it. Tasker watched him blur past the shoreline, pink capes, dark bush, onto the deep, blue-green water.

As Jim towed the Zodiac back, Tasker saw it was upside down, the bow collar riding oddly high, the whole length snapping side to side.

Everyone along the beach and on the bridge watched as Jim swung into the narrows. Everyone, including the marchers and the fishermen. It was about 7:00 in the evening.

Tasker observed too from his spot on the bridge. But it wasn't till Jim landed in the shelter of the ramp that he saw the form underwater behind the Zodiac. For a split second, Tasker figured his eyes were playing tricks – but then he knew.

He started to run down to the water. He recognized that form – it was a body, a rigid human body.

He scrambled over Jim into the stern of the canoe and over into the Zodiac. He pulled at the rope dragging out the back. Too heavy.

Tasker jumped into the frigid water, boots on. He and Jim jerked at the rope and finally up came heavy net. Slowly they hauled in the net and, tangled at the end, the body.

You could tell it was Blake McIntyre by the overalls and the beads around his neck, but not by the face. The face was a pale grey-blue with deep lines in the skin from the net. Blake's mouth was open, pulled over to one side, and his lips curled back in a grimace. His eyes stared wide, milky white. There was an obvious cut on the back of his head, but not much blood.

The fishermen on the bridge and the marchers all stared back as Jim cut the body from the net. Even the kid from Whitehorse gaped silently, his eyes riveted on Blake's blue, scratched and lined bare feet.

Peders walked past Tasker, mumbling in a tattletale voice, "The fool caught himself poaching."

Everyone stood around and watched as Jim helped Tasker lift the body into the back of his pickup. The whole town, it seemed, walked along beside as they drove to the cottage hospital, where Tasker placed Blake's body in the basement until the doctor could be tracked down.

When Jim and Tasker stepped outside, into the failing light, the crowd had dispersed, but Kay stood where the hospital steps met the boardwalk, waiting to keep Jim company for his drive home.

When he lay on his back, Tasker's shoulder wound hurt least, but it still felt like something was stuck in there. The hospital staff had assured him nothing was – it had passed right through him into the driver's seat. Another pellet, they said, went out the back of the cab, smashed the manifold and was found embedded in the pavement behind the pickup. Hard to believe for just a ball of lead. If the shotgun had been any closer, Tasker would be dead or he'd have no shoulder joint, no right arm. That's what they said – and Tasker believed them. But in the back of his mind somewhere, he had to hope the medical people were levelling with him. He'd known times when they hadn't.

Tasker got a bed in the men's surgical ward even though he'd been on the force more than thirteen years. There were apologies, but that was it. The head nurse wouldn't draw curtains between the beds unless the men were being examined, but if everyone was in the same shape he was, Tasker figured he needn't worry about privacy – he certainly had no idea what the man next to him even looked like. Whenever he raised his head off the pillow, Tasker trembled all over. And he couldn't get rid of a bitter taste inside his mouth and up the back of his nose.

Soon after he was admitted, the staff sergeant swam in and out of Tasker's consciousness and said, in a joking way, it served Tasker right for trying to do everyone's duty in the unit. Now he was forced to take time off and give others a chance to strut their stuff. Tasker didn't need to be told that – he knew he should have noticed, anticipated . . .

A nurse came by to offer him a drink of ginger ale. She flipped over his pillows and puffed them up. The cool feel of linen as he lay back down gave some relief from the light-headedness after holding himself up long enough for two sips.

The nurse's hands were gentle but firm and cool – they brought Ida's touch to mind. The only other time Tasker had been seriously injured in the line of duty, Ida was the one who had changed his dressings. It was shortly after the Tsehki case, but before he'd left the Yukon. Tasker got a knife wound accompanying a social worker on a child-neglect case. The father was a draft dodger homesteading it on the road to Atlin. His wife had walked out and he was reported to have gone crazy. As soon as they got there, the worker took custody of the children – no adults in sight and the cabin was in turmoil, with junk all over. The baby lay on the plank floor, trying to suck from a bottle milk so curdled he could draw nothing out. The social worker asked Tasker to carry the infant, and when they were partway to her car, the father rounded the cabin from between some partly constructed riverboats. He was roaring and swinging a chisel, which he planted in the palm of Tasker's held-up hand. All Tasker could think about was that one of the boats had a catamaran hull. It didn't seem a dumb thought then.

After he was released from the hospital that time, Tasker used to sit in the outpatient room, waiting for Ida to change the dressing on his hand. To touch him. Her lovely blue-black hair didn't shiver along his skin on these visits, though, because when she wore a uniform every strand was knotted back. That was after she'd started to see the other man – the one she'd met when Tasker went down to Tsehki and she started the rounds of her summer outpost clinics. And that was when Tasker stopped drinking beer and got a taste for whisky. He figured Seagram's 83 wouldn't smell bad on his breath, and he was taking a bit too much booze in his convalescence.

Tasker found himself in a foggy moment where past and present were blurring together. The duty nurse, not Ida, picked up his good wrist to take his pulse. She smiled, pleased, and then asked if he wanted the light off before she slipped away. Tasker felt a stab of loneliness, wanted her to stay, but couldn't say it. She disappeared into the shadows down the ward.

Jim was one person he'd like to see right now. He was never the kind to take charge and then disappear. Tasker had been. In the morgue, the night they carried Blake's body in, Jim was already planning how he could help Eve and the kids over the next winter. Tasker was out of their lives in less than a week. But he was young then, had so much to learn, even if he'd never have admitted it at the time.

Tasker hadn't kept up much with Jim since he'd left the north – maybe it was one way he had of stifling the bad memories of that summer, suspending the story that nearly overwhelmed him. He'd heard in one of Ida's letters that Jim wasn't living in Tsehki any more, but out of town at Kay's. Wherever he was, he was likely living the same as when Tasker had stayed over at his cabin occasionally, years ago, as a boy.

On a June morning, like the day Blake died, Jim would always lie back there in his bed, head on the pillow, and wait for the clear, ascending scale of the Swainson's thrush before opening his eyes to the moment of first light. He once told Tasker he loved to bunch his pillow under his head and lie there, listening, alert, grateful his hearing was still sharp. Even though Jim knew he should get moving, he always took a minute or two to just lie there considering the possibilities of today, denying himself the pleasures of stretching and standing up so he could savour instead the quiet transfusion of light and sound.

Jim never hesitated to tell anyone that Tsehki Junction commanded the most beautiful view on Earth. An untamed Switzerland of snow-capped mountains reflected in long, blue-green lakes. He'd travelled the world with the U.S. Army Engineering Corps and seen many spectacular places, but when he found Tsehki on the Alaska Highway job in '42, he'd decided to put down roots.

Back then, the town boasted a single row of buildings along the north shore of the narrows between Natasahin and Whitney lakes. "The Native side of the narrows was already cramped, but maybe they prefer it that way," Jim would say.

The first white settlers had come around the turn of the century, almost fifty years before the Alaska Highway. They aimed to catch the business of would-be millionaires hungrily chasing stories of gold nuggets over the mountains. Every tent-tired stampeder had to raft through these narrows; so the settlers busily laid out fine temptations – home-baked pie and white linen sheets at the hotel, tinned ham and woollen socks in the General Store, shot glasses of whisky and jellyroll music at Gypsy's.

When Jim moved down to Tsehki after the Second World War, those hustling settlers were mostly dead, reflections behind old river pilings. Except the hotel owner. There was an old man turned mean, someone who sold cheap whisky, bottles and bottles of it wrapped in brown paper bags, to people who were already reeling drunk. Jim said he felt no regrets when that old-timer finally died.

Jim cleared a lot on the north shore of the narrows where the morning sun came over Tagish Mountain first, and on the Natasahin side because Whitney Lake was reedy. He was about the only one who'd left space between his cabin and his neighbours' – and he never regretted it. The lake shivered blue-green in summer, there was plenty of firewood, and he could find all the companionship he needed with a little exercise.

His cabin wasn't fancy, but he'd fixed it right. A good little wood stove, lots of insulation, a comfy reading chair and one big thermopane window letting in that western view. The other three walls were floor-to-ceiling shelves for old gold rush bottles he'd collected, and books. Mostly books to feed his interest in the people and the wildlife of the north, like Britton and Brown's *An Illustrated Flora*, *The School at Mopass* and *Letters from Edith Josie*.

If it weren't for Jim, Tasker would never have known much about Blake. That's the way it was in the north back then: people didn't bother about anyone's life outside. Jim told Tasker more than once it was hard to believe this Blake, the homesteader, was the same man who had visited Tsehki years before as a university student – the carefree, laughing son of a wealthy Vancouver jeweller, he'd enchanted a score of local kids into helping him with his research on prehistoric trade routes. He'd mapped what they called the old "grease trails" – Jim liked the term – along which the barefoot coastal runners once backpacked seafish oil inland to trade for rich furs and native copper – and sometimes to steal back an elegant Athapaskan wife or leave behind a tent ring or a sleek obsidian flesher wedge, clues to a university trail-finder.

Now and then, when Tasker was a kid and spent the night with Jim, they'd go over the story of Tasker's dad. Jim told that terrible story well. He'd teamed with Paul Tasker in the 1950s, though Paul was a younger man, and they'd gone into contracting together. Paul knew what he was doing, having grown up on a homestead himself in New Brunswick. There'd been lots of work in Tsehki for two carpenters who also could do plumbing and wiring and run heavy equipment. They won tenders for the school, the police station, public housing, the roads maintenance shed. And they had fun. Paul sent back for his high school sweetheart, and Warren came along shortly after. Jim, he said he never could get Kay to marry him. But he'd say that with a twinkle in his eye.

Jim said he hardly felt his years till that one luckless March day on Natasahin Lake – 1963 it was. Jim and Paul had been hauling logs across the ice to build a little pioneer museum for the village. As they bucked each load, Paul belted out popular tunes like "Hound Dog" and "Blue Suede Shoes." Jim checked the ice and it was still over four feet thick. He drove the pickup in front and Paul followed in the flatbed, honking out the rhythms of his tunes for the mountains to absorb and echo.

Jim talked about the glare of the sun off the ice that day, about his eyes being sore from squinting. All the snow had melted from the shore and the sand benches behind. In fact, it was patchy till well up the mountainsides. He even thought he caught a smell of sage. Jim wore a T-shirt, his truck window open to let in the sun-warmed air of spring. He remembered noticing the show-off spins and rolls of mating ravens.

Close to the narrows he felt the back end of his pickup sag and he floored it. He honked loudly to warn Paul. Then, in his side-view mirror, he watched Paul's face, grinning and bobbing to one of his tunes, suddenly drop, disappear with the rig.

Jim ran back to look, but there was nothing. The ice was five feet thick beside the hole – but rotten into slivers, crystal shards, with no strength. Sucked dry by the March sun. The lake was three hundred feet deep to its stone-cold bottom.

Tasker's mother only once mentioned his father's death. Once. In fact, five years later, she stopped talking altogether. If Jim hadn't been around to tell the story, to talk to, Tasker might have ended up a horribly mixed-up kid.

Later, when Tasker and his mother moved up to Whitehorse for Warren to finish high school, Jim decided to sell the business and give them half. He didn't have the heart for it any more, he said. There were other hard-working men in the valley to take as a partner, but no one like Paul.

The town, particularly the side away from the Native village, changed a lot after that March day on the ice. The mine opened up on Crag Mountain. When Tasker and his mother moved out, their homestead disappeared, replaced by the trailer homes of more teachers, miners, nurses, RCMP; by newfangled – Jim's word – octagonal cabins built by the hippies who sold crafts to the tourists; and by the fancy bungalow built by the rich Native outfitter who'd even guided for an American vice-president.

In that makeshift hospital morgue, laying out Blake's body, Jim said it was hard to believe Warren had grown so fast, finished college and a year with the RCMP at twenty-two. He still thought of Warren as a kid, told him so too.

Ever since that night, Tasker felt he'd let Jim down, not in any particular way but generally, by not living up to what Jim had taught him, expected of him.

Tasker opened his eyes to find it was dark down the ward. One light glowed by the nurse's station. Something inside Tasker gave way. Blaming himself and blaming others, it never got him anywhere but deeper down. He didn't have the energy to crush it now. Jim could live and let live; if only Tasker could . . .

For the first time since he'd taken that shot, Tasker felt the linings of his cheeks contract, longing for a wash of a good whisky – even Seagram's 83 would do. His mind jumped at that distraction and he spent the next hour, before he fell asleep, plotting how to smuggle a bottle into this ward.

6. TSEHKI JUNCTION. June 1978. The morning after the fishing derby

Tasker turned hard right after the bridge and then left to the Native side of the village. He geared down for the potholes. Friday, he remembered scraping over can openers, real gas-tank punchers, here – it was better to rock slowly through the ruts. Tasker's only job, other than patrol, was to check in with Eve mid-morning and tell her Sergeant Flint had taken the police boat down the lake to look around. Jim went too because he knew the country so well. Besides, a stiff breeze had started out of the west and everyone knew Jim could handle a boat on Natasahin Lake in just about any kind of weather. As soon as they got back, the sergeant would speak to Eve himself.

Now, Tasker thought, if he were in that boat he might be sliding the throttle forward, feeling the surge of power in his lower spine, a shiver of excitement in the back of his legs. And he'd have company. Instead, he was manoeuvring through ruts in a dreary village.

Once he snuck Ida into a patrol cruiser – she sat right up beside him in the front seat, "two-headed" driver style, her straight, blue-black hair brushing his shoulder, and her Gwich'an eyes darkening with fun. It sure would be nice to have her with him now, Tasker thought. He couldn't have picked a worse time to get sucked into that fight. Yesterday she'd flown north for the summer-long clinics, starting in Old Crow.

Tasker had the feeling he'd spent most of this assignment alone with his thoughts. Still, he didn't want to make that visit to Eve. She'd had all night to think about Blake as he inhaled water, knowing he was dying. Tasker remembered when his own father drowned, his mother said only one thing – she was grateful he never wore a seatbelt, meaning, Tasker knew, he probably got knocked out on the roof of his cab and never suffered. But Tasker could tell, even though he was only a kid, that his mother despaired over her husband dying conscious, knowing he was drowning, gasping for the last bubble of air in the cab, sucking in water. Eve would have that same haunted look today, but at least she had a body to bury.

Tasker swerved around two husky mongrels curled in depressions on the side of the road, a third standing, its nose inside a pork-and-beans tin.

He pulled over at Howard's family place and turned off the motor. If he dropped in here he could kill time, let Eve sleep, he thought. Yes, and he could find out why Howard had gone out of his way to be curt at the roadblock and the ballgame – the fishing derby too. Friendships didn't just disappear like that. But on Tasker's part, there was his hard little suspicion in return – the feeling that Howard had something to do with the moose heads.

When he opened the door of the patrol car, a dog was already sniffing the tires. Tasker skirted round it and strode up the path, enjoying being outside, upright and swinging his arms. He double-jumped up the back steps, looking down at the garbage cans and old bicycles tidied away under the floorboards of the porch. The dog cocked his leg around the tires of the patrol car. Tasker knocked on the door and waited, looking down the village from the house.

Here you had a peaceful view: willows along the river, grey weathered shacks, other people's back porches, flowerbeds planted with radishes and lettuce, stray fireweed – no startling mountain peaks or expansive vistas of wild country like on the other side of the narrows. He heard someone moving in the house, but no answer. He knocked again.

Then Howard's mother, Rose Daniel, opened the back door, unsmiling.

Tasker took off his hat and held it in both hands. He said, "Hello, Mrs. Daniel. Warren Tasker. Could I speak to Howard?" He looked past her into the house he once knew well. It still smelled of wood smoke. On the kitchen counter he could see a digital clock and a food processor; they were new, and beyond, past the plaster archway his own father had been pleased to tell folks he knew how to construct, was the sitting room, with a big weaving frame hanging down the wall. Howard's family was working on another blanket; he could just make out the pattern, half-finished with white, blue and yellow balls of wool hanging down. One of those designs that had eyes within eyes.

"He's eating," Mrs. Daniel said.

"We're puzzled by some of the technical aspects of the accident yesterday. I thought maybe Howard could help." Not really a lie.

Howard's mother walked away from the door, not inviting Tasker in. He let it slide past and waited, rubbing his thumbs along the peak of his hat.

Being left back in town today was a deliberate putdown by the sergeant. The local doctor, Freeman Straun, had called Tasker "a smartass," and after that Sergeant Flint put the blame on Tasker for making things unnecessarily complicated. It made no sense. But, in the end, Tasker felt good he'd hung around last night and encouraged the doctor to keep looking at the cause of death.

Dr. Straun had been out of town at his fishing cabin when they tracked him down. Tasker recognized the resonant voice, the kind that carried, and the aging face – the same doctor who'd checked over Tasker's friend Gary Daniel, Howard's older brother, in the lockup years ago, leaving such a sketchy report (and not remembering anything but what was in that report) that Gary ended up a quadriplegic and no one got pinned with the blame. The way it all unfolded was one big reason Tasker went into the RCMP.

Tasker decided to hang around the hospital basement this time, especially since Flint didn't stay. He intended to be a quiet witness, standing out of the way, hands behind his back. He watched the doctor run his fingers over Blake's joints; examine the blood pooling behind the bony, white knees, look under Blake's fingernails, in the eyes and up the nostrils with a pencil light. Dr. Straun's hands shook. The doctor acknowledged Tasker's presence by carrying on a running commentary of his observations: "Body temperature that of surroundings; goose-flesh on the skin of both upper arms; skin on the palms and soles is uniformly thick and deeply furrowed, especially on the feet; recent lesions on the soles of the feet; semi-erect penis; tongue behind the jaws." There were pauses, but mostly the doctor's voice kept rumbling on and on. "The body has been on its back since death – liver mortis. Small amount of foam high in the nostrils; no ballooning of the lungs evident externally; no signs of struggle on the fingers, nothing under the nails. A somewhat atypical drowning, but it's a drowning all right. Took place about 10:00 a.m. – or an hour on either side."

That's when Tasker stepped forward and asked what made the cut in the back of Blake's head.

Dr. Straun shrugged. "A surface wound. The scalp will bleed a lot, especially in water, but it's nothing. There's still clotted blood even after hours in moving water – but it didn't kill him. It's not a textbook drowning though, Corporal."

The doctor pressed on Blake's chest and a small bubble of

white foam emerged from his nostrils. When the doctor released the pressure, the foam disappeared. "Odd how little foam. Usually more than a cupful comes out the nose and mouth," Straun mumbled. "I wonder if he had heart disease or if alcohol was involved. It's as if he were unconscious when he drowned." He lifted up Blake's head with two hands, felt through the hair from the crown down to the neck, then stopped and looked up at Tasker, holding Blake's head just above the spine. "Yes, three centimetres left and below the cut, a depressed fracture. Interesting." The doctor turned the head, parted Blake's matted hair and took a closer look.

After several long moments, Straun stared back up towards Tasker without looking at him. His eyes were thinking, solving a puzzle, his fingers encircling Blake's head. Tasker waited.

"Here's why we've got an incomplete picture of death by drowning. This fracture would have rendered the victim comatose before he submerged" – Straun was using his commentary voice again – "enough to kill him if left unattended on shore. He likely received the fracture as his boat flipped. The foaming is atypical because his vital functions were already failing." The doctor paused and then concluded with "No signs of a struggle to save himself. The coroner better have a look."

Flint walked back into the room. Straun lowered Blake's head gently and grinned not unpleasantly. "Your corporal may be wet behind the ears, Reg, but he's observant. Blake was unconscious when he was submerged. Head injury – likely an accident. He did die of drowning, however."

"So we'll have to identify what he hit himself on," Flint said impatiently. "What a bother."

The doctor looked at Tasker and said, "Since you're the smartass, Tasker, you put the body back in the cold room. We'll look over Blake's boat for edges that would cause that depressed fracture. Maybe the wooden platform the motor attaches to."

Tasker was left alone to work Blake into the bag, but that was OK. Dr. Straun would consult the coroner in Whitehorse, maybe even send the body outside to Vancouver for an autopsy. There'd be a better investigation than Gary ever got, a documentation of all the injuries.

Not that this helped Gary any, or that Straun had done anything wrong. But Tasker felt better – the down side was that Flint shut him out of the rest . . .

Tasker wasn't part of the investigation, that was plain, but he could talk to Howard. He wanted to clear up the thing with the moose heads. The last time he'd seen Blake alive, he'd been crying and it had to do with those moose heads. What a way to remember a guy.

Tasker startled from his thoughts when Howard appeared on the other side of the screen.

"Morning, Howard," Tasker began. "Can I talk to you about what's been going on the last couple of days?" Tasker bent his head and moved his hand to open the screen door.

But Howard pulled it shut and held it. He looked back through the screen at Tasker and muttered, "I can't help, Warren, I don't think."

Howard had stayed short, Tasker noticed, with broad shoulders and thick black hair pulled back in his braid. He had a way of holding his shoulders square and his elbows out from his body that made him look unusually powerful. His face was round, eyes dark and he had a straggly moustache. The hand on the door had wide brown fingernails.

"Any ideas how Blake had that commercial net without a licence, for instance?" As Tasker asked, the sun broke through behind his back and shone off the metal screen so he couldn't see Howard's face clearly.

"He probably bought it." Howard's voice was flat.

"Did you know he used one?"

Howard shrugged.

"Who sells nets around here?"

"Beats me."

This conversation was going nowhere. Tasker couldn't see Howard's eyes and that bothered him. "When did you last see him?"

"Baseball, probably."

"Any theories how he died?"

No answer.

"A guess?"

"The lake's not for outsiders, Warren, you know that," Howard said. "A Zodiac can flip easy anywhere along the shore."

"But on a calm day, with a local? Howard, can I come in and talk to you?"

"Not now. My mother doesn't ask RCMP in our house, ever since Gary's trouble."

Howard cocked his head so it fell into Tasker's shadow. Now Tasker could see Howard's eyes looking over the RCMP uniform. He seemed to be smirking.

"Where were you Saturday morning about 9:00?" Tasker asked, feeling suddenly quite annoyed.

"Kakhteyi."

"What about after baseball Friday night?"

"Around."

"What do you know about the moose heads in Blake's lane?"

"Moose heads?" Howard laughed and backed away from the screen. "Warren, you get off on being a cop?" Then, "Look, I gotta go. I don't know anything that could help."

Howard shut the back door and left Tasker standing alone on the porch, holding his hat.

Tasker stared at the door, at the cracks in the varnish by the hinges. What was eating Howard? His chest tightened with a helpless frustration. He thought of Gary Daniel, in the lockup years ago. He remembered peering into that stinking cell and seeing his friend lying flat, prone, in a stain of urine, a dark stain that spread on the concrete in a circle around Gary's body from his knees to his armpits. The thought made him squirm inside all over again. He remembered thinking Gary was sickening. Then he realized something was wrong – Gary Daniel wasn't a lousy drunk. It was as much a feeling of having no say, no control, as concern for his friend. His voice was panicked when he'd shouted for the officer, for the doctor.

Now he was the cop, but still wasn't in the driver's seat. Maybe he'd better forget it, just go get his job done with Eve.

Tasker looked up and down the row of houses. His father, Paul Tasker, had helped build them all. As a boy he'd thought they literally glowed with his craftsmanship. A tin scraped on a rock as the dog nosed through more garbage. There was something familiar and welcoming in the sound.

Staring at a hinge and pulling his field cap back onto his head, Tasker couldn't stop a grin spreading across his face. Yes, maybe he did get off on being a cop. He scratched his moustache. No way was he going to let the underside of this town, what it used to be or what was simmering now, get the better of him. So what if Howard had a problem, he'd come around. So what if Flint tried to shut him out – he'd find what happened to Blake and why. No big deal.

As he returned to his cruiser, Tasker saw Albert Daniel, the band chief, disappear into the Cultural Centre. There was a place to start.

Tasker rolled forward the short distance and stopped again at the side of the road.

Friday, he and Flint had tried to get in to look around, but it was locked. The building was definitely designed to assert its aboriginal roots: built like one of those old meeting houses with logs crosscut in planks and set vertically into slots on a square frame, with large log supports at the corners and in the centre of the front and back. Not many trees around that size. The supports were carved in a natural way with the usual Native symbols, traditional crest figures, but abstract, suggestive of knots on a tree trunk.

Tasker followed the chief up the steps and got right inside this time. It was all fresh-smelling wood, and the space was divided into offices with low, movable walls. It felt official, modern, competent and not smoky or prehistoric. But it had an old meeting-house feeling too, with a skylight in the roof like the traditional smokehole letting daylight filter into each room.

In the foyer, Tasker's eyes were drawn to a carving high on the wall. A crudely rendered grizzly bear, a grizzly that seemed to be dancing. Tasker had seen it somewhere before. The dancer's posture was strange, sort of feminine and alluring. Grizzly were supposed to represent the elemental wilderness somehow – unpredictable, solitary, cruel – and not be seductive.

The chief strode out of one of the rooms and up to Tasker. "Yes, Officer?" His face was closed in a bland expression like yesterday on the bridge.

Albert had only recently been named chief, and moved back from Prince George, where he'd been an instructor in the vocational school. He looked like he was a relative of Howard's – powerful, stocky shoulders kind of rounded forward, big face, mid-length black hair slicked under a headband.

"I was just admiring the plank house," Tasker answered casually.

"Yes, we packed these in from the coast." The chief spoke slowly. "Not many trees this size inland."

"I guess that's why you locals want to save the spruces." It sounded lame, Tasker knew.

"Yes." Albert started to walk away. "Look around. We're just moving in."

"There's something I'm curious about. Not very important." Tasker's neck felt hot and his cheekbones prickled, but he ignored the sensation. "Why wasn't Blake helping at your road-block? He wanted to save the big trees too, didn't he?"

The chief's mouth tightened slightly, but his voice stayed flat. "He came, but I told him we didn't need him."

"Can I ask why?"

"Our people claim Kakhteyi. We've got our own ideas for its future."

"Oh. I thought Blake would be useful . . ." Tasker was genuinely surprised.

"Blake wanted it declared a wilderness park run by government officials. That's no different for us than a Kakhteyi run by corporate managers for a mining company."

"But you both wanted it protected?"

"We set watchmen all day at the big spruces to protect our heritage from people who want to use it for their own ends like Blake. Government's no different." Albert's voice quivered with rage now, but his words still came slowly, deliberately. "Poverty, booze, stolen land, broken promises – that's what we thank government for. They took our children away to residential schools, tried to rub out our language, our way of life. They think of it as management." He pointed his finger at Tasker. "I am thinking you're here for no good reason. Our people don't want you and your self-serving laws."

Tasker looked up at the carving on the wall. He let out a

humourless laugh. "Chief, I was born here too, as you know. Gary Daniel was my best friend when he carved that story mask, before he lost the use of his hands. I know he never got justice. But your people, most of them never opened their mouths to help him. You're all part of the system, part of the problem too."

Tasker turned and walked out of the foyer – and into sunshine.

It was late morning on the road north out of town when Tasker saw Ivan Peders's approaching van lurch to the right. Peders compensated left, but then it pulled stronger – the van was all over the road. Tasker veered as far as he could over on the shoulder to get out of its way.

Peders finally got the van stopped and, as he was climbing out, Tasker heard him call to Larissa sitting in the passenger seat, "I'm going to check the tires."

She smiled, looking ahead out the windshield. Peders didn't pay attention to Tasker watching on the other side of the road, but Larissa did. Her eyes rested on Tasker's for several long moments.

Peders's right front tire was flabby. When he found the problem, he flung open the back doors of his van irritably. There was quiet talk between Larissa and Peders that Tasker couldn't hear distinctly, but from the rhythms of what he did hear, he knew it wasn't pleasant. They were likely angry at getting a flat so close to, but too far from, the Chevron station at the north end of town. Tasker turned off his motor and sat waiting for them to cool off. He didn't feel like walking into an argument. Then he caught Larissa's eyes on him again and met her stare.

"Plug this in the cigarette lighter. The flat's on your side," Peders ordered Larissa loudly as he came around to the passenger door, carrying a pump, a crowbar and a star wrench. But instead

Larissa slipped out, jumped into the ditch, and started picking bluebell stalks, her back to the van. Her jeans were tight, so tight Tasker could see the line of her underpants showing through.

"Hey, I asked for help!" Peders called. "When you call, I come."

She ignored Peders. Tasker watched Larissa's large hands when they stretched from her side with their bony knuckles – their light, competent movements as she snapped the stems. He glanced down at his own smaller hands. When he looked up again, Larissa was facing the van. Now he saw her stained white T-shirt and the outline of her breasts. It didn't look like she was wearing a bra.

"Don't bring those weeds back here," Tasker heard Peders call after Larissa. "They're caked in dust." His high voice was echoed and hollow from the inside of the van, but there was something about the tone – complaining and powerless – that made Tasker uncomfortable.

Then Peders scrabbled back out the open passenger door with the tire pump and clamped the hose onto the tire valve. The pump vibrated on the gravel, dancing and shaking around.

Peders squatted, put down the tools and ran his hands lightly around the tire, feeling for the leak. He stopped and ran one finger up and down the wall.

Larissa walked on into the bush, bending over now and then to touch the small flowers on the moss.

Peders loosened the nuts before getting the jack out of the back. One nut was on too tight. He held the crowbar on a line with the bolt and banged it with a rock, sending a shiver down the shaft.

It was only then that Peders's eye caught Tasker stopped on the other side of the road. Tasker got out of his cruiser and asked, "Need any help?"

"No." Peders didn't look at him. "I don't like that attitude, like anything alive is precious. There is too much life – everything breeds and populates all over the place . . ."

Tasker figured the man was really just talking to himself, and stood watching. He looked over the kiddie figures on the side of Peders's van. They were in odd positions, as if they'd been blown out of the mouth of a cannon. That's what was weird about them, Tasker realized, and suppressed a laugh.

"That homesteader poached, you know. Not that poaching bothers me much, but since he preached conservation and all the preciousness of life, he got what he deserved," Peders said, still looking at his work.

"You mean Blake?"

"I seen him cleaning big catches of fish on the riverbank and his pickup full of dark meat out of season – seven times since he moved here." Peders worked off the tire and rolled it round to the back of the van. "Most of those save-the-trees guys, they're liars," he continued. "You got to think what's in it for them."

Tasker laughed aloud and said, "Those are serious allegations. Any evidence – or just your say-so?"

"Natives are the same." Peders ignored Tasker's question and carried on. "Take either side of the road, travel a thousand kilometres, and there's nothing of value – just bush. So why do they always claim the land next door?" Peders put the spare on the wheel casing and looked around for the hubcap and nuts. "So they can mooch off other people's sweat, that's why. Only the Natives don't call it mooching, they got a fancy word for it – sovereignty."

Tasker said, "Not many people 'round here'd agree with you." Not caring to give Peders the chance for a comeback, he pointed to the fender. "I see you worked that dent out. Your flat probably got started when you bashed into the pickup."

At first, Peders didn't seem to hear. He was watching Larissa walk back out of the bush. She carried a large bouquet of blue-bell and lupine. Peders said, "They were obstructing the road. I have a right to get to work, fulfil my contract. They're lucky I didn't blow them through the middle."

Tasker said, "You're lucky you didn't." Fed up and turning away from Peders, Tasker found he was facing Larissa and said, "Hello."

She walked past Tasker and smiled, the smell of cigarette smoke drifting past with her. Her eyes didn't connect with his this time, so it was easy to take in her whole face. He was surprised to notice the skin under her eyes was finely lined. She looked tired, stressed maybe. Tasker wanted to look closely at her hands again, but one was hidden by the flower stems and the other stuffed casually in her back jeans pocket. Her breasts moved loosely in her shirt as she reached into the van to lay down her flowers and pick up a beaded moosehide jacket off the front seat.

Tasker put his hands in his pockets, followed Peders around the back of the van and watched him put away the jack and lock the door. He asked, "Where were you between 8:00 and 10:00 yesterday morning?"

Peders grinned. He seemed to like the question. "I was fishing in the derby, wasn't I? Got there pretty early too."

Peders got into the van and started it without looking at the key. His eyes watched Larissa sitting beside him in the passenger seat.

Tasker suddenly understood what was going on. Those two went back a long way; they knew each other really well.

Tasker pulled out first to get a jump on the dust, but he looked over his shoulder to make sure they had no problems. He caught Larissa, her head twisted out the van window and looking back at him with intent eyes and a funny smile.

Larissa, now she had possibilities! Her dark hair, white face was . . . beautiful. But . . . different.

The jacket she put on, the one she wore at the roadblock protest, was something. Smoke-tanned leather – pale brown, not the rich medium brown of factory-tanned hide – with long fringes that swung at her breast and hips when she walked, and beadwork of local flowers – lots of stalk and leaves with little blossoms, not the usual big flat, stylized flowers. Her T-shirt and tight jeans, they just didn't go with it. How'd she ever get stuck on Ivan Peders?

Tasker swung into Eve's lane, scanning for the moose heads. Funny. They were farther along than he remembered. He smiled, the way he'd smile back at Larissa – next time.

Tasker slowed for the wheels to bump over a texas gate. The lane broke into a meadow with a fence around the outside. Hard work fencing in this country. No postholes. Too many rocks and patches of permafrost. Tasker remembered the work as a boy, the strain in his lower back, the smell of his own sun-warmed sweat. He'd cut plenty of spindly aspen, nick off the branches with an axe and sit for hours peeling the stick trunks with a drawknife. And the aspen always had lots of knots, so the drawknife never pulled smooth. That meant sticky fingers and yellow zigzag stains that turned black on his hands and pants, and jugs of drink. His mother used to send out lemonade. Then, when the trunks were all white and clean, he'd cut them into posts, cross them in threes and bind them with wire or spruce root to make upright teepee supports for the rails. A lot of cutting and peeling. It was on soft summer evenings after working all day with the drawknife that Tasker and Gary Daniel used to like cruising in town, talking to the girls, sharing a smoke, sneaking a beer and getting away with it.

At the far end of the clearing Tasker spotted the moose heads in the bush. He stepped out of his car to look, carelessly slamming the door. It was then he was hit with the stench of rotting flesh. It burned the back of his throat. Listening, he held his breath and stretched his eyes painfully to the right and left, looking to see if any scavenger or predator had been attracted by that smell.

Tasker heard a thump. He jumped back into the car, and rolled up the window. His breath came fast and a pulse throbbed in his ears. He gripped the steering wheel with two hands and floored the pedal.

Inhaling deeply down his dry throat, he tried to force himself to calm down. Spruce trees choked the lane, the trunks scrawny, and dead grey branches fingering awkwardly out at the car. He was going too fast.

Tasker eased up on the accelerator. No point scratching the paint. He laughed out loud at that thought. One thing, no one had seen him, sensed his groundless fear.

He peered into the dense underbrush, darkly tangling for sun and air. Second growth. Not like the lane in sight of his old homestead where the trees had breathing space, green shining patches of moss, red kinnikinnick berries and sprays of false camas lilies between trunks. He used to hide in the shadows and jump out to surprise his father when he heard the truck coming. Never here. Too claustrophobic, grey, strangling.

As he calmed down, Tasker knew, suddenly, what it was about Larissa. She looked white, was probably brought up white, but had some Native somewhere in her background, or wanted to. Maybe she was cultivating her Native side. The jacket was part of it. He conjured an image of her – tired face, grubby T-shirt and tight jeans, gasping for air inside an oversized, overelaborate beaded jacket.

Tasker's thoughts were interrupted by the first signs of the homestead and he knew he'd better slow down. A couple of sheds spilling out equipment; logs dumped beside a sawhorse ready for bucking; and an old rusting beige Volkswagen van, windshield wipers askew, stripped of tires and engine, even the back seat hauled out and rotting beside the body. Homestead clutter, he remembered, looks better covered in snow.

The lane opened into a large turning area littered with old tires, orange and yellow plastic balls, and a wagging, barking dog – one of those tiny, yappy herding dogs. The cabin stood on the left, a huge vegetable garden on the right, and ahead, free-range chickens pecking in the yard.

No matter how you looked at it, Tasker thought, land claims made losers. No treaty had been signed in the Yukon, so everything was up for grabs. For the white settlers, all that hard work clearing the best land and then it might not be theirs any more. The talk had been going on for years – it was getting fruitless, boring and academic. Self-government, nationhood, self-policing – some of the issues were mind-boggling. Tasker couldn't see two police forces, two sets of laws, two courts of justice. On the other hand, things couldn't keep going on as they had. If Blake were alive, he'd likely be making representations to the commission because his homestead land bordered on the Tsehki claim. Tasker and most of the people he knew had tuned out, however, leaving it to the politicians and bureaucrats, even when they were affected. Some people had a nagging sense that once there was a settlement, there wasn't going to be an end anyway. The process would self-perpetuate.

Funny, Blake chose an isolated, wild lot with spectacular scenery and then plopped his cabin where you couldn't see a thing, not even a gentle view. Blake was different all right. But that didn't explain why no one – Howard, the chief, Ivan Peders

– trusted him. This poaching business, it didn't wash somehow. As he turned off the car, Tasker felt a low tug in his gut. Well, here he was. It was time to talk to Eve.

Stepping out, he heard the distant swish of the river. That was one good thing about summer, the silence of frozen rivers could get unbearable. Maybe for Eve, though, that summer river rushing would remind her of Blake's watery death.

Nearly lunchtime. He'd put this visit off too long.

When Tasker slammed the car door, Eve stood up in the vegetable patch, startled, her hands clutching weeds. Even from the distance he could sense her pain, her jaw hanging suspended, her dazed eyes too large with their dark rings, her straight hair dragging down the sides of her face accentuating old acne scars, a homeliness he'd never noticed before. Incredibly sad. She slumped over to the compost pile, dropped in the stringy greens, and stood staring at them as if she'd forgotten what to do next.

Tasker didn't know how to handle this. He walked over and put his arm around her shoulders, and sensing her tense body, realized how wrong his gesture was. He awkwardly dropped his hand by his side and she kept staring at the ground. Tasker mumbled the sergeant's message. She responded with a nod and then, "Thanks . . . Tea?"

Inside, the black cooking stove stood between a kitchen and sitting room. The kitchen, near the windows and daylight, had red gingham curtain panels drawn tidily across all the shelving. The gaiety of the print and gathers seemed out of place today. The pine table was still cluttered with dishes and crumbs from breakfast. On the other side of the stove and away from the light was the sitting room, dark, heavy with bookshelves, Eve's piano, a green chair and horsehair sofa. The sofa Tasker had helped Blake onto only two nights ago.

Tasker tried to think of something to say while the tea brewed.

Eve scrubbed her hands at the sink and then stood slouched, her hip leaning against the counter, her arms hanging at her sides.

She asked if he liked milk and honey in his, and then she kept on talking, no eye contact. "I haven't seen him since baseball. He was up and gone at dawn in the camper, saying he was going fishing away from the derby. His note said he'd be back in the afternoon." She sighed, the sound coming from listless depths. There was a short pause and then she added, her voice low, "It seems random . . ."

"Who's got your kids?" Tasker asked. He couldn't think what else to say, still standing awkwardly in front of the stove.

"The twins are sleeping and Jessica's in her room. She hasn't said a word" – Eve paused. "It's the second . . . for her."

Tasker remembered part of that story – Jessica's mother had dropped out on Granville Street in Vancouver. Eve was her younger sister, a lot younger. Jessica's mother sent Eve postcards now and then from remote places in Asia . . . maybe it was islands in the South Pacific . . . as she drifted farther and farther away. Tasker once heard the postmaster make a big thing of it: "Eve, you've got a stamp from Katmandu." Jessica would have been six when her mother left.

Eve was saying, "You know, my last talk with him was an argument." She shook her head and turned around to pour the tea into mugs. Tasker sat down at the table and shoved away a bowl of cold porridge to make room.

"I've been worried about Jessica," Eve continued, her voice hushed. "She lost the twins in the bush and ended up slapping Sheila. They were up fencing. He won't talk about it, so we argue . . ."

Eve dropped down beside Tasker, leaving the tea on the counter, and said, staring at the table top, "His parents aren't coming. They never liked me, approved of me . . . wouldn't even come down off the mighty British Properties for our wedding."

Jessica ran into the kitchen with a handful of papers and stopped in front of the stove. She stared wildly at Tasker, her face white and tear-stained, her hair unbrushed, and she lifted the lid of the stove, pushed in the papers and ran back upstairs while the lid clattered back into place.

Eve didn't seem to notice. She said, "We lost two cows last month. He found a hole in the fence up back. He has a lot on his mind."

Tasker stood up and carried the mugs of tea over to the table. Inside his head he kept correcting what Eve said: "He *had* a lot on his mind . . . He *wouldn't* talk about it," and wishing she'd stop making those mistakes in tense.

The stove roared as the paper caught fire and the chimney made familiar sifting noises.

"While he was out fishing, I went berry picking with the twins. We knew a couple of early strawberry patches. He said he wanted one of my pies, so we went picking near the river mouth. We could have been a few feet from him when – just on the lee side of the dunes . . ."

Jessica ran in again, her face even paler, eyes wilder, and rammed wads of paper in the fire. The lid slipped and crashed as she lowered it. She didn't hear Eve ask, "Tea?"

Eve apologized to Tasker and followed her upstairs, each step heavy on the wood.

Tasker took a sip of his tea and listened for the paper to catch. His eyes caught one piece lying on the floor that hadn't made it into the fire. It was a watercolour – a close-up of a face, Howard's face. It looked like him – she'd even caught his smirk.

Tasker suddenly heard, "Oh! Jessica!" in a panicked voice from the second floor. Then the roar. Flames curled around the lid and the whole top of the stove rattled. Tasker could just hear Eve's shocked voice, "What happened!"

Tasker ran upstairs and stopped in Jessica's doorway. Eve and Jessica were on the floor, surrounded by thin artist's sketchbooks, only blank paper remained on the wire coils.

Jessica had pressed her face into Eve's shoulder. Eve looked bewildered and cradled Jessica in her arms.

"Warren, she's burned all her drawings. I'm going to sit here for a while."

One of the twins started to whimper in another room. Tasker mumbled, "I'll stop by later," and backed out the door. Eve stared back at him with a puzzled look in her eyes. That's when Tasker realized he'd been too familiar, running upstairs. Funny, he had to remind himself, he should know to keep his distance; that was his job.

As he coasted down the driveway, Tasker thought about his own sketching. He thought, that's what he'd like to be doing now – losing himself in a puzzle of line and colour. Maybe he could see his way easier through all this if he got into a cross-section, dorsal view, detail of parts . . .

When Tasker was almost at the highway, a coyote loped across the lane in front of his car. He'd want to sketch something simpler than a coyote.

It was a good hour after the lake search returned before Jim teamed up with Tasker and they set out in Tasker's cruiser for the big spruces. One of the good things about assignments in remote towns was the way a trusted local could come along for the ride without anyone asking questions. Jim, navigating from the passenger seat, suggested they turn into an older, back road, not the well-graded one that climbed up to treeline and then down past the mill and around into the Henderson valley. That new road passed by ugly piles of rock left over from the concentrating plant and near the site of the proposed acid-effluent lake. He had to drive it every day, Jim complained, and to make it worse, last year the mine had logged some mature spruce along the roadside for braces in the pit and the remaining stumps still bled sap. He said he tried to avoid that end of the road when he could. Jim accepted harvesting logs in the ordinary way – he'd done plenty of it in his time – but felt uneasy about this job. The crew, brought in from outside, took the giants because they were closer when ordinary black spruce would have done the job. It was a senseless, violent sacrifice.

The older road was rough and Tasker took it slow. He was more than content they avoided the scarred landscape around the mine. Besides, he liked Jim's company, so the pace didn't matter. In fact, going slow because he chose to felt good. They bumped along easy and talked for the good eight kilometres before the road got really bad as it dipped down into the Henderson River valley and the untouched climax forest.

Even though his travels today had been for a sadder mission, Jim said, he took pleasure in them. The country endured with a harsh beauty of its own, despite everything. The lake search had produced nothing but calm water coldly reflecting back grey cloud; the striated white, brown and green of mountainsides; and a golden eagle wheeling through the thermals high overhead, screaming its own land claim. It was spectacular, even though it was commonplace around here. "Not many places in the world you can count on an eagle any day." Jim smiled.

He said he was grateful to whatever quirk of drainage, shelter and soil it was that had created the Henderson valley, harbouring its treasure of spruce and fir, the haunt of thrush and bear and wild orchid. The trees may not be nearly as big as those on the Charlottes or Alaska side, but they were twice as big as any others in the area. And they provided a rich green core to the otherwise grey hard lines of the rugged landscape.

The trees grew along the banks, but where the river emptied into the lake, they were replaced abruptly by sand dunes and brush. It was as if, Jim said, the land, exhausted, simply gave up everything it had to support the big spruces. The only attraction at the sand dunes were dwarf strawberries, in abundance about this time of year.

"I hope you're getting some pleasure from this ride. I am," Jim said as Tasker turned the steering wheel sharply to avoid a big rock. "We all need to lighten up."

Jim's reference to the world outside the forest reminded Tasker of the irritants he'd faced through the morning. "Flint hasn't made my day," he grumbled.

Jim had been there when Tasker made his move, tried to get onto the investigation. Flint had asked, "Any new information?" He was stepping out of the police boat, so Tasker found himself answering into the top of Flint's head.

"Concerns, sir. Some things don't sit right: the commercial net, the moose heads, the dislike some people had of Blake . . ."

The sergeant brushed off Tasker's concerns, "We'll leave spec-ulations in their place for now. Let's concentrate on fact, on objects, on finding the hard edge that made that depressed frac-ture. Let's not make work for ourselves!"

Jim nodded, remembering. "It's not easy, but Flint may have a point." Funny, Jim could say things like that and it didn't feel like criticism.

Sergeant Flint, looking through his notebook, had said, "Someone should check out the Henderson after lunch. I don't want anything thrown back at me. Tasker, that one's for you. There won't be anything there, but we'd better cover all bases."

When Flint said that, Jim spoke up, "I'd like to join Warren," and it felt good.

In the car, Tasker said, "Well, I was as much as told to take a hike. We're going where there's nothing to be found."

But Jim said it just might be productive on the Henderson after all. Out on the lake in the morning, he had this hunch, never voiced to Flint: maybe Blake was in a Zodiac because he'd been up the river. If Blake had planned to fish the lake, he'd likely have taken his bigger freighter canoe. Yes, the more he thought about it, Jim said, the more it made sense. The river was high and milky with runoff, and he'd seen traces of that silt in the unusually calm, clear water of Natasahin Lake yesterday, streaming in a ribbon from the Henderson right up to the narrows. Today, like most days, that silty ribbon was chopped up along the beach and spread out through the lake, but yesterday there were no waves and the course of the current was strong. So if Blake had been on the river when the accident happened, then that current would have carried him just about to where he was found.

Even if there was nothing there, Jim said, it would be a fitting way to spend the afternoon after Blake died, hiking through a place he loved.

The road got rougher, corduroyed and then spongy in parts with runoff mixing black soil into the gravel. Finally it washed right out and Tasker had to pull over.

"Hasn't been a grader down here in a while. We'd better walk."

The sun took the chill off their backs when they stood outside the cruiser. The air was rich with the organic smells of water and soil. Jim said the meltwater from the mountain, seeping through the forest litter and decay, was releasing memories of last summer's warmth. "I guess that's getting a bit too poetic." He laughed.

"Need any bug juice?" Tasker smiled. "Not much poetry in a whining mosquito."

"No, I'm immune." Jim laughed and led the way.

"Or deaf." Tasker laughed too.

Tasker had on tough, RCMP-issue boots that could walk through anything, and he was looking forward to doing just that. Soon he took the lead from Jim.

"Does Sergeant Flint always want minimal fact, that's all?" he asked after a while, feeling the morning's putdown again. "No wonder he's stationed in this backwater."

Jim nodded. "Yes, but it's wise to move cautiously in a small town."

"He's more concerned about covering his backside than protecting townsfolk, *I* think!"

"In a place as small as Tsehki, people are close to events. The police have to move thoughtfully – or people get hurt."

Tasker stopped abruptly. "Hey, someone bottomed out here in the last couple of days." He squatted on his heels to examine the ruts. "I bet it was Ivan Peders. His lugs were foreign like that – Japanese, I think."

"He covers a lot of country. Knows what's going on." Jim was a little breathless.

They started walking again, but Tasker set a slower pace. Jim kept scanning the forest floor, saying he hoped to see a lingering calypso orchid. He pointed out a patch of pipsissewa, nodding at their saw-toothed leaves. The tiny pink blooms looked delicate, and Jim wondered aloud if their frailty wasn't spreading out from the forest, even into the way of life in Tsehki itself. Maybe he should speak to his friends in Whitehorse, speak to the Commissioner in defence of all this, instead of keeping mostly to himself, leaving it to others. "It's getting serious," Jim said and smiled. "Not just romance. Now Blake is gone, the wilderness has lost a real crusader. But whether you leave everything be, or struggle to keep it as it was, you lose something either way in the end."

After a long stretch of hard walking, Jim stopped. "Let's take a rest," he said and leaned up against a tree trunk, breathing heavily. "I never told you about Blake's and my trip down Natasahin Lake five years ago. Remembering the good things about him – the value of all this – brings that story to mind." Jim looked at Tasker with the intense, thinking look in his dark eyes that Tasker knew so well. It meant a good story coming. "One I never told before," Jim said, his breathing easier now.

Tasker propped his arm on the other side of the trunk and smiled, ready for the rest and the story.

"Five years ago this fall, Blake and I worked together bringing in the buoys and channel markers on all these lakes before ice-up. A friend had the contract with the coast guard, but he died over the summer and his widow asked me to cover because she needed the last cheque, she said. Blake offered to help and I could sure use another pair of hands. We borrowed a wide, open riverboat from her because the buoys were big – it was late in the season and we had to round them up all at once.

"Well, the winds blew up when we were at the far end of Natasahin Lake. It was dangerous – that shallow hull with the big swells and the ice-cold spray. In fact, the ice must've formed in our wake because kids were skating on Whitney Lake next day – you know, black ice where you chase fish below as you skate above them. Blake and I pulled the last marker from Maltby Inlet and both got drenched – hair, jackets, belts, everything. We knew if we tried to make it back across the lake without warming up and drying out some we'd be in trouble. So we beached for a cup of tea and a change before ploughing across the open water to Tsehki. Blake started a fire and I hung the pot. It was on that tongue of scrub lowland this side of Watson Ridge.

"We were sitting on the smoky side to catch all the warmth we could when a large, white owl landed on a stump on the other side of the fire, ruffled out its feathers and stared at us. It was like the big, barrel-shaped kind – you know, a snowy owl. Except it wasn't quite a snowy owl.

"Blake started talking to it, telling it how cold we were and how we'd be lucky to get back home alive. I was surprised, it was so out of character for Blake. The bird seemed to listen. I didn't realize how scared Blake was by our trip, but he sure told the owl all about it. When we finished our tea, I stood up but that owl didn't fly away. Blake kept talking to it – about how many tourists are lost each summer on these lakes – and I said we had to get going, night was coming. Blake kept right on with the owl; he told the story of that Olympic swimmer in the wetsuit going down two years ago, while I kicked sand onto the coals. Finally I had to lead Blake to the boat – it was starting to freeze rain. As we pushed off, Blake huddled into the bow, but then he sat upright and said, 'Look!'

"I twisted around. The owl had dropped down from its stump and was sitting on the sand where the fire had been, still looking at us. It was ruffling up its feathers again and settling down to soak in all the warmth of our coals. Blake called back, 'Have a warm night, my friend.'

"Blake and I couldn't talk until we landed in Tsehki because the wind and the bashing of the boat on the swells drowned everything out. It was a bad ride – a couple of times the waves swung us sideways and we took on water. Once the motor even conked out. But we were lucky.

"When we were back safely in the Grizzly Den and warming up Blake said, 'You know, Native people have stories of visits by animal spirits in times of trouble – wolves, raven, lynx. They say you can tell a spirit because it sits on the other side of the fire from you, in the smoke. So now I have my story – in the same genre.' He had real wonder in his voice.

"Since he felt it was his story, I never told it until now. The funny thing is, I never heard him tell anyone else either. We both sort of respected it – it was a nice, unspoken connection between us and that day on the wild water."

Jim stepped forward from the trunk and started to walk again. After a while he said, "Blake was usually opinioned, not the kind to get caught up with wonder . . . it's sure something he died on the lake in the end."

"Ivan Peders told me he'd seen Blake cleaning large catches of fish, carrying around loads of fresh meat in the back of his pickup off season. Says he poached," Tasker said.

Jim stopped again at the butt of a tree, about a metre in diameter, one of the biggest. "Yes, he poached now and then, fish mostly."

"What?"

"He had a tough time making ends meet. A lot of mouths to feed." Jim shrugged. It was a lame excuse and he obviously knew it.

"But that's opposite to what he preached, all his talk about conservation and saving the forest."

Jim looked at the trickles of black earth on the ground. He didn't say anything, probably knew Tasker wouldn't accept just any explanation.

"No wonder the chief and Howard didn't trust him. Jerk!" Tasker muttered. "Ivan Peders thought he was a hypocrite and he was. What about Eve?"

"He told her he got road kills and confiscations from the game warden. In fact, he did get most of his red meat that way

– he poached very little, just fish. Netting isn't very productive since there are no migratory fish here like salmon. Netting lake trout or even grayling is almost as sporting as rod and reel." Then Jim added, "Don't be too tough on Blake. There's another story there, but I don't know it all. I think his family in Vancouver cut him out entirely when he married Eve. He could talk a good line about environmental homesteading, but his lifestyle had always been subsidized. Poor little rich boy, sort of. When Eve got pregnant with the twins, he bottomed out – started drinking more, lost much of the humour and charm he'd had, got really judgmental with his opinions. People say he was unfaithful, even, to Eve." Jim started walking again slowly. "A good woman like Eve. Something like that happened when I was a kid in Cleveland. My father found out my mother fooled around with his partner and the breadman and the clerk in the dry-goods store. I remember I didn't feel angry so much at her as I did at him. He'd never let grass grow under his feet before, but he let this happen without a fight, sitting in his armchair, listening to the ballgame on the radio, drinking beer. He was about the same age as Blake."

Jim let his point drift away and Tasker didn't want to push it. He didn't see the connections. The story about the owl was good, but not this one.

After a stretch of quiet, Jim stopped walking again. They'd come to the heart of the big spruces and he said he wanted to accustom his eyes to the pale green light of the climax forest. It always felt like a sanctuary, he said, even at this time of year when the swish of high water intruded. Following the sound of the river, they walked through trees so tall the lower boughs had broken off for lack of sun. It was something, Jim marvelled, to walk in forest in these parts and not scratch against lower branches. Eventually the forest opened up around huge moss-covered deadfalls into a flat area of new lime green deciduous growth.

At the edge of the river, the high water was eating away part of the gravel bar. And there were Blake McIntyre's leather boots. On the bank, beside an elbow snag. Placed there, together, standing upright. Jim clearly wasn't surprised. He said he could see Blake taking them off to wade in and stretch out his net from the snag to – yes, there was a stake driven into the clean gravel of the riverbed a net length out and across the mouth of a deeper pool. It would have been an aching-cold wade but quick. The boots were quality leather and new.

Tasker held up his hand to stop Jim from touching them. He took out his notebook and pencil and started to take notes, walking around, looking up the river and down. But there was really nothing to write down except finding the boots neatly placed on the riverbank.

"I'll go back and radio in," Jim offered.

"Wait, I'll finish it off first."

Tasker pulled a plastic evidence bag out of his breast pocket, lifted the boots one at a time by the laces and carefully lowered them into the bag. He wrote his name and the date on the label – he'd have to add the occurrence number back at the station. He said, "We'll walk downstream to the mouth of the river. After, we'll check upstream. Shouldn't take long."

Jim followed Tasker, who carefully carried the plastic bag. The boots were heavy, dead weight. Jim looked worried and mumbled that he hoped they wouldn't find anything more.

They covered the downstream part quickly and found nothing, just pristine grayling habitat, but upstream was different. There they came across a new tent on a platform about a hundred metres from where the boots had been. Jim figured it must be for the band watchman. The Natives had talked about setting up a "watch" to protect Kakhteyi, he said.

Tasker threw up the canvas flap. On the left stretched a cot with a blanket, a swatch of leather partly beaded, and little tins of beads and quills lined up along the pillow. On the other side stood a table with a camp stove, a pot for tea, an ashtray and, under it, a large locked trunk. In the corner, a radio, batteries and a coil of electrical cord spilled onto the plywood platform.

"Yes?" they heard behind them. Larissa was walking up with a backpack, her strong thumbs locked under the shoulder straps. She looked briefly at Jim, then at the evidence bag sagging in the shape of Blake's boots, and then her eyes settled on Tasker's.

Tasker, abashed, knowing he was literally red in the face, stuttered, "Can I help with that?"

Larissa said, "No," swung off the pack at the door of the tent and, standing on tiptoe, yanked down the door flap. Tasker noticed her jeans were short in the leg.

"Are you watchman?" he asked.

She nodded her head and lifted one elbow up so her hand lazily touched the back of her neck at the top of her braid. The fringes on her jacket swayed. "For now. The chief offered me use of the tent for keeping watch." Larissa's voice was naturally low, and it made her sound assured.

"Were you here Saturday morning?" Tasker asked.

"I've been here all week." She pulled a loose twig from her hair and flicked it behind her back with her thumb.

"Anyone else here Saturday?"

"Howard and Jessica." She let her arms down heavily and Tasker looked at the fringes settle along the line across her breasts. "I only saw Howard."

"What was he doing here, do you know?"

"Out looking for wood with the grain he likes for carving. He said Jessica was with him to learn some sketching tips but she was busy somewhere deeper in the forest." Larissa's eyes found

Tasker's, raised them and held them. "It's something good when one person shares a skill with another."

Again Tasker noticed the fine lines cupping her eyes. They made her look tired, but this time he read something else there too. Was it fear? She wasn't acting scared; in fact, she had volunteered lots of information. Tasker looked at the ground and said, formally, "Did you see anyone else here Saturday morning?"

"No."

Tasker thought of Blake's body in that net. Then, it suddenly didn't make sense. There was no way Blake could accidentally fall, severely injure himself and get all tied up like that in a net under his boat, fishing up here by himself.

He felt a rush in his gut – everything else felt very still. "No one else?"

Larissa closed her eyes slowly and opened them again. "Not Saturday, not here." Tasker tried to decide if she was lying or not. He was uncertain, the slowness of her eye movement could've been weariness . . .

"We'd better carry on, Jim," Tasker said, trying to sound casual. "Check out the other parking area by the mine road. It's late."

Jim cleared his throat and followed. He was making twitching movements with his head and the colour had gone from his face. He was clearly fussed.

When they were out of Larissa's hearing, Jim muttered, "Sometimes it's better not to draw conclusions. Not to try too much, too quickly. Things are better left be . . ."

"Hey, Jim" – Tasker found his voice rising – "we can't just ignore what we've seen."

Jim was staring dully ahead. "I know," he said. "But everything's changing, isn't it, and I don't like what I see. There's no time to work things out between folks. That's all."

For Tasker, Jim might as well have said it would be better if he just drove back to Whitehorse.

Tasker looked his old friend up and down. Jim was staring at the ground ahead of him, his shoulders and arms hanging without tone down to his thin, blue-veined hands. His profile looked pinched, with his roman nose more hooked than usual and deep lines sinking into his cheek. Jim was looking old and acting old. Part of Tasker felt sorry for him, for the crushing conservatism of his old age. But part wanted to be more like him.

Tasker finished his third solid meal in hospital and actually liked it. Institutional food, nothing fancy – Swiss steak, mashed potatoes, overcooked Brussels sprouts, canned pineapple slices – but it didn't leave him dizzy with the effort of sitting up to eat. He was starting to feel better, but he wasn't fooling himself; he wouldn't be better until he was sitting at the bar of a quiet little establishment eating chicken wings with a spicy, double diablo sauce and sipping a smooth single malt, maybe Macallan. There was a combination that would electrify his purist friends, of both the chicken-wing and the single-malt persuasion – but he loved it.

He could shuffle to the toilet alone now, and draw the curtains down the sides of his bed, past the bedside table anyway, to give himself some privacy when he slept. He didn't mind people hearing him snore, but the idea of someone watching his slack face made him worry he was beginning to look old. He'd ordered a phone, at his own expense, but it wasn't hooked up yet.

His partner from the stakeout had come to visit. She said they figured Tasker was hit with a semi-automatic Remington, SSG shot, the kind of rifle found in every farmer's barn in the province. She also reported they had a few leads on that white camper – first letter and last digit on the licence plate. The gun was going to be harder to trace, though, probably sawed off. They'd detained the boy on a B and E charge, figuring he knew more than he was saying.

The corporal brought the daily newspaper to show Tasker. She pointed out a printed correction – the games editor was apologizing for a misprint on the last chess problem, checkmate in four moves not five. The corporal joked, suggested he sue the paper for his injury, and that made Tasker want to laugh – he had to be getting better.

The newspaper front page had a detailed account of the shooting. The city was outraged a cop was hit, and door-to-door searches in the suburbs and surrounding industrial parks were still going on. Tasker read it all, said it was nice to be appreciated, and then his eye caught something else. In the "News In Brief" column there was a note about the takeover of an historic hotel near the Yukon–B.C. border. Land claims again – maybe his old Grizzly Den friends weren't buying the government's latest promises, Tasker thought.

The corporal stood up to leave and Tasker knew he'd stopped giving his visitor the attention he should. When the young woman slipped Tasker a brown bag with a bottle of Glenfarclas "from all of us." Tasker said, "Thanks. Things are looking up now."

Later, when he was alone and had wrung the newspaper dry of news, he remembered the feeling of being ambitious and eager – and getting his report ignored by a jaded old sergeant. He hoped he hadn't left his corporal with that feeling. He remembered walking into the police station with Jim, Blake's boots and the story of their trip to the big spruces. Flint was behind his desk, emptying a brown paper bag onto the desktop. Shorty, bent over beside him, was picking through the contents.

It had been a quiet ride back to town. Tasker and Jim had had time to build back some excitement about their find. "Hey, look what we stumbled on!" Tasker called out, waving the bag with Blake's boots.

But Flint and Shorty looked up only briefly from the desk. Flint said, "Kay was by, Jim, and wants you to drive with her out to Eve's. She's going to stay there for a while."

Jim was immediately heading for the door.

"She's waiting at your place." Flint called after, "Tell her thanks too. She gets my first big catch."

Tasker sensed, with Jim gone, his discovery wasn't going to get much attention. He walked closer to the desk to see what was absorbing the men. He found they were sorting a collection of feathers – mostly grouse and ptarmigan, but there were a few vibrant red and yellow songbird primaries and an iridescent magpie tail there too. They were beautiful, was his first thought, but they were for making fish flies and had nothing to do with police business at all.

Tasker started telling his story quickly, speeding in a kind of nervous reaction, to keep Flint from cutting him off. "We found Blake's boots by the river where he took them off to set his net. And we found the stake the net was hooked on. But the water is too shallow there, the banks too low, for anyone to get a severe head injury, snagged and accidentally drowned all by themselves. Not easily anyway."

Shorty's head snapped right up, interested, but Flint's didn't. Shorty looked across at Flint, then crouched over again, busy with the feathers.

Flint braced his hands on the desk, admiring the collection laid out under his arms. He said pleasantly, still looking at his feathers, "And who was in the forest Saturday morning?"

"We saw the girl, Larissa. She said she was there and so was Howard Daniel and Jessica Weiss, Blake McIntyre's niece."

Flint, his voice less pleasant now, said, "We've gone and put Eve through a formal autopsy. We'll wait until we get results from that. Coroners usually have a good idea what kind of object makes a specific fracture." He looked wearily at Tasker. "Log in the boots and secure them in the evidence locker. Then type up a report of what you saw on your walk. That's all we have to do; anything more is unwarranted. Homicides don't come our way often. It's going to be an accident."

Tasker lay back heavily into the depths of the Regina hospital pillow. That was a conversation, he thought, that shouldn't have made him as angry as it had. But he'd always had a problem when he had a story to tell and was put off.

Tasker unwound the foil on the Glenfarclas cap, pulled the cork and sniffed the vapours. He could smell the peat and maybe the sherry from the Spanish oak casks, but the harshness of the alcohol was too much. He pushed the cork back in and decided to wait until his stomach was ready for diablo chicken wings too.

8. TSEHKI JUNCTION. June 1978

While the sergeant occupied himself with his fly feathers, Tasker added the occurrence number to the label on the evidence bag and started typing up his report. The office was quiet and soon pleasantly filled with the smell of freshly brewed coffee. Shorty carried in two mugs just as the phone rang.

Sergeant Flint lay down a partially tied trout fly to answer it. "Yes . . . Yes . . . I'll send Tasker over right away. I'm just back from a difficult talk with Eve." In the same movement of hanging up the phone, his hands shifted back to the hook and spool of thread. Flint said, "There's a job for you and not me. Get over to Freeman Straun's office. He had a break-in at his clinic last night. You can leave typing up that report until later."

Tasker grabbed his notebook, field cap and the fresh mug of coffee.

He was at the door when Sergeant Flint called, "Don't get too eager. It's best to take it easy with Freeman."

Dr. Straun was waiting for Tasker at the door of his clinic, a trailer unit that stood in front of a two-storey clapboard house and beside the country hospital. All three buildings backed onto the beach along the main street of town. The hospital had been moved in on a couple of flatbeds and sat on a permanent foundation. It could be activated as an emergency facility, surgery, three-bed ward, and morgue (as it had been the night before), but it usually waited empty, locked up. The Red Cross sign hung over the smaller, office trailer unit. Potted plants were set out on the dirt along the trailer wall towards the hospital, and with fireweed blooming in between, the town's medical facilities looked almost welcoming.

Dr. Straun stood squinting in a pale grey gentleman's smoking jacket that sagged over baggy flannel pants. His hands were pushing down the front pockets.

He opened the clinic door for Tasker. "It's not robbery, I see, it's only vandalism," he mumbled and then made a guttural sound that was a mix of laugh and sob. Tasker stepped into the cold, disinfectant-smelling trailer.

Inside, the floor of the small waiting area was littered with papers. A drawer of the filing cabinet hung open, and patient files were strewn everywhere. The reception desk, however, seemed untouched, as did the side table with copies of *The Angler*, *Steelhead News* and *The American Fisherman* magazines neatly displayed in a fan across the top.

"Take me through so I can get an overview, please," Tasker said and took off his hat. The ceiling was low, and the floor, as he walked, had a thin, insubstantial sound to it. What he expected in a trailer.

The dead, disinfectant smell was even stronger in the hallway. Dr. Straun, with another suppressed grunt, directed Tasker to the examining room first.

The paper for covering the examining table was unrolled all over the furniture and floor, ripped and scuffed with shoe prints. Prints with circles on the sole. Dumped on the paper were disposable plastic gloves, microscope slides, a metal clamp-like tool and blobs of clear ointment or jelly. Untouched, on the shelves behind, lay assorted stethoscopes, tongue depressors and other instruments that Tasker recognized for peering into mouths and ears and eyes. He wondered what random chance had kept them from being flung around too.

Farther down the hall, in the bathroom, the floor was covered in broken glass from bottles that had mostly rested on a tray on the back of the toilet.

In the small lab beside the bathroom, nothing was touched, and Tasker saw that it would have been easy to smash into the glass cupboard displaying its wide range of drugs and samples.

Across the hall from the examining room, in the doctor's personal office, textbooks were pulled from the shelves and pages ripped. The top of Dr. Straun's desk had been swept clean of photos, curios, and ashtrays, which lay smashed altogether on the floor.

Dr. Straun made no sensible comment through the tour, but kept up continual guttural rumbles of contempt and anger.

Tasker suggested, "Let's step outside and talk about this."

"What's there to talk about?"

"We should establish how they got in, when it happened and who are the most likely suspects."

"Through that back door." The doctor pointed to a door beside the filing cabinet and behind the reception desk. "It was ajar – they could have used a credit card."

Dr. Straun's voice was forceful, but his eyes weren't. They looked washed out and reflected back a flat gaze to Tasker. The doctor seemed small, caved in under the frame of his wide shoulders.

"It could have been anytime since Friday. My nurse went home at five, and I gave her Saturday off for the fishing derby. I haven't been in since Friday either."

"You didn't come in briefly before or after examining Blake next door?" Tasker asked.

"No, everything I need for that kind of examination is in the basement over there. Last time I was in here was about 4:00 p.m. Friday."

Tasker pulled out his notebook and started to write.

"Put your scribbling away," the doctor grunted, jamming his hands deeper into his pockets. "I'm going to clean up and have done with it."

"Do you know who did it?"

"Someone with no respect –" His voice cracked.

Tasker wondered if Straun was going to get difficult now. He said, "It should be looked into, sir."

"You have until six to look for whatever you want here. I'll have my nurse come in after dinner to clean up for Monday's clinic." Dr. Straun shook his head. "I won't press charges. I don't want to know who did this." He twisted around, took his hands out of his smoking-jacket pockets, pulling out a pair of sunglasses, and went to let himself out the back door. Tasker noticed it took him several tries to grasp the doorknob, and when he did, Dr. Straun put on the sunglasses as he stepped outside.

Tasker went out the front to his car and radioed to update Sergeant Flint. Since the doctor wasn't going to press charges, he'd need Flint to be part of a decision to carry any investigation past dinner. Then he returned to the office and strode over to examine the filing cabinet. The top drawer, ajar, was labelled A – M; the bottom drawer, N – Z, was empty. He circled around the files on the floor and saw they were from both drawers – "Johnny, Angie"; "Johnny, Joseph"; "Peters, Joseph" . . . It would take time to figure out who or what was missing, if anything. He made a note to ask the nurse to do that in her clean-up.

In the examining room Tasker looked closely at the footprints on the floor. None was complete, but he could see they weren't large – likely a kid's. Definitely sports shoes. And only one pair.

A bang on the outside door brought Tasker back to the waiting room. He found Howard in the doorway, carrying the skinny, gangly boy who'd been with Reggie at the ball diamond.

The boy was pale and lay limp across Howard's chest with a bloody leg – a twisted, rusty rod jutted out from below his knee through a tear in his jeans. It was one of those reinforcing rods at least a centimetre thick, with a solid core and coiled ribs like a screw. Tasker felt sick to his stomach and forced his eyes away from the injury. He stared into the boy's impassive face – there was something about his expression: all the mischief gone. Reggie lurked behind, down the path.

"We need the doctor," Howard said.

Sergeant Flint's cruiser drew up behind.

Tasker said, "Sit down while I get him. He's out back."

Tasker turned for the rear door, stepping around the files, relieved to be heading for air, shoving away thoughts of cold iron screwing into hot bone . . .

As he wrenched the door open, Tasker heard Sergeant Flint speaking from the waiting-room front door. "Howard, take him right across to surgery. I'll get Freeman, Corporal, and the hospital key." Sergeant Flint strode past Tasker and pushed the back door out to the doctor's house.

Tasker stood collecting himself while Howard carried the boy back down the walkway to the road. As he turned right to the hospital, Tasker looked again at the back of the boy's head, the stoic way he held his neck stiff, and his limp legs. It likely happened some time ago, Tasker thought. The pain would be unbelievable. Then he noticed, not really looking, that the soles of the boy's sneakers were worn to a shine.

Tasker heard Sergeant Flint's voice out back. "Isabel's boy's inside with a hunk of metal in his leg, Freeman, just under the kneecap. I've sent them across to surgery."

Then he heard Dr. Straun reply, "Tell them to go to Whitehorse. The office is closed."

"He's in pain. You'd better take a look."

"No."

"Whitehorse is two hours away!" Sergeant Flint was shouting now. "This kid has lost blood. It happened some time ago from what I can see."

"I am not available."

There was a long silence and then Sergeant Flint was back with Tasker. "Have a quick look around and then leave it," he snapped. "He can clean up himself. I'll be back in a couple of hours. You'll have to cover the office until I get back – record it a 'call out.' Sorry to cut into your leave, but I'd better do this run personally."

Sergeant Flint strode back to his cruiser without another word, coasted down to the hospital, and in moments his siren was screaming north out of town, with the boy in the passenger seat beside him.

Tasker walked to the rear door of the trailer and looked out past Dr. Straun's dark Buick to his house. The doctor was nowhere to be seen. Tasker grabbed the door handle and pulled the trailer door hard shut. The cheap sheet metal frame shook and the roof seemed to shift overhead. Tasker was shocked, his insides nagging. Why did Flint let Straun get away with it?

Tasker left Tsehki late Sunday evening after Flint got back. His reports on the break-in and the circumstances of finding Blake's boots had long been typed up. There was no message from Ida waiting when he got into the Whitehorse barracks, not that he liked to admit he cared, but he did. He visited his mother and told her the news from Tsehki. She listened to his story with vacant eyes, and when he'd finished, passed him a letter from her sister in Vancouver inviting her to move down to share an apartment. The best Tasker could make out, his mother was interested, and so he offered to write and find out more about it.

He decided not to write Ida too, although he had the time, and tried to kill his bitterness by following the news from Tsehki Junction on local radio. It gave him some satisfaction to hear that Blake McIntyre's autopsy pointed to murder. To be more precise, the coroner said homicide had to be presumed until it was ruled out. Slivers of bark were found in Blake's skin as if he'd been clubbed from the horizontal swing of a stick or he'd been travelling at high speed and hit himself on an overhang. The report said Blake had taken two blows to the head about an hour before he drowned, but the second one, the depressed fracture, was the serious one. He might've died of the depressed fracture even if he'd got hit on a neurosurgeon's doorstep. Sergeant Flint apparently found a club that likely did the job by the river in Kakhteyi forest. There were no obvious overhangs along the river. Tasker didn't want credit for his little part in the case, but he found it interesting that Flint took it all for himself. Flint was well spoken in the interviews, Tasker thought; he even handled himself with flourish.

Tasker listened to eulogies broadcast from environmentalists in Vancouver and Ottawa and a chief in Alaska. All of them were using Blake's murder to elbow in a few points for their causes – but knowing Blake, he wouldn't mind.

When Tasker reported for duty at dawn Wednesday, he was dispatched right back down to Tsehki again. On the drive, the radio reported that Flint had slapped Howard Daniel with the murder charge. Tasker wondered what exactly Flint had on him.

It was late morning when he rolled into Tsehki. Every car in town, it seemed, was parked at the local Anglican church – Tasker had missed the start of the memorial service. There was no point walking in late, so he headed for the detachment kitchen and grabbed a frypan and got two eggs from the fridge. Good plain food, his mother's remedy for everything.

He cracked an egg and watched the white slither across the black bottom of the pan and up one side. The white spread quickly and the yolk broke on its own. Tasker guessed Shorty wouldn't pay the cost of fresh local eggs and settled for a case trucked in from Edmonton.

He opened the cupboard and took down a coffee mug. The perking coffee cut the smell of Pine-Sol and was warming up the kitchen some. Things were getting better already – at least in small detachments, you could raid the kitchen.

Tasker cracked a second egg as the phone rang. He turned down the heat before he picked up the receiver, wanting his eggs just crispy round the edges.

Tasker recognized the voice. "Warren, it's Eve." She sounded miles away.

"Yes. How are you?" Why was she calling? It must be just after the memorial service . . .

"Warren, I'm glad you're the one I got. Jim told me you'd be there."

He mumbled an embarrassed apology about not getting to the church.

"Don't worry. I understand," she replied. "What matters to me is – they arrested Howard."

"Yeah. I heard over the radio." Tasker was cautious.

"I can't believe Howard did it. And Jessica keeps saying he's innocent."

"That's right, Jessica was there with Howard on Saturday, wasn't she?"

"Yes, sketching with Howard. She's got some story that she shoved Blake, he fell towards Howard's collection of wood and she ran away." Eve paused and then said huskily, "She's in rough shape. She says it's all her fault."

"Have you talked to Sergeant Flint about this?"

"Yes. Jessica and Howard were separated several times in the forest, including when Jessica pushed Blake, and the sergeant figures Howard could've fought with Blake after she ran away, knocked him out and set it up to look like a drowning while Jessica was off deeper in the forest."

"Well, if she only pushed him once, maybe she didn't cause the more serious injury. One injury was just a surface cut, I remember. And he did die drowning – he was unconscious when he went into the water. Tell her that." Tasker could smell his eggs.

"But it's not right – for the Daniel family. There's no way Howard would ever do such a cold-blooded thing, deliberately put an unconscious man, a man he knew to be a husband and a father, where he'd drown. I don't believe it for one moment."

Eve had put her finger on something that didn't sit right with Tasker either. The RCMP had already taken its part in messing up the life of Howard's family – the business with his brother Gary. Then he thought of the evidence . . . "But they've got the murder weapon and he must be able to connect Howard with it."

"Of course. He was out there collecting and stacking the wood to carve. Some thread from Howard's jacket was on it. So what?" She paused and then said forcefully, "Warren, I want the right person found. Howard – it's ridiculous – and it's destroying Jessica. How could Blake be dragged underwater down the length of that river, anyway. It's got too many shallow sections between the deeper pools. You tell that to Sergeant Flint for me?"

Shorty walked into the kitchen, coughing, and glared at Tasker. He switched off the stove and flapped the eggs onto a plate. His hair was slicked back and he wore a shirt, sweater and tie – probably just back from church himself. He reached up behind the door, took down his apron and started to pull it on.

Tasker watched, not hungry any more, finding himself promising Eve he'd see what he could do, agreeing to visit Howard in jail.

He hung up and reached for his coffee.

Shorty snapped, "Don't forget to clean up. I got enough to do," as he disappeared into the next room. He returned carrying a pack of cold cuts and a loaf of bread. He didn't look at Tasker and had a grim set to his jaw. As he was in no hurry and wanted to keep good relations with the cook, Tasker hung around to let him begin the conversation again.

Shorty started to deal out slices of bread on the countertop and then stopped to go back to the fridge. Tasker thought he'd help and carried on laying down a few more sandwich pairs.

As he worked, Tasker's mind reviewed who was on the scene in the forest Saturday morning. Howard and Jessica had been there – no one was denying that. So was Larissa, and maybe Ivan Peders too, if the tire tracks he'd found told the story. Tasker had made some enquiries about the latter two in Whitehorse over the last couple of days, just to satisfy his curiosity.

Peders had no record. When Tasker checked into his employment, he found he had a blasting permit. The blasting inspector said he'd never been reported or suspended. In fact he was the best in the territory. He could estimate everything for his contracts instantly, on site, in his head – volume of rock, size of charge to move it, safe distance – accurate to the second decimal point. He'd dropped into the Whitehorse office early last Tuesday on his way to a job west of Dawson City to report a length of primer missing or misplaced from the Tsehki job. No other blasters reported little things like that. Only Peders.

Larissa Stanley, however, had been on probation and spent time in the Juvenile Detention Centre. She'd lived in Tsehki as a kid, but Tasker could conjure only a sketchy memory of her parents. Her father was grossly fat, a miner who came up from Toronto or Hamilton, sometimes drove a truck. Her mother was a part-time waitress in the hotel coffee shop. They kept going on binges, and when she was five or six, Larissa was removed to a receiving home, then placed in a group home in Whitehorse. Her mother didn't stand up to the father. Larissa came back once or twice, but that never worked out for long. Finally there were charges of promiscuity and she ended up on probation and even spent time in the Detention Centre. While she was there she was accused of lifting other people's personal things. The list was something – a damaged locket, an old signet ring, letters, a grandmother's diary, family portraits: all hoarded in a shoebox under her bed. At sixteen, she was let out and lived in Whitehorse. No record after that, only picked up a few times for suspected soliciting. No convictions. No reason to link her to serious crime.

Shorty said, "The problem with Yukoners, they're all out for themselves. Never think of the other guy."

Tasker let that sit before he asked, "Why would a kid in a detention centre steal trinkets, personal mementos, and then hide them under her bed?"

Shorty was at the sink now. "Probably for the love in 'em. You know, poets write feelings into things like that. You read poetry, eh?"

Tasker remembered from school, "Symbolism?" and laughed. He swiped two slices of bread, made a sandwich with his eggs and took a bite. "Ever know Larissa Stanley?"

"Smart girl. Bad spell for a while at Bear Creek Detention Centre," Shorty replied. He was in a better mood now. "Gimme a minute while I get the mayo."

Tasker took another bite – it tasted leathery. "You worked at Bear Creek?"

Shorty nodded, sat down and unscrewed the mayonnaise lid. "Medical problems, I think."

"Any idea what?" Tasker watched the deft back-and-forth twist of Shorty's wrist as he spread the mayonnaise with a knife.

"She had bad problems gettin' to sleep — that was part of it. Kept herself awake so she wouldn't have to face night terrors. She needed to see a psycho doctor — you know the kind. There was woman's stuff too. Maybe VD. Couldn't have been that bad 'cause, once out, she got herself laid non-stop. Lots of customers, a pretty thing like that. I'd see her in the Whitehorse Laundromat warmin' her hands on winter nights. Then the layin' around, it stopped for a while."

"Know why?"

"Only that she finally came back to Tsehki after her parents died in that accident. Ivan Peders gave her the lift back down in the first place, I think. She cleaned up her life overnight. Just like that. Don't see her with him much any more, though. On her own a lot now, I guess. And I saw her with a miner at the bar the other night and it looked to me she was back to her old tricks."

"What made her get into laying around so young, I wonder?"

"I figure she was just workin' out the Detention Centre — the kids hated it there, most came out angry, hatin' even themselves. Only place I cooked as bad as that was the residential school. The government hired the teachers and the Church hired the rest. Came to be that servin' two masters was more important than servin' the kids. They finally realized the whole thing was bad and closed the mission down."

Tasker stood up. He said out loud, but not to Shorty in particular, "People do things for reasons. Maybe Eve's right. There's no motive. And how the hell did Blake get out onto the lake riding under that boat?"

"I'd agree there's no motive, if you're talkin' about Howard.

But it's not my business. Makin' soup is," Shorty said. "Want an apron?"

Tasker moved towards the door. "There has to be a motive. Someone has it." His thoughts weren't slipping into gear, it was like trying to accelerate in neutral. "Don't count me in the supper pot. I think I'll look into the prison when I'm finished with my orders for the day. Howard said something about boats flipping easy along the shore."

"OK," Shorty muttered. "But don't come in here snackin' again if you're goin' to leave it half-finished. I got budgets, you know."

Tasker turned and nodded to thank Shorty before he shut the kitchen door behind him. He was trying to be concerned about what Shorty had to say, but he was thinking how he was getting himself deeper in, but still with no authority. He'd like to be able to show Flint that a little effort digging around the corners of his case was worth while. He'd already decided Howard was innocent – and he knew that wouldn't necessarily help.

The other question bothering him was, what, if anything, did the doctor's clinic break-in have to do with this?

Yukon Medium Security was a new facility, the inside corridors all lined and sealed with brushed-steel doors that rolled on ball bearings and locked with randomized codes – a long way from the squeaky hinges, echoing halls and rattling keys in old westerns. Tasker had only to adjust to changing air pressures as he penetrated through the security layers towards Howard. It crossed Tasker's mind how odd it was that the inside was so modern, but the outside still looked medieval. There were even glass shards spiking up on the top of the walls, and piles of rock and logs in the yard for hard labour.

Tasker hadn't told Sergeant Flint he was coming here. No point in that. He'd spent all afternoon chasing down a reported B and E at a prospector's cabin – a pile of tanned hides taken, but the dynamite stored in the loft wasn't – and was partway to the jail anyway at quitting time. He just slipped into his civvies and showed up for visiting hour.

Tasker's ears sensed each door seal behind him before the next tracked noiselessly open. The guard murmured that Howard had a small knife for whittling, on the request of the Native Brotherhood, so he had to stay in the cell for Tasker's own protection.

Howard's back was to the door and he didn't acknowledge Tasker's entrance, just sat on his stool whittling a length of one-by-six. No windows. And the room had a stale, smoky smell.

"A mask?" Tasker asked.

Howard startled, turned and then smiled humourlessly. "Thought you were the social worker lady, going to ask me the spiritual significance of this . . ."

"Well, has it got any?" Tasker laughed.

"No," Howard murmured, his eyes taking in Tasker's civvies.

"I'm here on a personal visit." Tasker tried to pick it up. "Eve phoned me, said she was sure you weren't guilty." That came out too loud, considering the guard was still in the room.

Howard started to whittle again, the shavings falling in curls on the hard floor around his workboots. His toes were braced solidly, giving his knees some spring to respond to his knife strokes. And his carving posture, with his head, shoulders and arms all turned to his work, gave his body that powerful, self-contained stance. It was like his presence in the prison was incidental, he could have been anywhere.

"Eve's upset you've been charged . . ." Tasker started again, keeping his voice low this time.

"My lawyer said watch out for undercover cops coaxing me

to talk," Howard interrupted. "I've got no confessions or slip-ups."

Tasker was pissed off. "I came to help," he said, unable to keep the edge out of his voice. "We go back a long way, Howard."

"Yeah, but I didn't ask for your help," Howard answered. "Look, Warren, you may have good intentions, but I've got people working for me and I want to rely on them. I just don't have any reason on earth to trust RCMP."

"They can connect you to the murder weapon, apparently, but there are problems I see with the murder happening upriver." Tasker wasn't going to stop, even though he heard Howard loud and clear.

Howard brushed woodchips from his knee and then pushed his black braid from his shoulder to his back.

"Eve says Jessica's upset." Tasker would try that one.

No response.

"OK." Time for a wild card. "Tell me about Larissa Stanley. Why'd she come back to Tsehki?"

"Maybe she can't get no Whitehorse man."

"She had all the men she wanted there."

"She couldn't keep any."

"Why not?"

"Maybe they like a woman can get their babies."

"She's too young to get into that yet."

Howard didn't answer.

"What about Peders, what she see in him?"

Howard shook his head. "I don't want to know nothing about that one."

"Would Larissa or Peders want to kill Blake?"

Howard shrugged.

"What about Jessica? How'd she feel about all this?"

Howard mumbled, "Best help would be if you get outta

here." Then he turned his back on Tasker and bent farther into his carving.

Tasker looked at the keen knife blade.

"Howard, if you killed Blake in anger, you'd have used your knife, not a stick. Point that out to your fancy lawyer."

As he worked back out through the prison security, Tasker was seething with frustration again. He'd got nowhere and he'd used his own time getting there.

Late that evening, back at the barracks, Tasker dialled the nursing station in Old Crow. It was a spur-of-the-moment decision. Ida answered with her nurse-in-command voice, making her sound her full three years older than Tasker.

"Hey, I missed you this week," he said. "What you up to?"

"The usual." And then he heard her whisper, "A friend from Whitehorse," to someone at the other end.

"Keeping you busy?"

"Yes, mostly short-term hearing loss, a bad winter for ear infections. From what I read, you've had plenty to do," she answered.

"Yes, it's kept me out of trouble."

"It said an arrest's been made." Her voice sounded flat – or maybe it was the interference in their connection.

"Yes, but you'll like this: I don't think they picked the right guy."

"Oh, I see, you didn't make the arrest."

"Not this one." Tasker didn't catch her dig at first, and then decided to ignore it. "You ever heard the Gary Daniel story?"

"Yes. I've sort of forgotten . . . Howard related?"

"Brother."

"That's too bad," she replied and sounded like she meant it.

"If Howard isn't the one, who is?"

"Well, I've just spent the evening running through options. There were three other people in the vicinity at the right time, and Blake's wife was not far away."

"Got a favourite?"

"No – Blake's niece was there with Howard and reported to her aunt she scuffled with Blake, he fell and she ran. That doesn't account for how he got all wrapped up in the net and set adrift. Larissa Stanley, well, she was there in a tent, but says she saw nothing. I think I believe her. Ivan Peders, another local, hasn't been asked, but I found his tire tracks the next day on the road in. I'm going to find more out about them all."

"I've had dealings with some you've mentioned . . . How do you know it's not Howard?"

"I don't but . . . Howard isn't cooperating, mind you. The sergeant down here acted quickly – I guess I want to be convinced we got the right man."

"Sounds like you're playing a one-man police force."

"Thanks, Ida." He had to smile – he liked the pepper in her. The way she was talking, he could picture her, hands on her small hips, head to one side, a little smile on her lips, eyes narrowed and laughing, foot tapping.

"I'd like to see Howard cleared." She paused. "I remember him, always thought he'd go places if he could get his act under control."

"Well, I'd rest easier if I understood how the body got under the boat in the net – the mechanics part – and if we had motive. All we got now is a couple of squabbles between Howard and Blake. Blake argued with everybody."

Ida said, "Excuse me," and talked to someone else in the room again, muffling the phone. Then she said, "Listen, Warren, is there a reason you called?"

"Nothing special."

There was a pause and then she said, "You had some nasty things to say last week . . ."

"Correction – we both did."

"Well, yours are still ringing in my ears . . . and I have to clear the line."

"I'll call another time."

"If you like . . . Goodbye."

"Hey – looks like we both got some fight left."

"You said it." Ida laughed. "OK, call again."

Then she hung up. Tasker knew she'd be laughing on and off for a while yet.

9. TSEHKI JUNCTION. June 1978

It was 10:00 a.m., dull and overcast, when Tasker got the call. He sped to the new mine road and then turned left, past a "Danger Explosives" sign, towards the mine magazine. There were only two pickups parked in the small turning area in front of the explosives storehouse: one was Jim Weatherby's green Chevy and the other had the mine decal on its door. Good, he thought, he'd got there first, before Sergeant Flint.

Tasker sprinted from his car towards the squat, windowless structure. He could see Joseph Peters, the assistant custodian, the one who'd phoned in, crouching tenderly over a prone body just inside the open door. The victim had fallen into the concrete storehouse, so Tasker couldn't make out the condition, the face – but it had to be a man with those workboots. Surely not Jim – Tasker's throat went dry and he ran faster.

Joseph had draped his maintenance jacket over the victim's shoulders, and as he got closer, Tasker saw Joseph stroking a hand. The person, then, was still alive.

When Tasker finally lunged into the dark room, he flinched. It was Jim, unconscious. Tasker felt sick.

Dry, brown blood caked Jim's cheeks and lay thickly congealed along the lines of his forehead and down the side of his nose – all coming from a clotted cut on the right side of his head. Jim's eyes were shut. Unconscious, and still breathing, but not in good shape at all.

Tasker didn't crouch down with Joseph. He didn't want to

touch Jim. He felt shocked, hollow, apart. He shivered and his eyes darted around the dark room. A thick, blunt stick, one end rounded in a burl, lay left of the magazine door. A natural club like the one that killed Blake McIntyre. Shit!

"Called the doctor too?" he whispered to Joseph.

"On his way," Joseph whispered back. "Told me not to move him."

"Seen anyone else?"

Joseph shook his head, "Jim come up an hour ago to replace the lock on the door. When he don't get back, I come looking. When I find him and go down to phone at the gate, the keeper say he seen no one else come this way."

"Anything missing?" Tasker asked, conscious his voice wavered. His eyes scanned the shelves neatly lined with brown boxes, all labelled with the names and addresses of companies, and dates of manufacture. There were also official signs posted: "British Table of Distances," "Permission to Erect a Magazine," "Regulations Governing the Care and Use of Explosives in the Yukon Territory." Rules that didn't help Jim.

Joseph pointed to a clipboard lying on the floor beyond Jim's outstretched left arm.

Tasker deliberately avoided staring at the limp, blue-veined wrist as he picked his way around to the clipboard. It listed inventory, using technical terms and abbreviations he didn't understand. Impatiently, he waved it at Joseph and asked him if anything was missing.

Joseph looked puzzled and said, "I plan to check, as soon as we get Jim taken care of."

Tasker had to get outside. He was claustrophobic. His body twitched, jittery with shock. He said he was going to take a quick look around. Somehow all his training hadn't prepared him to see Jim like this.

He stepped out the door and immediately felt relief, even though the sky threatened rain and the forest had turned a dull green with weather rolling down the mountain. The magazine was a cold, featureless block structure, and for a distance of at least fifteen metres in all directions, the yard was clear of brush and covered with rock chips. Hard to track in gravel.

Tasker quickly walked over to the sandy parking area. No tracks but those from the three parked vehicles. Then he skirted the edge of the rock-chip yard where it met the damp, scrub forest floor, tracing a large circle round the storehouse.

Only at the very back could he spot where the meeting of the gravel and the brush had been disturbed. There, a narrow ribbon of gravel pressed on the moss for a ways into the bush, evidence of a little-used trail. Could be a game trail, but maybe more. Tasker bent over to touch the soft grey-green path. His fingers felt indentations like human heel prints. A chill ran up his arm.

Tasker kept his hand on the moss, determined to keep calm, inhaling the earthy, spruce smell. He had to figure how all this fit together. A piece was missing. If only he knew what to look for. Maybe it was more than a piece – like a dark, menacing presence that was setting good people up.

Tasker heard a truck roaring uphill. He swivelled to take a bearing of where he was relative to the magazine, and walked back across the gravel. Tasker spotted a faded cigarette butt lying partway over. Rothmans. A sense of desperation swept over him. He'd found nothing.

The big RCMP four-wheel-drive wagon rumbled to a stop in the turning area. Sergeant Flint climbed out one side and Freeman Straun, with his aging, florid face and leather doctor's bag, the other.

Without looking at Tasker, Sergeant Flint said, "How's Jim?" and he strode towards the magazine.

"Unconscious." Tasker's answer drained from him. "Looks like he was hit on the side of the head with a club. It was left lying there. Joseph will check, see if explosives are missing."

The doctor stopped behind them and started to dig in his leather bag.

"Forget something?" Sergeant Flint called back.

"Got your tool kit in the back?" the doctor asked in his distinctive, resonant voice.

When the sergeant nodded, Dr. Straun closed his bag and hurried to catch up.

At the magazine door, Joseph met them and said, "Three sticks of dynamite gone. Old stuff from that crate near the door. And it looks like someone's tried to pick the lock . . ."

Dr. Straun knelt down beside Jim's head. He pulled up Jim's eyelids one at a time and directed the narrow beam of his flashlight into each eye.

"Corporal, come here," he ordered Tasker who'd been trying to focus on the picked lock.

Tasker turned and saw the doctor wink at Sergeant Flint. What is with this doctor? Tasker thought. He quelled a rush of anger and approached, determined to control his feelings and help out if he could.

"I need your young eyes," the doctor said. Tasker kneeled beside Dr. Straun and looked into Jim's flaccid face. "When I shine the light, tell me what you see."

Dr. Straun shakily lifted up Jim's left eyelid and shone in the light. It looked dead, sightless, Tasker thought. "His eye is staring at me. Wait, the pupil is shrinking. Now it's stopped."

Dr. Straun grunted and lifted the right eyelid. "Now this side."

Tasker's face pressed the cold concrete floor as he manoeuvred to look. "Same thing. But the pupil is staying big." Something in Tasker's stomach gave way. "What's that mean?"

"Would you describe the right pupil as fully dilated and fixed?"

"Yes, is that bad?" Tasker asked.

"Yes, fixed pupil is bad. If we don't act, he'll be dead in a couple of hours. When did Jim come up here, Joseph?"

"More'n an hour ago, I guess."

"So we have less than I thought. I'll have to make a burr hole."

"What can you do?" Tasker's knew his voice sounded agitated. He didn't like the sound of "burr hole."

"Plainly, his skull has been fractured." Dr. Straun's voice reverberated with irritation, but his hands locked in an explanatory gesture, as if he were squeezing something with his palms. "The middle meningeal artery has ruptured and is spurting blood into the brain box. The blood buildup is applying pressure on the brain stem, including the cranial nerve, which serves the pupil of the eye." The doctor unlocked his fingers and jabbed them up and down, pointing at Tasker. "Fixed, dilated pupil is a cardinal sign of pressure on the brain stem. We have to relieve that pressure before it cuts off more vital functions – breathing, circulation . . ." He paused, then said to the sergeant, "I'll need some tools. A brace and bit, needle-nosed pliers, masking tape."

Sergeant Flint jerked his thumb to indicate Tasker was to go back for them. Tasker hesitated only a moment.

"Three-quarter-inch bit," the doctor called. "Three-quarter-inch, and needle-nosed pliers, Corporal."

Tasker was at a loss why the doctor would want carpenter's tools. But he ran to the tool box in the back of the RCMP wagon. As his fingers and thumbs fumbled through screwdrivers and wrenches, fear about the doctor's competence stabbed at his gut. Jim's life was in this older man's hands.

"Three-quarter-inch, yes," Dr. Straun checked each piece as Tasker handed it to him.

The doctor lay out his other instruments on a clean, ironed handkerchief on the floor – gauze, scissors, tape, string. "I'll need a hacksaw too."

Joseph ran to get it and the doctor chuckled, "Flint, watch out for 'pliers.' That's a fine Scrabble word!"

This was too much for Tasker, who blurted out, "What about an ambulance?"

"Corporal," the doctor growled unpleasantly, "minutes count." He rolled Jim over onto his back. Jim's left arm slithered across his thigh and thumped onto the floor.

Tasker watched in horror as the doctor picked up the brace and bit and placed it on the top of Jim's right temple, where the temple met the forehead, within the hairline. As he started to turn the brace, Sergeant Flint stepped out the door.

Tasker's horror was so intense, his breath came shallow. He wanted to lunge forward to grab the tool from the doctor, but his body wouldn't obey. His voice squeaked out, "You know what you're doing?"

"I've done all the explaining I'm going to do! Quiet or out!"

Blood streamed from Jim's scalp, and its rich, warm smell filled the room. Tasker wretched. Dr. Straun pulled away the brace and held the bloody bit out to Tasker. "Be useful. Cut off the tip with the hacksaw. I've got enough bite now."

Tasker was able to take the tool, but Joseph relieved him of it and carried it out the door. Stunned, Tasker watched the doctor dab gauze from his leather bag in the wound and sop up the blood. In a minute, the circle where the bit cut was a clean, bloodless wound, but Jim's hair glistened with sticky red blood. Even his eyelashes.

From outside Tasker could hear the rasping pulses as the hacksaw cut.

"Yesterday, I used these pliers pulling quills out of Flint's dog!" Dr. Straun laughed. "He couldn't watch that either!"

He took the bit back from Joseph and wiped the saw filings off with another folded cotton handkerchief from his bag.

"What about germs?" Tasker gasped.

"What's infection compared to your brain stem!" Dr. Straun placed the bit back on top of his cut. "They'll have hours to spare in Whitehorse to tidy this up. Antibiotics. Anti-tetanus. Besides, with no tip left, I'll not pierce the dura."

Then he started to drill very slowly. No shake to his hands at all. It took one turn, and a backwards turn, to get the bit to grip again. But in a moment he pulled away the tool and a great gush of blood poured out the hole.

This time, he let it bleed. He sat back on his heels and nodded. "That's it. Nothing we've done here can't be cleaned up and sterilized in a couple of hours!" and he expelled a long breath. For some reason, Tasker felt relief too.

Bending forward again as the blood flow diminished, Dr. Straun carefully started to pack the neat hole with gauze. Then Tasker saw a bright red spurt of blood pulse out. "There's the bleeder," the doctor said as he poked in the pliers and pulled out a small blood vessel. He clamped the pliers tight on the artery and taped the grip of the pliers shut and flat against Jim's scalp. Then he finished packing the hole and wrapped a wide, white bandage around both Jim's head and the pliers.

Jim suddenly opened his eyes and flung up his arm. Dr. Straun put his hand on Jim's wrist and gently said, "Take it easy. You're OK. Try not to move too much."

Tasker could see there was a moment of recognition in Jim's stare.

Sergeant Flint walked back in the door and said loudly, "The ambulance has started south. Kay will be at her gate to meet it on the way down." Then he turned to Tasker. "Corporal, you and Joseph carry him to the truck. Straun and I aren't as young as we used to be."

Tasker managed to find his fireman's hold with Joseph, and gingerly they lifted up Jim.

"Watch the head," the doctor warned, uttering another deep rich laugh, and put a hand on Sergeant Flint's shoulder. "By the way, he'll not be able to tell who hit him. Post-traumatic amnesia."

Tasker could feel Jim's body respond weakly to the lift and carry. He'd made it. And Dr. Straun had done it.

Dr. Straun settled Jim into the back of the RCMP wagon with a bedroll to cushion his head. Jim stared out and seemed to smile as Tasker carefully shut the tailgate.

Pulling himself into the driver's seat, Sergeant Flint issued orders. "Tasker, you and Joseph see the road is cordoned off and the magazine secure until I get back." Then Flint slammed his door and Tasker winced. The poor suspension of the four-wheel-drive would make the ride painful for Jim, even with the doctor in the back keeping him steady.

Tasker would lock up, all right, but not without poking around some. A cold, hard knot was tightening in his stomach and he knew it would keep tightening until he had his hands on who was making the moves. There was no way whoever did this to Jim was going to get away with it – it was too much, too personal. It wasn't going to be another Flint-centred investigation.

"Let's take a look at that lock." Tasker put his hand on Joseph's back and nudged him towards the magazine. "See if it was a professional job."

But it was clearly amateur. The keyhole was all scratched and the doorframe bent weakly where someone had tried to pry back the metal to release the bolt. There'd been no such marks on Dr. Straun's clinic door.

"If they'd had a crowbar," Joseph said, "it'd be nothin' to get in."

"Jim must've noticed . . .," Tasker was thinking as he talked. "He'd have to report and secure it the day he found it. So he'd have seen it first just before he was hit. When was the shed last opened?"

"Peders got charges out Monday."

"Picked in the last four days, then," Tasker calculated. "I'll take another look outside. Give me the keys. You cordon off the road down at the bottom, and tell Flint I'm out back if need be."

Tasker circled the magazine, thinking it wasn't just any time in the last four days someone tried to get into the magazine. It could have been less than two hours ago too. The assailant could've been waiting inside. A search for tracks could be dangerous. He'd keep cool. Freeman Straun was incredibly cool. Tasker had to give him that.

He made a careful study of the whole gravelled yard and walked the circumference again. No tracks, nothing out of place except the one suggestion of the trail he'd found before with a little gravel worked in at the mouth.

Tasker followed the trail and after a few metres, it swung left and up an incline. The bush was open, approaching treeline, and he found only two snapped twigs about chest high, not enough to give an idea of height. It had to be a game trail, woodland caribou probably. Too narrow for bear. And still mossy green. Not used often enough to kill vegetation.

The trail turned left once more and opened to a small clearing, padded and worn, with dozens of cigarette butts pressed into the moss. Different brands too. Rothmans, Du Maurier, Belmont. Tasker looked downhill. A clear view of the magazine, the turning area, and well down the road past the sign.

Someone had watched the magazine, had lain in wait, smoking, right here.

The small hairs on Tasker's neck prickled. How far behind this person, these persons, was he? He glanced around the clearing and focused on the continuation of the trail, now well used, heading back down towards the big spruces. So they'd come that way. Often. Watched the magazine, and only occasionally gone over to it.

The knot in his stomach tightened harder, and faintness overcame Tasker. He had to sit down.

He looked back to the magazine and saw Joseph climb into his cab and coast slowly downhill to the mine road cutoff.

Tasker was alone. He felt shaky and sick. He placed his head down between his knees.

His mind threw out questions that muddled in his dizziness. Who'd been sitting here, right where he sat? The lock picker? The one who assaulted Jim and stole the explosives? Was it two people? Three?

The dizziness subsided and he lifted his chin. The trouble with dynamite was it was easy to detonate. He'd better check the cap and fuse shed anyway.

But then he sat upright and clear-headed. He heard the blasting inspector's words: "Peders reported a length of primer missing Monday."

Tasker was appalled. This was more than an assault. This was premeditated. Someone had stolen a significant length of fuse, and dynamite, and had committed assault, maybe murder too, to get them.

What were the explosives for? To blow up the mine office? Shit!

Had Jim just been in the way? And Blake McIntyre? Was Blake's death connected to this? Maybe Blake stumbled onto the plot. Or was he part of the plot and disposed of? What about the B and E at the trapper's cabin and the vandalism at the doctor's office?

Tension was high in the community. But that high? The two sides seemed to be the mine and the Native band, but the victims had been Blake and Jim. Agitated third parties. Like himself, if he took off his uniform.

Then Tasker realized another victim, the real and intended victim, might yet be attacked. With the stolen explosives.

What if Sergeant Flint was keeping something from him? Why was Flint always leaving him on his own?

His breath came fast. The armed thief, the killer, was not Howard, who was in jail, or Peders, now allegedly in Dawson City, or Jim. The killer lurked in the bush ahead. In the dark forest.

Tasker jumped to his feet, taut with nervous energy. He would track like a predator. The killer might be less than an hour ahead.

Tasker stole up the trail, acutely alert to sight and smell. He followed the path as it crept over the crest and then switch-backed down into the Henderson valley. The trees got bigger and farther apart. The forest floor sprung underfoot when he strayed off the narrow trail. Faded brown needles concentrated in the path, some broken by footfall, and fragments of bone here and there, including a flat, lichen-crusted shoulderblade – moose, probably. There was no sound. The lowering clouds held each twig separate from every other, paralysed in noiseless mist. Thick with possible sound, but hushed. Tasker could hear the humming in his own brain.

On the valley floor Tasker lost the one distinct trail. He back-tracked and cut circles around the big trees, trying to find it again, but it seemed to come to one point and then fan in several directions. He checked down the old road to the highway, but he found no tracks at all. Even Peders's tire marks from last Sunday were washed away.

He searched towards the river, driving himself, holding his fatigue at bay, ignoring the iron-rod feeling between his shoulders, the knot in his gut.

On the way he looked into the watchman's tent, but no one was there. He smelled the damp canvas and noticed the floor was swept, the beads put away. Tidier than last time, Tasker thought.

He dropped the tent flap and crept along towards the spot where he'd found Blake's boots. His eyes rarely stopped sweeping the dark, gently undulating forest floor. He hadn't reached the river yet, but suddenly its rush filled his head.

Tasker stopped to listen. Was that a motor? Were his ears playing tricks on him? He backed up against a large tree. If Blake could come upriver in a Zodiac, so could anyone else. He'd not thought of the river for escape!

Then he heard a low grunt to the right. He steadied himself by putting his left hand on the trunk and leaned forward, his eyes searching the shadows. There was movement.

About thirty metres to the right, staring back towards him, was the dish face of a huge bear, swinging its head from the hump on its back, moist snout up, trying to catch his scent. Grizzly.

Tasker froze. His hand edged across his chest and down to the holster on his hip. His right hand closed on the cold steel, and his forefinger snapped the release. He knew he'd be a fool to pull the trigger unless the bear charged – an injured bear was a hell of lot more dangerous than a scouting one. Tasker pressed his left hand harder onto the bark.

The bear lifted its muzzle high to the left and lumbered towards Tasker. The tips of its black fur flashed golden as it approached, flat-footed, through a patch of light. Tasker caught the heavy smell. Bear sweat. It stopped again directly ahead, swinging its head and sniffing, this time closer to the ground. Tasker watched, feeling oddly calm in the centre of his fear. It was the biggest bear he'd ever seen, its eyes and ears tiny, inadequate. The bear lifted up his left paw and swiped inwards at a pile of logs and then suddenly swung around and bounded, incredibly light-footed for its weight, down to the river and disappeared. Tasker heard splashing. It was crossing the water in the shallow spot below the bend in the river where Blake's net stake had been.

He waited a long minute before he pulled his hand off the tree beside him. His palm was bruised blue and imprinted with the pattern of the bark.

He stepped carefully forward to examine the bear's track, but it didn't show. The moss and litter had bounced back. No wonder he'd lost that trail earlier.

Then Tasker checked out the little log pile the bear had upended. It was a stack of freshly sawn clubs, some splintered now, like the ones that killed Blake and nearly killed Jim. It must be Howard's collection of burls for his carving. Anyone could have taken one or two from here.

A pulse throbbed in his ears again, drowning out the sound of the river. Part of the plot may have been to lay a false trail to Howard . . . or to free him.

The river filled the woods with sound, but Tasker felt only intense aloneness. He turned and ran back through the forest. He had to be with someone, anyone, even Sergeant Flint.

The sergeant hadn't returned when Tasker scrambled into view of the magazine. Exhausted, he climbed into his own cruiser and lay across the front seat on his back, his feet dangling out the driver's door. His body sank heavily into the cushions and he breathed deeply, inhaling the sweet, oily smell of takeout fries and onion rings that saturated the upholstery. He had to fight off sleep.

Tasker became aware of rain splattering on the windshield above his face and zigzagging in channels down the dusty glass. He felt tingling in his feet and calves.

When he sat up, thick-headed, he saw that heavy rainclouds now completely shrouded Crag Mountain. Any tracks he'd missed would be gone soon. He had to search one more time.

Tasker stepped stiffly out of the cab, the cold drizzle striking his face, clearing his head some.

He looked around. Jim's truck sat empty, two rifles mounted in the back window. Knowing Jim, it was probably unlocked, and with no ammunition handy.

Tasker crouched to study the tracks in the turning area again. He found evidence of four vehicles, all of which he could account for – Jim's, his own, the RCMP wagon, Joseph's.

The rain started drumming hard into the back of Jim's pickup. Tasker checked to see if he had left anything there that could get ruined by rain. Sure enough, he found the tea thermos and, up against the cab, two cardboard cartons with their flaps neatly tucked shut.

Tasker took a look inside the boxes and saw they were full of clothing – overalls, bush shirts, and a hand-embroidered, white cowboy shirt he recognized. They were Blake McIntyre's clothes. Looked like Eve had already passed on the usable stuff – that would be like her, thinking that somebody else could use them. Tasker's mother had hung onto his father's clothes for years till she'd packed up to move to Whitehorse, and sorting through it all then, still maintaining her near-total silence, made the move all the more difficult for them both.

Tasker decided he should move the boxes into the cab, and as he refolded the box flaps, he spotted Jim's keys in the ignition. He took them out, locked up the cab and pocketed the keys.

He shivered. The jacket he was wearing was soaking wet. He went to sit in his own car with the heater on until Sergeant Flint showed up.

Staring through the swimming windshield, past the magazine, up above treeline to the slide scar and the mine, now lost in cloud, he wondered if the mill sat on the spot where legend said the dancing-bear feasthouse once stood. He peered into the mist swirls, thinking of sensual bears beckoning men and women who abused wild things, who wasted the plenty of nature.

Sergeant Flint's rumbling wagon brought Tasker back. The rain had stopped. The sergeant looked tired climbing down from his seat. In fact, he looked quite old and stooped taking off his hat and running his fingers absently through his grey, lengthening crewcut.

Sergeant Flint had that way of never looking right at Tasker, always finding some point to stare at to the left or right of Tasker's face. Tasker sensed, standing there, that that was what made him so uneasy with Flint: there was never any connection.

"Had a good sleep?" Sergeant Flint's tone put Tasker on edge.

"I locked up." Tasker held his impatience in his gut – it wasn't going to get in his way. "I looked around outside some. Found a trail behind that heads to the river with a clearing." Tasker pointed. "Right over there. Could've been used as a lookout. There were cigarettes butted into the moss. And no unaccounted-for tracks in the drive or turning area."

"So what are you speculating?" the sergeant challenged, raising his eyebrows, but still not looking directly at Tasker.

"Someone, maybe more than one, lay in wait till the magazine was opened. Hit Jim to get explosives." Tasker spoke quickly and with relief that he didn't feel he had to fight, like before, for a hearing. "I followed the trail but found no one. Down by the river, though, I did find a pile of clubs. Like the one used here and on Blake. Probably the collection Howard said he was making for carving." When Sergeant Flint said nothing, Tasker added lamely, "I watched a grizzly swat them around a bit. That's how I noticed them in the first place."

The sergeant rubbed a hand along his forehead and then held it out in front and seemed to examine his own fingernails. He looked old again, a grey face with deep lines. "So what do you make of it?"

"A number of things. Someone used the club as a weapon on Jim to confuse us. Make us think the assault was connected with Blake McIntyre's death. Or maybe they were just trying to take the heat off Howard." Tasker paused and let it sink into his own head as much as Flint's. "On the other hand, the two crimes may be unrelated." Flint pulled his keys out of his pocket and put them back. "Or, Howard is innocent of Blake's murder as he claims, and the same person who hit Jim killed Blake. Maybe Blake's killer was wanting to plant the club in the munitions shed – and Jim was just in the way."

"Not likely, but go on," Sergeant Flint said harshly, his hands moving towards his hips.

"This possibility – it's no good. I want to know why the explosives were stolen. And then I want to know if another crime will be committed with them. Maybe Blake and Jim were just in the way." Tasker stuck his neck right out. "I want to know if the explosives are related to the political situation in town."

"You know, I just don't get too concerned about three sticks of dynamite." The sergeant sounded tired now, as well as a little sarcastic. He leaned against the hood of his wagon and, with exaggerated patience, said, "Someone may have taken them to move a stump weeks ago, and it never got noted. Why weren't the canisters of, say, ammonium nitrate lifted? The thief probably got scared and ran before taking anything." Sergeant Flint shook his head grimly. "Let's see what we find inside."

It sounded to Tasker like the sergeant had dismissed his summary. But then he thought, so what, that wasn't his problem. It probably wasn't even personal – Flint had forgotten he was human just like every other cop. When the stakes rise, private life, feelings, disappear. Where was his private life anyway? In a nursing station in Old Crow? Not likely.

The sergeant lifted the fingerprint briefcase out of the wagon, handed Tasker a pair of white cotton gloves and slammed the door. They walked up the path and Tasker unlocked the magazine.

The door opened and with it came the dry, chemical smell from inside. Tasker thought out loud, "I wonder what Jim does remember?"

The sergeant held up a gloved hand and pointed to a clear thumbprint on the right side of the metal doorframe, just inside. He turned and grinned broadly. Tasker grinned back, feeling for the first time a kind of partnership with the man.

They worked in silence, carefully dusting the frame, the dynamite crate, the club.

When they finished the dusting and Tasker was cleaning the brushes, Sergeant Flint said, "The inspector in Whitehorse tells me the environment minister has brought his visit forward, is coming here from Ottawa Sunday, to make some pronouncement." He paused to lay tape over the dust-blackened print. Tasker watched Flint lift the print – the older man actually did it well.

"Good. We've got clear definition here," Flint continued,

holding the tape at arm's length. "There'll be a lot of security, but I can't afford to ignore your theory." Then he walked from the doorframe and carefully placed the print on a prepared sheet beside his case. When it was filed in the briefcase he continued, "I want to find the person who swung the club and I want to account for the explosives before he gets here. You can follow up your conspiracy idea. But no sneaking around, like visiting Howard in jail out of uniform, without reporting to me. I want a written report on my desk twice a day telling me where you've been and what you actually know."

"OK! I'll backtrack, start by finding out where all the locals were at the time of both crimes. Look for a common thread."

"You got more energy than I do," Sergeant Flint mumbled into his briefcase. "In my experience, there's no reward in overextending yourself." Straightening up he said, "Myself, I think the crimes are unrelated and I'll follow up that angle. I think the answer is in here." He tapped his briefcase with the fingerprint filed in it. "I'll run the names of any recently hired miners through when I take this print up to the lab. See if we got any haywires moving in."

"I'll start by collecting that pile of clubs by the river. I'd like to send them in with you."

Sergeant Flint began labelling a plastic evidence bag for the club left in the magazine. "OK. And I'll have to visit the crown attorney's office." His eyes narrowed and he let the bag drop to his side. "He may want to let Howard Daniel out. One thread from the suspect's jacket on a club may not be enough to convict Howard any more, not after this attack, but I'm going to push for keeping him in, at least over the weekend." He frowned. "The way I see it, Howard Daniel caught Blake poaching, they scuffled, Blake got so badly injured he was near death and Daniel tried to make it look like an accident or that it took place somewhere else. He probably thought Blake was already dead. He's no good, that kid. Bad family."

Tasker said, "But it doesn't paste together for me – the mechanics of it. If Howard killed Blake, how and when did he get the Zodiac and the body to the mouth of the river? The body would've looked a lot different if it had bumped through all that shallower water on its own. More than a few lesions on the feet. Maybe someone in another boat towed them down. There wasn't enough time for Howard . . ."

"No, Blake's motor was turned on – in Whitehorse they think he was thrown into the Zodiac after he was in a coma. The motor was set on low throttle and the boat sent downriver where the lake overturned it somewhere by the dunes, choking the motor. Makes sense. With no steering, it would've drifted sideways to the breakers. Blake was near death from the head injury – the fact that he drowned is a smokescreen. If he wasn't a dying man already, his drowning would've shown more exaggerated signs, like a mushroom of foam all over his face. They are saying in Vancouver that Freeman was pretty slick to see signs of drowning at all. And here" – Sergeant Flint pointed to where Jim's body had lain – "I think what happened was a thief got spooked. Now, let's go find your wood pile. We'd better collect those cigarette butts too." Then Flint added, "This isn't all fancy, glamour and cracking conspiracies, you know. It's just police work."

As if I don't know the humdrum already, Tasker thought. Eve's theory to clear Howard wasn't going to work, but there were other considerations now, a little lifting of the fog.

"Sergeant's still to Whitehorse," Shorty said and indicated with his fork for Tasker to sit down at the mess table to eat.

"Bad day," Tasker mumbled, "but good-looking food." His mouth was already watering with the rich gravy smells. He never had a problem with his appetite, he thought grimly, even when things weren't going well.

"I wish I got more notice who's eatin' in or out around here. Everyone's a no-show at the last minute. You all think if you miss you can come and gobble off hours. Eat up my budget."

Tasker had never met a cook who didn't need time to grumble. Figuring the best way to appease him was to eat up, Tasker dug into his hot turkey sandwich.

The two men ate in silence for a while.

"I don't get it," Shorty started again. "The two most unlikely in town."

It took a moment for Tasker to realize Shorty had changed the subject. He felt like talking about Jim himself.

"Must've been an outsider," Shorty continued.

"Flint thinks it's a miner."

"Most of them are outsiders. There are so many new guys up there. Summer workers. Never can keep the kitchen staff, even. All from Edmonton or Vancouver or Anchorage. Bringin' in drugs."

"What about Howard killing Blake?"

"No. The Daniels aren't that way."

"Flint doesn't agree with you on that."

Shorty coughed and made an impatient gesture with his hand. "Ah! He always had it in for the Daniels. Spent too much of his first year here defendin' hisself for what happened to the older boy, Gary. Got his back up. Now he's less than a year away from full pension and all the old chippiness is comin' back." Shorty took another bite and finished his thought after swallowing. "Anyway, Howard'll get off."

Tasker took a drink of milk. The talk was getting interesting.

At another time, he'd find it comfortable even, chewing through low-key police politics.

Shorty cleared his throat and continued, "Yukoners, Native, white, they're a good lot. Crimes of drink, but that's all. And you can count on most of them – you know, park a cruiser outside Harry's house the night after the welfare cheques come in, and that stops him beatin' on his wife . . ."

"What about up at Raven Creek, that business last year? The assault and rape with the broken beer bottle."

"Drink."

"Yes, but more than that too. So much bad feeling – the young couple dead, the brother and an uncle with broken bones, the grandmother beaten . . ." Tasker shuddered. "The community bulldozed both houses. That got rid of the memory for them!"

"It was alcohol brought out that violence. Just you watch. The sergeant'll find the outsider who got Jim, and likely he'll have the one who killed Blake McIntyre. He'll know it. Howard'll be released, wait and see."

Shorty carefully wiped the corners of his mouth and then dropped the napkin onto his empty plate. His fancy eating manners, Tasker thought, didn't go with the yellow teeth and stubbly chin. Tasker used to mull over possibilities with Ida. She had insight. With the public health records at her fingertips, she'd know what the chances were that violence – "trauma" was their word for it – was local and alcohol-related. She wouldn't be making guesses – she'd have statistics. That crazy from nowhere really only hits once in a hundred times, she'd confirm, or a thousand times. It was usually local, domestic – Tasker knew that for sure but wasn't going to argue it out with Shorty.

Shorty coughed and stood up to clear the table. "I bet this is an outsider. No one 'round here, drunk or sober, would want to hurt Jim. Blake, well – but not Jim."

"I agree the crimes are connected. If Ivan Peders hadn't been out of town and at a job up north, I'd be sniffing around him," Tasker said and then as an afterthought added, "What d'you know about Peders?"

"The only times I had direct dealings with him didn't work out too good." Shorty was rinsing the dishes at the sink. "Last winter, I asked if he'd volunteer to help us put the roof on the curlin' rink. But he said no. Didn't make sense. It was goin' to be a good time, a bunch of guys with a case or two." Shorty came back to the table and sat down with two cups of coffee, obviously with more to say. "His parents died when he was young – Danish, I think, tuberculosis – and he was brought up by the Catholic brothers or fathers in Watson Lake. People have stories about what went on in places like that. Some can't say anythin' but bad things about other folks tryin' to do good . . . I don't put much store in them. Anyway, Peders took summer jobs with the crews straightenin' the Alaska Highway south of there. Found he had a way with explosives. Deaf a bit, from the blastin'." Shorty lit a cigarette with his lower lip extended and talked on, the ash collecting on the end and looking like it would fall off with each word. "He'd have been better off a sign painter. Has a real flair for it – just look at the side of his van." Shorty took the cigarette out of his mouth in time to catch the ashtray and stuffed it back in before he added, "Father Leonard tells me Peders tithes to the church every month. Says he wants to apprentice with an organ maker somewhere on the lower mainland. Wants to leave the north. I knew he had a flair for makin' things – but makin' organs, that's skill."

"Well, we're going to nail the guy who hit Jim," Tasker said to wind up the conversation. He drained his coffee, feeling a little better for the food and company, and stood up to leave. "We have fingerprints. I'll look into the bar tonight. Maybe I'll get a fix on some of the characters who're moving through."

Shorty called after him, obviously pleased Tasker was acting on his suggestion, adding a little more advice, "Look for a real greenhorn. Most locals know where to get dynamite easy – road crew, prospector's shacks. You don't have to go assaultin' old-timers, part-time carpenters, for dynamite."

When Shorty finished talking, his chest heaved into a rolling smoker's cough that sounded to Tasker like he would heave out his lungs.

When Ivan Peders drove into town that night, he headed for the hotel bar. That's where Tasker was when he walked in. It would be fourteen hours straight from Dawson, including stops for fill-ups, and the only place to go that late in the evening for food was the Grizzly Den.

Peders ordered a platter of french fries with double gravy and a can of 7Up. He sat in the corner near the dartboard, opened his logbook and made like he was planning. Tasker watched him for a minute, and noticed that, with his head bent forward, Peders's sausage neck actually looked smooth and soft. His blond hair still spiked straight out from it though.

Tasker moved over to Peders's table uninvited. "You just get in?"

Peders nodded, shut his book, but didn't speak. In the dim light his eyes looked colourless they were so pale.

"You keep an hourly record of your work?" Tasker asked.

Peders put his hand over his logbook. He still said nothing.

"I got a question." Tasker smiled, his eyes on Peders's hand. "You got a record of when you took explosives out of the magazine here last Monday? And detonators from the fuse shed?"

"Joseph keeps the schedule and register," Peders answered in his high, cold voice.

"I thought I'd ask you." Tasker kept smiling. "And the exact time you noticed the fuse missing later on that day?"

"I already reported that and I plan to get it back." Peders rubbed his temple with his hand. The gesture wasn't unusual in itself except the way Peders's shoulders moved back and forth as he rubbed.

"So do I," Tasker said, keeping it polite. "Any leads?"

Peders was looking at the door when Larissa walked in. Tasker followed his stare. Larissa glanced in their direction, levelled her dark eyes with Peders's and then looked away quickly. She stepped over to the table closest to the door and smiled awkwardly at the men sitting there, her left hand on her hip and forward slightly. She was wearing an oversized bush jacket so it was hard to see her hand movements, but it looked to Tasker like she moved her right hand over to her left hip and held it out. One of the men tipped his chair and grinned up at her. She smiled back quickly. Then he took out his cigarette package and offered it to her. She took two, tucked one in the breast pocket of the jacket and bent over for a light of the other. She dragged in deeply, smiled and shuffled back outside as she exhaled.

Before the door swung shut, the waitress walked in front of Tasker and placed Peders's fries on the table. They smelled warm and sweet, making Tasker's saliva pump. Peders jabbed in his fork.

Tasker asked, "Would the missing fuse be what you'd normally use to set off dynamite?"

Peders ignored him and stuffed the fries in his mouth. They looked plump and crisp, and Tasker swallowed hard. He wasn't getting anything from Peders – he decided to be more direct.

"Jim was nearly killed by a thief at the magazine this morning, and three sticks are missing."

Peders spat the fries in his mouth onto his plate and then sucked in hard. He took a quick drink of 7Up and shoved back his plate. "You give someone a big hand and then they let on you're nothing," he mumbled. Then he shouted, "These are the worst fries I ever tasted," stood up from the table and bolted out the door.

Tasker pushed back his chair, feeling stupid, aware that everyone in the bar was staring at him. He'd expected Peders to get riled but not like this. He placed his hands on the edge of the table, ready to get up and away from the mess of fries, when he noticed the log lying there. Tasker grabbed it, opened it up. It was a diary with business and personal entries in a thin, spidery hand – numbers, short notes. Tasker knew he had no right to take a good look, so he closed it and followed Peders outside. As he walked past the table of men by the door, he saw the one who'd given Larissa the cigarettes had left.

Ivan Peders was sitting in his van, gripping the steering wheel and staring doggedly at his dashboard. Tasker tapped on the driver's window and held up the log. Peders's eyes jerked up alarmed and he rolled down his window. Then, without a word, Peders accepted the log and backed his van out. Tasker, watching the van's rear lights as they glowed north into the night, sensed Peders had reacted to Larissa's sidling up to the miner and not to Tasker's update on Jim at all.

The van lights had disappeared. Maybe Peders was lonely, Tasker thought. Maybe his attraction to Larissa was what they had in common – they were both orphans in their own way. Tasker could relate to that a little – he was lucky he had Jim.

He remembered going with Ida to visit one of her aunts in a cabin by the river in Whitehorse. There were many older women Ida called "Auntie." This one sat in a straight-backed wooden chair, one hand on a cane, the other holding a glass bottle of Orange Crush. She was a powerful presence. There was nothing haggard about her old, wrinkled face with its few good teeth and arched nostrils — all her features added up to an incredibly alive smile. Although she wore workboots under her long, dark dress and a camper's scarf crushing down her white hair, she was an elegant woman. In all the silences of the visit, so much was said. Old Auntie, ninety at least, had one interest in that half-hour and it was Ida — and Tasker because he was Ida's friend. The few breaks in the silence came when she referred to the loss of her three sisters in the epidemic of 1918 and when she told the story of the birth of her son, premature, on the shores of an unnamed long lake east of the Chilkat Glacier. Her first husband, now long dead, delivered the baby, cut the cord, and buried the afterbirth in the shallow, gravelly soil.

Tasker was shaken by the power of what was and what wasn't said in that room. He'd been in similar company before, but this was a time that made him miss his own broken roots, his father's interrupted story.

Deep roots and stories. Peders probably didn't have many, nor did Larissa. Some people just don't recognize the strength passed-down stories give them. Peders maybe felt the hollowness of having few — felt he shared that with Larissa. But it sure wasn't mutual.

The van was gone from sight now, but Tasker could still feel the rumble of the engine.

He inhaled the cool spruce air — it cleared his thoughts. A brisk walk back to the detachment was what he needed before sleep.

Next morning Tasker was up before sunrise, driving over to Jim's place. He'd woken up suddenly during the night, worrying that whoever hit Jim might have also rummaged through his cabin. After that, he lay there, his mind circling, thinking he'd pushed his way into the case and now he just wasn't getting a handle on his conspiracy idea. At 6:00 a.m. he was dressed and ready to go.

Sergeant Flint had got in late from Whitehorse the night before and had left a written order for Tasker to locate the whereabouts of Larissa Stanley, and report back for a briefing at 10:00 a.m.

Tasker decided he'd check Jim's, poke around town to see if he could get any leads on the missing explosives and talk to Peders because he might be more cooperative now. Larissa would be easy to find.

Tasker opened Jim's cabin door and walked in. He spun on his heel in the centre of the room and looked at the shelves. Everything seemed to be there: all those old bottles Jim had found in ghost towns — Dawson, Conrad, Lindeman. Whisky bottles, inkpots, sarsaparilla jars, even an old Worcestershire sauce bottle with a glass stopper. Brown, green, white and purple — so valuable to collectors now.

A new short-wave radio crackled in the corner, and Tasker recognized the rhythms of the Whitehorse police dispatch. Tasker hadn't thought of Jim as a hack before — especially one of those so fascinated by the police they monitored police radio. Tasker didn't know why it surprised him, though. There was one in just about every community – might as well be Jim here. Usually their benign snooping proved helpful.

Things seemed in order in the cabin, but there was a rotten-food smell. Tasker looked in the fridge, found it sweet in there and cut off a hunk of cheddar cheese. He started hunting for the garbage, and was thinking he should phone Whitehorse at 8:00 a.m. to find out how Jim was doing, when he heard the first blast. Loud and close. He was dashing out the door when the next four or five went off in a sharp cluster. Wasn't that too many? And he'd rounded the corner, in sight of Ivan Peders's house, when he realized they were firecrackers, cherry bombs probably, and nothing more.

Down the lane he saw Peders fling open his front door. He was all tight-fleshed, bare pink except for the white boxer shorts. And he pointed and squealed at two boys in the street. The boys danced, long legs stiff around a can on the gravel and then shot off between the houses as the can broke apart with a multiple blast. One of the boys dragged his leg in a funny way.

Tasker kept running. Peders disappeared into his cabin, slamming his door against the settling dust. The boys were nowhere to be seen. Tasker got to the remains of the can and called, "Come out, guys! I wanna talk to you."

Silence. The sun was just rising over Tagish Mountain, a snowy thread on the ridge, leaving the houses in the valley with long, clean shadows. A dry, blue-sky day, except for the puff of smoke rising over Peders's house and the warm, sharp smell of gunpowder.

A garbage can clattered down the road. "Reggie, get over here," Tasker called. A good guess. Reggie swaggered out, grinning, stuffing dirty hands in his jeans pockets.

"Isn't it a little early in the day to be letting off cherry bombs?" Tasker asked, smiling back, his voice filling with indulgent good humour despite himself.

The second boy, the one who'd been injured by the rod in the knee five days ago, limped out of the shadows on the other side of the road and joined Reggie, shuffling, a safe distance from Tasker.

A loud blast of music – precise, staccato, classical – swelled out of Peders's cabin, and the boys exchanged glances and then snickered together.

Tasker joined their laughter. "You guys. You always get a reaction from him?"

"He's a weirdo!" Reggie answered. He had a great big, coarse-looking mouth for a kid. And ears that stuck out.

"What sort of things does he do?" Tasker put his hands in his pockets like Reggie.

"Always put his music on loud." Reggie laughed. "Bach and Beethoven." He pronounced the names awkwardly. "Not many people stay up all night listening to that stuff on loud and drinking 7Up." He pointed to the stacks of empty pop cans in among firewood and what looked like furniture crates and metal housings along the side of Peders's cabin.

"Yeah, too many boom booms! He don't hear nothing on low volume," the other boy added from behind.

While Reggie was sturdy like Howard, the other boy was tall and scrawny. His arms swung loose from his shoulders, clown-like.

"I had no idea. Really strange, eh? Like?" Tasker invited . . .

"Yeah. Last week he was at the dump, pullin' out old moose heads and sneakin' them into the back of his van." Reggie laughed again.

The other boy added, "And being real picky about finding

clean sheets of newspaper" – the boy made exaggerated movements with his body – "to lay on the floor of his van to protect it from moose guts."

Tasker kept his tone casual. "What were you guys doing at the dump?"

"Shooting ravens – target practice. We hear this van comin' and hide to watch." Reggie stuck out his chin. He was proud of the story.

"Do you keep an eye on him?"

"You bet," the other said and they both laughed.

"I have an idea he went out to the big spruces during the fishing derby. I saw his tire marks there. Did you notice him take off from the narrows?" Tasker realized his tone got too serious because the boys started to shuffle. So he added, "No. I guess you were busy that day, eh?"

Reggie shrugged and the other one drifted backwards.

Tasker thought he'd try another tack. "You guys good shots? Hit any ravens?"

Reggie grinned, pleased. "The buckshot ruffles up their feathers, that's all."

"Maybe you boys could help me. I'd like to help Howard, if I can . . ."

Reggie stopped still and serious. His friend whispered, "We got stuff to do . . .," but Reggie was intent on Tasker's remark.

Tasker asked, "When did you last see Blake, not counting Friday's baseball game."

"I went up with him the day before to fix a fence back of his place. We went up in the pickup."

Tasker looked hard at Reggie. "Anything happen up there?"

The other boy started to snigger. Reggie swung around to grin at him.

"Tell me, guys. What happened?"

"I was hidin' in the back of the pickup, waitin' to see what Blake'd do to her!" Reggie said, still grinning, looking at his pal.

"Oh yeah!" the other shouted.

"What d'you mean?" Tasker asked, trying to sound like he was having fun.

"You know, see how he'd touch Jessica," Reggie answered, dancing back and forth on his feet and working his hands and fingers in front of his chest as if he were fondling breasts.

Then they both collapsed with laughter. Tasker stuttered, unbelieving, "Jessica?" And then he asked, "How many people know?"

The skinny boy drawled, "Everybody. Even his old lady." Then he nudged Reggie. "Come on. We gotta go."

Tasker sputtered, a kind of humourless, hollow laugh, his mind a jumble. He was aware of loud organ music, from Peders's, building to a dull crescendo, and a chill wind off Tagish Ridge. He knew the boys were sneaking off but he didn't stop them.

Maybe there was no grand plot, just dirty, family violence. Here was a motive for Howard to kill Blake, if Howard knew. Maybe Jessica did shove Blake at the big spruces like she said, and maybe Howard finished him off. No wonder Jessica . . .

Yet it seemed mean and cold-blooded. And Jim didn't fit in. There had to be another angle.

And there was Eve too. Did she really know? It was just her word where she was that morning of the fishing derby – so close, by the sand dunes, the mouth of the Henderson, near the big spruces. And her husband fooling around with her niece, her adoptive daughter. "Christ," Tasker said out loud.

And what the hell was Peders doing with the moose heads?

More questions, but a little closer, Tasker sensed without much satisfaction. The bit about Blake and Jessica was a twist.

Suddenly he thought, it really was Bach that Peders was listening to. Tasker smiled to himself. Reggie was no fool. How'd he know about Bach? Read something at the dump, he bet. Reggie and his friend probably knew more about people in Tsehki than anyone would ever expect. And scrambling through the garbage had probably cost Reggie's friend that knee injury.

Tasker trudged back to Jim's cabin, wanting to think about what else Reggie might know, but actually just staring at the dirt road in front of him. His eyes followed the hard edges of his own shadow and those cast from an occasional stone in the gravel. The sun warmed his back right through his jacket and shirt, but the air was cool. The spruce trees even smelled cool.

He would delay talking with Ivan Peders until the guy had a chance to settle down from the cherry bombs, Tasker decided. Besides, he didn't know all he wanted to get from Peders yet. Instead, he'd look into Eve's claim she'd gone berry picking the morning Blake was killed. The dunes was country he hadn't visited in some time, but it wasn't far from the sites of both crimes. Getting to the dunes wasn't easy any more, unless there was some new road. And it seemed early for strawberries yet. But Tasker had enough respect for Eve to look into her story first rather than accuse and bully to get at the facts fast.

Then he'd take on Peders.

Once back at Jim's cabin, Tasker dialled the Whitehorse hospital. The nurse on the men's ward said she wasn't permitted to release patient information to the public. When Tasker explained he'd assisted with the emergency procedure, she allowed that he could phone tomorrow and speak to the patient himself.

Tasker counted out eighty-five cents and placed it beside the phone to pay for the call. He looked west out Jim's window, over towards Natasahin Lake and the border range beyond. The view was spectacular.

Yesterday's rain had fallen as snow farther up, dusting the mountains down to treeline, but most of that wouldn't last today's sun. A huge eagle rose over the lake, stretching out at least a two-metre wingspan and flashing gold off its neck as it wheeled around. It had to be a mature golden, maybe the one Jim talked about. The creature passed low enough for Tasker to see it manipulate individual primaries to catch the breeze like a priest with raised arms, pulsing them slowly, seeking to strike the right gesture, fingers poised, ready to accept prayer from below. Today's sun would warm layer after layer of thermals, allowing the eagle to climb high with little effort, until it became only a dark speck soaring in the midday sky.

Another predator, an unholy one, stalked on the valley floor, and he was going to find him – or her.

Tasker turned his back on the view to shut the door of the cabin. It came to him suddenly why Jim used no locks to protect his artifacts inside, even after someone swiped the pair of pearl-handled throwing knives he'd found at Fort Selkirk. Jim wanted to trust people in return for the view. He would see the view as a gift, not personal property, and far more valuable than any treasure inside. Without locks, Jim kept his priorities straight. Tasker smiled – was he imposing his own values and motivations on Jim because he liked his old friend so much?

Tasker climbed into his cruiser, trying to imagine an eagle's-eye view of the Henderson River delta and the tracks and trails that went in there. His parents used to drive to the dunes, bumping along the shore from the village, but no one did that any more. It tore the beach up too much. Eve wouldn't have boated down to the dunes either, because landing would be risky, and even on calm days there could be rolling, ice-cold breakers if you got close to shore. When Tasker was a kid, when he could fill his outboard for twenty-five cents, he and Gary left their old freighter canoe on that stretch of beach once, and the breakers smashed it up overnight. Not one piece of wood remained attached to another in the morning. The motor was mangled beyond repair. He'd kept the cotter pin for a while, beaten flat, as a souvenir.

Tasker drove north out of town, past the Chevron station, looking down a number of turnoffs to the left before the main mine road. He decided the only one that might get close to the dunes was that old road into the big spruces – the one he and Jim used when they found Blake's boots. Maybe there was a new cutoff to the south into the dunes that Tasker hadn't noticed going in that time.

He turned around at the main mine entrance, drove back towards town and eased right down that old road. It wasn't far before he found the suggestion of a cutoff to the left. Not what you'd call well used. Poplar seedlings sprung from the rise between two tracks, short enough to be missed by the high carriage of a pickup. Tasker turned and followed the track. It was the sort of trail that would be great for dirt biking and it was heading for the dunes. Tasker kept his speed down so the scraping young trees and sagebrush wouldn't damage his undercarriage.

It was slow, and as he watched for potholes he thought about Reggie and his firecrackers. That could've been him ten years ago – even ten days ago. A small-town joker knowing his little world so well he could dance circles around it. Tasker remembered losing most of his confidence when he moved to White-horse, but keeping up the banter around a hollow core. The city kids encouraged his strut, and so the game went on. Like with Ida, until she said she'd tired of it all. And he had too. Somehow the events of the last week had pared it all away and he was having to stand with his pockets empty of cherry bombs. It was a shock to find himself thin-skinned and vulnerable. Having just been in Jim's cabin made it worse.

The dunes came in sight, first the old ones colonized with jack pine and shrubs. Tasker stopped his car and got out to walk. He'd finish this up quickly and get back to town to work on what the sergeant wanted. Finding Larissa's whereabouts made no more sense than anything else. Maybe he should just do it.

With the engine off, he heard distant breakers pounding the shore. Yesterday's windstorm. Yet off to the right, around to the side of the lake and sheltered from the prevailing wind, lay the lush valley of the big spruces. So close, but here the land was dry and the trees grew stunted on either side of the track. The hard sand dirtied Tasker's boots. Made of heavy minerals, not quartz. There were lines of black sand, too, that attracted prospectors every year – with no strike yet.

Tasker smelled smoke, faintly, from the village. He walked up and down the steep sand-dune ridges that lay like frozen waves, running north–south, parallel to the beach. The trees gave way to brush and shrub. Finally, from a tall ridge, he saw the spread of the lake and its long arm slashed into the mountains to the west – towards Maltby Inlet. That was the arm of the lake that tunnelled the wind between the mountains and whipped it up to carve these dunes, down near where Blake and Jim must have seen that snowy owl.

The east-facing slopes were already warm to touch – it was still before 9:00 a.m. – while the west slopes remained shaded and night-cool. The smell of smoke got stronger.

The scrub mostly disappeared, leaving only tendrils of plants running along the sand and tufts of bright blue lupin with hairy, pale green leaves. There were a few berries. And those were no bigger than a fingernail. Tasker picked a vivid red one and popped it into his mouth, tiny green cap and all. His tongue and the linings of his cheeks smarted with the tart, sweet flavour and he thought immediately of his mother's summer pies. Seems Eve's alibi checked out.

Suddenly, just back to the right, on a little wooded plateau, Tasker found himself almost on top of a smoking campfire and a lean-to. The poles of the low structure were poplar and looked to be cut with a hatchet and lashed with spruce root in the traditional way. The opening faced east, and the west side was thickly woven with spruce boughs. Quite serviceable and well used–looking, with a stack of firewood, kindling, a stump table and bucket in front. Tasker circled around and peeked into the opening. There were a few blankets neatly laid out with a copy of *Valley of the Dolls* open, face down, on top and a backpack that looked heavy, like the one Larissa had at the big spruces. It was no kid's fort; it was like a fish or hunting camp, but too far from any game.

Then he heard a moaning sound. West of the lean-to and over another sand-dune ridge.

Tasker edged behind to a clump of scrubby pine. He looked down and there was Larissa picking strawberries in the sun. A huge patch. She had an old evaporated-milk can half full and was duck-waddling along in a squat position, picking and singing as she worked. Not really singing, sort of humming out long, tune-less notes.

Tasker crouched too, his right knee on the sand and the other jutting up to rest his arms across. He thought of Ida and how they sometimes took summer picnics along the sandy bluffs of Miles Canyon just outside Whitehorse. In such a sunny place Ida would have her shirt off by now, her bra off too. She'd let Tasker rub on the Coppertone, massage it into her dark skin and darker nipples. And she'd kiss him. A peck. Sunbathing was too serious for more than a peck. Her skin would glow warmly and his desire would heat up too, mount and stretch. Ida had absorbed some interesting habits when she went outside to finish her training.

Larissa kept picking the tiny red fruit. It was hot now, and she wore layers of long-sleeved shirts under her jacket. Tasker counted two shirttails at least hanging over her jeans under her jacket. And her dark hair fell forward hiding her face. Tasker was fascinated by the way she swung her duck walk with a thrusting movement of her shoulders.

Her hands picked in turns, rhythmically. In the sun, she must be a sweatbox. The skin on those working shoulders and thighs would be slipping with sweat.

He watched expectantly, waiting for her next move. But Larissa didn't break the rhythm of her berry picking. She worked slowly across a sand valley that warmed to the colour of honey against an intense blue sky. The young green leaves of a poplar tree quivered as she passed underneath.

Finally, the can overfull, Larissa unzipped her fringed jacket, laid it quilted side down on the sand and sat on it. Tasker shifted his weight to his left foot.

Larissa sat with her legs outstretched and crossed, her palms flat on the gritty sand, propping her up from behind, and lifted her chin to the hot sun. Same tight, short-in-the-leg jeans she wore yesterday. Tasker waited, but that was it. She didn't even open her top button.

Several long minutes passed. Shifting her hips, Larissa pulled a cigarette pack out of her jacket pocket and lit one, drawing in hard so that her cheeks dimpled and then exhaling slowly with her mouth slack. All the while she kept her face tilted to the sun. She seemed to be happy, enjoying her cigarette and the heat of the sun. Tasker wondered what she might be daydreaming. He missed Ida.

Tasker's feet suddenly cramped in the chill of the shade. He looked at Larissa's strawberries, and the aftertaste of the one he ate was strong in his mouth. Larissa slowly turned her head and looked straight at Tasker. He stared back, unable to move his eyes. He felt caught out, embarrassed. But Larissa's stare didn't judge him. She looked matter-of-factly, as if she knew what he'd been thinking, completely unsurprised.

Tasker made a wry face and eased backwards, ankles stiff from the crouch. He had nothing to say to Larissa. It was a public place, after all, even if he had intruded on her private moment. What had he expected? Maybe he was just no better than Blake, he thought. He dusted off his knees and turned away. He didn't look to see when she stopped watching him.

Well, he thought as he strode back to his car, he'd come to check out Eve's story, and that he'd done. If he talked to Eve up front, maybe she'd lead him to some link between the two crimes. And he could tell Sergeant Flint he knew exactly where Larissa Stanley was.

Tasker started to drive off slowly, but was soon speeding along the track, ignoring the loud scratching from under the floor. As he approached the old forest road, still hidden by the bush, he caught a glimpse of the brake lights of a van heading into the big spruces. Ivan Peders! What was he up to?

Tasker turned off his engine and coasted. The van's steady rumble grew fainter and farther away. Peders probably hadn't seen him.

Rather than spend the next hour chasing him in the bush, Tasker decided to talk to Eve and then report in. He'd get to Peders later.

Partway down Eve's lane Tasker slowed and pulled over, grazing the underbrush. A car was approaching from the homestead, a beat-up, wide-bodied Oldsmobile. The back end swung low, its suspension shot.

As it drew alongside, Tasker recognized the driver as Albert Daniel, the band chief, with his left elbow resting on the frame of his open window. The chief looked serious, even sullen, but he rocked to a stop beside Tasker.

Tasker wound down his window, letting in the roar of the powerful old V8 and that smell of heated oil and grease mixed with road dust. He waited for Albert to speak first.

Albert pulled in his elbow slowly. His face looked darker in the shade than Tasker remembered and his eyes and nose seemed flatter and wider.

Finally Albert said in a deep voice, "Eve says you're working to get Howard out."

"Not exactly. I'm collecting all the facts I can," Tasker called back over the roar of Albert's engine. "Some things don't sit right for me yet."

"No one wants facts in Whitehorse, or truth for that matter. We been negotiating for years and got nowhere."

Tasker wanted to hang onto the opener, about getting Howard out. It was just possible Albert knew something – it was worth a try. "You see any link between what happened to Jim yesterday and Blake's death?"

The chief looked ahead out his spider-cracked windshield and down the lane. "Jim's a good man." He was hard to hear. "I can't think of him with Blake any more than Eve with Blake. She's a good woman."

Tasker could hear no cadence in the voice, no way of telling if the chief was surly or being cooperative. He took a deep breath in preparation for shouting another question, and then irritably exhaled, put out by the engine noise. He turned off his cruiser and waited.

"What did the doctor actually do to Jim?" the chief asked.

Tasker didn't yell this time, just answered in his normal voice,

"He used carpenter's tools to open up Jim's temple, let out the buildup of blood inside."

The chief's eyes rolled and he shook his head, "Man!"

"But it worked, a nurse says I can speak to Jim tomorrow," Tasker finished. If he wanted to get out of his car on the driver's side to talk above the noise, he couldn't. The Olds was too close and the smell of exhaust was filling his cruiser.

"Trouble with him, he practises cowboy medicine in every situation."

"He's got a peculiar bedside manner," Tasker agreed and added lamely, "But he saved Jim."

"More like no bedside manner – no ethics either. The way he treats Native people, like Isabel's son with the rod in his knee . . ." Albert seemed to drift off in thought.

The fumes from the Olds were getting unbearable now. Tasker squeezed the steering wheel with his left hand and, turning the key, said briskly, "Let me know if you can figure why someone would want to hurt both Blake and Jim. I'm looking for anything."

Albert put his elbow back on the door and his car started to roll past Tasker. "Your guys put Howard in there. You're going to want to let him out."

With a shriek from a tight fanbelt hugging his engine and a dismissing wave, Albert accelerated off towards the highway.

Tasker coughed with a burning throat. He wanted that lead to clear Howard and make it up to Jim – badly. He mumbled, "Fuck them all." Then he shouted it out into the bush as he rolled up his window.

Tasker heard "Come in!" but waited stubbornly outside anyway, rubbing the sand off his boots. He recognized the smell coming from indoors – a steamy, pungent smell that went along with jam making. This was a professional visit; he wasn't going to let old memories suck him into getting too friendly again.

Eve finally came to the door. She said, "Oh! It's you. I'm sorry about Jim, Warren. It's lucky he got help in time. Come on in." Her voice had some life in it and her arms swung with more of their old lilt as she let him in.

Tasker saw they weren't putting down fruit preserves, though a pot of water did bubble on the stove, heating the can of paraffin wax. Eve was tending the hot wax while Jessica and the twins drew on paper at the table. A bolt of unbleached factory cotton lay across two empty kitchen chairs.

Tasker felt his sinuses prickle and dilate with the moist air.

Eve smiled warmly and, putting her hand on his shoulder, invited Tasker to sit at the table. Tasker kept standing and said he had to get on with business. Eve said she'd like to help, but needed a minute to get the temperature right on the stove.

Jessica was working on some lettering and seemed too shy to acknowledge Tasker standing there beside her at all. While Eve finished up at the stove, Tasker watched Jessica. She was running the fingers of her left hand under her long red-brown hair as she drew, a child's movement. Her pale complexion was flushed in the moist air – she was one beautiful girl. Tasker could picture Blake watching her, fingers itching to touch those small breasts. Too young to touch, Tasker thought, and involuntarily shivered with disgust at his image of Blake. Then he shook his head; he sure hadn't been disgusted with himself when he was peeping at Larissa.

"Albert dropped by with the cloth and asked us to make signs for the minister's visit," Eve said by way of explanation. "For the roadsides, you know."

"I didn't think they wanted our kind of help."

"Well, they're in a rush. They've got a potlatch to organize and the date's pushed forward. The runners from the Alaska coast bringing the grease may not get here in time now." Eve shrugged. "Actually, I do a lot with the band, set up their accounts – taught the local bookkeeper some modern tricks when they got big." She scraped the saucepan along to the left side of the stove, away from the direct heat, and while rummaging in the cutlery drawer, called over her shoulder, "I usually help pre-audit every year, too. Did a lot of that before the twins came along." The noise of banging cutlery stopped when Eve dug out a pair of rubberized tongs and returned to the stove.

"I guess the band knows what talent you got here!" Tasker said lightly and let his hand fall on Jessica's paper. She snapped it away quickly and didn't look up.

Eve lifted the can of wax out of the water with tongs and placed it on the counter. Then she swung the bolt of unbleached cotton onto the counter and unrolled about two metres of it along to the right of the can.

Tasker was getting impatient – obviously he'd have to remind her he'd come with a purpose. He glanced back at Jessica and said, "I have some questions for you, Eve. Perhaps we could step into the next room."

Eve looked at Jessica too, pressed the palms of her hands together and then touched Tasker's shoulder quickly. "There's nothing she can't hear." Jessica kept her eyes on her work, but moved her left hand over to her mouth and started chewing her nails.

Tasker said, "OK, but it may get uncomfortable." When there was no response, he took out his pad and pencil and, still standing, continued, "Let's start with what happened to Jim. Know of any link between Blake and Jim that may have led to both attacks?"

Eve was leaning over the sink, twisting a window lock. "I've been thinking about that," she replied. "They were together twice on the Friday. Jim came by and told us about the road-block in the morning and then later took Blake to the bar after the ballgame – both were out of the ordinary, but nothing special." She shoved the window open, and immediately a blast of dry air cut the steam in the room.

"Scissors?" Eve asked whomever, and Tasker pointed to the pair in front of him on the table. Eve took them and leaned over Jessica's work, straddling it with her hands on the tabletop. Her voice took on a detached quality. "Jim and Blake had such different ideas. Blake was off on his own park idea, while Jim's more like me – wanting respect for locally determined needs . . . I can't see a link there . . ." Her voice faded away.

The twins had finished their scribbling and, in getting down from the table, jiggled it. Jessica said, "Hey! Watch out!" in a testy voice, drawing Tasker to look irritably back at her. One of his instructors once said questioning witnesses in their workplace can provide a lot of useful information, but this kitchen sure wasn't ideal. Jessica seemed to sense Tasker's hostility and stiffened more, continuing to ignore him, even turning her shoulder so he had to lean forward to see her work. Her paper read "Listen to Us."

"Any ideas who might want to hurt Jim or steal explosives?" Tasker turned back to Eve who was rounding up toy cars from under the table with her foot. The twins started to roll them noisily along the smooth plank floor.

Eve answered, "No. Makes no sense to me." She carried the scissors over to the counter, snipped into the edge of the material and, as she ripped off a length of cloth, asked, "Was the operation necessary? Albert and I were just saying he's knife-happy."

Jessica stood up and carried the bolt back over to the chairs. She smoothed the length of cut cotton banner along the counter before she started to transfer her letters in a light but steady motion.

Eve cupped both hands around the can of wax and, as it had cooled with the open window, moved it back onto the stove. She said, "Dr. Straun wanted Jessica and I to take pills this past week to stifle everything. He's like that – with women especially. He goes ahead and does what he thinks is right and doesn't discuss options or procedures with his patients. No way he'd agree to natural childbirth. I went to Whitehorse to have the twins." Her voice trailed off again and she stood behind Jessica, admiring her work. "I was once told he studied and interned in Alberta, but was so disliked he could only get a job through Northern Health. That's why he ended up here. A big fish . . ."

Tasker had stopped taking notes. They were off topic now as well as surrounded by all the distracting activity. He let anger slip into his voice. Maybe Eve would take him more seriously then. "What about enemies? Blake have any enemies, particularly ones he shared with Jim?"

"Not enemies – a few people wished he'd keep his mouth shut –"

"Any liaisons that were a concern to you?" Tasker let it drop hard.

Jessica lurched upright from her work and stared into Eve's shocked eyes. Eve turned and looked hard at Tasker.

He thought, she knows . . . Each of them knows that the other knows. He pushed harder. "A girlfriend? – shared with Jim perhaps?"

"Shared with Jim?" Eve cleared her throat and said, "The woman who runs an environmental group out of Toronto, but I don't know if she knew Jim much." Her voice sounded pinched.

"He told me she called the morning of the memorial service . . ."

Eve's hand twitched and hit the can of hot wax and a blob splashed on her hand. She stared down as it whitened on her skin.

Tasker stood watching it too as he considered. He didn't need to dig any more – they knew. And it didn't seem to link the two cases. All it did was leave Tasker with a stronger distaste for Blake. He let the silence widen.

Jessica snatched the tongs and carried the wax over to the counter, manoeuvring between Eve and Tasker without looking at either of them. She dipped in a wide brush, as wide as the can top, and firmly started to paint in her outlines with wax.

Standing aimlessly in the middle of the room, Eve said, her voice shrill, "Isn't it possible that whoever killed Blake and hit Jim were up to something else altogether? Blake and Jim were just in the way?"

"In the way of what?" Tasker asked. But there was no answer. He turned to Jessica and asked with little energy, "And that's where you may be able to help, Jessica."

Jessica's body startled, but she kept right on applying the wax.

Tasker continued, "What happened *after* you shoved Blake? Like – how long before you caught up to Howard?" Tasker felt Eve hovering behind him. "Did you notice anything?"

Jessica flashed a quick glare at Tasker. "I don't remember much. I told the police already."

"Try to remember. It could help Howard," Eve encouraged.

"No, nothing!" It was so final, so obviously a lie.

Tasker looked at his watch and said to Eve, "I have to report to Flint in a few minutes, but I'd like to come back later and get a statement from Jessica."

"Right." Eve seemed out of breath. "I want you to take something back. Hang on." She hurried out of the room.

Tasker found himself alone with Jessica and said gently to her,

"If you have anything to tell me without Eve hearing – about how Blake bothered you – anything that might help Howard . . ."

Jessica kept looking at her work, but said in a low voice, "I'm not doing any more talking. Not until Howard is out." It came out cool and deliberate. Funny, Tasker thought, but he wasn't shocked. It made sense somehow. Jessica could be pretty tough underneath.

Eve walked back into the room with a dish and a large pail. She handed the plate to Tasker. "Homemade wild strawberry pie. Shorty can serve it at the barracks."

Tasker took the cold pie in his hands. Blake's pie.

"Tell Shorty to send me back the dish when he's finished," Eve called as Tasker walked to the door and then she turned to the sink and started to fill her pail with water.

Outside at the car, Tasker slipped the pie onto the passenger seat. He felt an incredible silence all around. It had been strange: Jessica hiding information but not too concerned about his knowing it, and Eve seeming relieved – yes, relieved – that Blake was dead.

It took Tasker a good five minutes while Sergeant Flint ate breakfast to describe what he had. All through the part about Peders – the logbook, the cherry bombs, the moose heads – the sergeant shovelled in bacon and eggs. Shorty stood, his back to the conversation, slowly scraping the scales off a large lake trout with a camp tool made from six beer caps nailed on a wooden handle.

Tasker couldn't tell whether Sergeant Flint was even interested he'd stumbled on Larissa at the dunes. And Flint only nodded over his coffee as Tasker explained about Blake's pressure on Jessica. Shorty grunted sounds of recognition during that part. This business of reporting to an audience whose attention was on food didn't encourage Tasker to tell all. He felt no need to mention that Jessica would talk if Howard were released – it wouldn't sit well that he didn't get it out of her anyway.

Sergeant Flint's expression seemed harsher than usual. He had a fresh Whitehorse haircut – a crewcut of thinning grey hair that exposed liver-coloured spots on his scalp.

Only when he'd finished eating and Shorty carried Eve's pie out of the kitchen to the freezer did Sergeant Flint start to engage. He bent forward, looking at Tasker directly, and said like a conspirator, "It was Larissa Stanley's thumbprint on the door-frame." Then, "I want to go carefully with this. Find out if she was with Peders when he got the explosives out Monday."

"His logbook may say . . ." Tasker couldn't finish his sentence. He was trying to imagine Larissa swinging a club.

"I can get a court order on that if we have to. But try not to show our hand, eh? See if you can get Peders to cooperate." He paused and then finished, "The print could've been there for weeks, they tell me. There's no way to date it. The door jamb was too clean, sheltered, recently painted – the oils in the print wouldn't dry out quickly. So I don't want to jump too fast."

"She doesn't look that strong . . ."

"She's a tough one. Don't let a face kid you. What I can't figure is motive. We get motive or any other supporting evidence, and we pick her up fast," Sergeant Flint said. "But, that's not all the news. Two types of blood on the club that hit Jim. Two! One matches Jim, the other Blake. And Blake had unusual blood. There were spatters of it on several of the sticks in your pile. But the worst is, there's a knob on the club that hit Jim that may match up with the depression on Blake's skull better than the club we are holding already as the murder weapon. They're checking to see if any of hairs and skin samples on the club that hit Jim were Blake's too."

Tasker, trying to register the scope of what he was hearing, thought out loud, "Blake bled some because he didn't die until he drowned, the coroner's report said. So . . . Blake bled all over the woodpile then. That blood could've come from an injury caused by Jessica's push! The second injury didn't bleed externally, right? Could he have got both from one push, sort of bounced on the woodpile, whiplashed?"

"No one's suggested that." The sergeant chewed the last crust of his toast, his eyes losing their sharpness again. "The crown attorney has ordered more tests on the club we originally thought hit Blake. It looks like she'll let Howard Daniel out, or at least take it easier on the bail set."

"Where'd you find the club you thought was the murder weapon?" It crossed Tasker's mind, just for a moment, that Flint had messed with the evidence to frame Howard. But Tasker knew that Flint was lazy, not crooked.

"Near your pile, closer to the river. It was lying there by itself – stood out because of the thread from Howard's jacket on it. I still say Howard did it – saw Jessica's push and finished him off." Sergeant Flint was twisting around in his chair, looking for Shorty. "Especially if what you say is true about Blake and Jessica. A boyfriend could get pretty angry at a 'father' who sexually abused his girlfriend."

"So, you figure Howard wrapped an unconscious Blake up in the net and sent him downriver in his boat to die of a head wound."

"Sure, but he probably thought Blake was already dead. It almost worked. We'd never have connected the murder to Howard and the forest, except Howard forgot to throw in Blake's boots. Maybe we'd still be thinking Blake died in some sort of accident out fishing on the lake, injured himself, maybe drowned himself."

"Except Jessica would have placed Blake in the forest, and Howard knew that. What you're saying is that Howard acted not just in anger, but in a premeditated, cold-blooded way – forgetting about two really important things: the boots and Jessica. And if he cared for Jessica, he'd be leaving her with the guilt of that push . . ." Tasker knew the case against Howard was unravelling. There was no way. There had to be an easier explanation.

Before Sergeant Flint had time to answer, Shorty returned to the kitchen. Flint pushed back his chair and held his cup up for a refill. "Shorty, I'm going to the mine in a few minutes. Why don't I take you up so you can drive Jim's truck back down. Lock it up in the compound."

Shorty nodded in agreement, a little smile playing on his lips, and filled up Flint's cup. "Food warmed you up, eh?" he said.

Sergeant Flint mumbled, "Always does." Then he said, "OK, Tasker, let's talk about your day."

"I'd like to speak to Peders, see if I can get in to talk to Jim," Tasker said. He was beginning to feel uneasy and excited, like something was about to happen.

"Track down those explosives before Sunday. Maybe someone wanted to break up a beaver dam when Joseph was off duty." The sergeant was at the door with his coffee. "Whitehorse is sending down extra security – they expect outsiders, professional protesters. And the top executives of the mine. I don't want them nosing around for a couple of sticks of dynamite too."

Shorty snorted. "The top brass of the mine will be more interested in what the mine kitchen is servin' than any missin' sticks of dynamite."

"What will Whitehorse think if we got one murder and an attempted murder and no suspects?" Tasker asked.

Shorty coughed loudly.

"We got a suspect – Howard. We can always haul in Larissa

about that thumbprint, but I'd rather have more. They'll just have to take what we got. Come on, let's go." With that the sergeant stepped into the hall doorway. "Meet me out front in five minutes with the keys to Jim's truck," he called to Shorty.

Tasker sat in silence, staring at the empty doorway.

Shorty joined Tasker and looked steadily at him.

"Yes?" Tasker said.

"Keep your eye on Larissa." Shorty grinned and then winked.

"You!" Tasker found a laugh. "Sometimes you're incredible!" Even though his laugh was hollow, it was a release. It let him welcome the inevitable, accept that resolution was near.

Tasker shook off Shorty's remark. The sense of resolution was too great. He used to get the same feeling out moose hunting. After he and Gary had rubbed an old piece of antler on the bark of a tree, the way a male moose would, sometimes they'd hear a rival grunt from some distance. Then there'd be silence. But they knew a bull moose was on its way, even though they couldn't hear it. He and Gary would stand silent – alert, tense, stomachs knotted, guns cocked, watching for which way the bull would charge. There was no way to stop a bull once it was aroused.

It was like Tasker had heard the grunt, and the final move would be any minute. Maybe Flint was feeling that too.

It was almost noon when Tasker spotted Ivan Peders driving down Main Street. He followed the van as it turned past Jim's place and rolled to park in front of his cabin. Tasker didn't have to drive out to the big spruces after all. He let his cruiser roll forward until it almost touched the van's rear bumper. At another time he'd enjoy a big confrontation, but right now, well, it could be interesting.

Peders snatched a quick glance at Tasker through his rear-view mirror. He took a moment, preoccupied with straightening stuff on his front seat. Then he climbed out and locked the driver's door, sending no nod of recognition Tasker's way. But as he walked towards the back of his van, Peders's pale eyes shifted to Tasker again. The cruiser was so close he couldn't cut between the vehicles.

Tasker turned down his window, waiting for a good moment to connect with Peders.

Peders called out, "Can you back up? I need to get in here." He pointed across Tasker's hood.

Tasker obliged by coasting backwards. He'd like to know what made Peders tick. Not every hard-working explosives man listened to Bach. Tasker stepped out of the cruiser, pulled his pad and pen from his inside jacket pocket, and walked forward. "I have a few questions you can help me with."

Peders turned the key in the back doors of the van and swung them open. Tasker moved in and stationed himself with his shoulder touching one door, so close Peders might back away a step. He could see little beads of moisture on the pale hairs above Peders's lip and smelled a workingman's sweat partly masked by scented deodorant. Peders's blond hair spiked out from under a stained ball cap that advertised "Yamaha Pianos and Organs."

As Peders leaned forward and stretched into the back of the van, his left leg lifted up and showed black soil on his leather workboot and the cuff of his otherwise clean and freshly ironed green coveralls. Then he pulled two small cardboard cartons out the back and placed them carefully on the ground beside the rear fender.

"If you'll just stand back, I can shut this," Peders said.

Tasker obliged again and moved to the far side of the boxes, his back to Peders's cabin. He figured he had cooperation from

Peders now, what Sergeant Flint wanted. He said, "I want you to help me pin down some times and give me advice about handling dynamite."

"Found them?" Peders stood back abruptly from his van doors.

"No, but when I do . . ."

"I'll give you a hand."

"Good. I'll remember that! I'll be only too glad for you to dismantle them."

Peders smiled a little and put his hands on his hips, his long index fingers slipping into the side pockets of his coveralls.

"What were the times you were last in the magazine and the cap and fuse shed, and who was with you?" Tasker held his pen poised to record Peders's answer.

"Joseph and I were at both locations by 7:30 Monday morning."

"Just you and Joseph?"

"Correct."

Tasker lifted a foot to rest on one of the cartons between them. "What was the job?"

"Two jobs. One was to move a jam in the hopper at the mill. I just did that because I was here; they usually handle those on their own. Jim helps. The main job was running a test bore at the pit as part of an investigation on an option to tunnel."

Tasker wrote that down and looked at the box his black boot rested on. The top flaps, he noticed, were open, but they were bent where they'd been tucked in earlier. "Who was with you at the job sites?" he asked.

"Joseph. Jim was there at the hopper job too."

"No other millhands, miners nearby?"

"No. We cleared them out. Breaking up a jam can get loud in an enclosed building space." Peders bent forward to pick up the boxes. "Now, if you'll excuse me . . ."

"One or two quickies," Tasker said, leaving his boot on the carton. "You've been known to take Larissa with you to jobs. This time?" Tasker watched Peders's eyes turn wary as he straightened back up.

"No." The answer was aggressive. Then, "I stopped taking her along three weeks to a month ago."

"Wasn't that kind of unusual, her coming to your blasting jobs?"

"No. People get interested in the trade – like Jim too. She wanted me to teach her some of the things I know, some basic physics and mechanics. I saw no harm in that," Peders answered, clearly trying to hold his patience.

"The fuse?" Tasker backtracked. "Any idea how it went missing."

"No."

"Any chance there was a mistake in the records and no dynamite was stolen?"

"Not the way Joseph runs things."

"Any suspicions?"

"Reggie and them know something." Peders spat out his answer and bent over to place the one box onto Tasker's foot, which was still resting on the second. Tasker noted how light it was and slipped his foot from between as Peders hoisted them and finished, "Didn't you put that together after the cherry bombs? Those little punks, they know I'm watching them!"

Tasker moved in closer to Peders. "What were you doing just now at the big spruces?" He looked down at the dirty cuffs.

Peders shifted the boxes to his left side and rested them on his hip.

"Looking for Larissa?"

"That's my business."

"Is that her stuff in those cartons?" Tasker tapped one.

"No."

Suddenly Tasker knew the cartons were the ones he'd locked in the cab of Jim's pickup the day before. Blake's clothing. He was so sure his back shivered involuntarily.

Peders had swiped them. He'd followed the trail from the end of the old spruces' trail road to the explosives shed that morning and stolen the boxes right out of Jim's locked pickup.

His fingers still touching the side of one carton, Tasker asked, "Did you go anywhere else in your van this morning besides down that old road to the big spruces?"

"No – and I have work to do." Peders swung around Tasker and headed for his cabin.

It made sense Peders would want to check out the explosives shed for himself after the theft. It would be very interesting if he walked up that trail from the old road to get there. Tasker would be able to doublecheck the boxes were Jim's – Shorty would be driving down the pickup any minute. He could also check if Peders used the old mine road; the keeper would know if he went through the main gate.

It was a strange thing to do, steal cartons out of a locked pickup. What did the guy have in mind for Blake's clothes? Like the moose heads. Tasker called after Peders, "I won't forget your offer to dismantle the dynamite!"

Peders didn't turn to acknowledge, but fumbled at his door with keys, juggling the boxes on his left hip. Tasker made a note to ask Eve if the clothes were intended for Peders – if they were gone from Jim's truck, that is. There could be a logical explanation.

Tasker suddenly felt tired. His shoulders were heavy, and he had a headache. Maybe he was seeing things that weren't there, trying too hard, taking this all too seriously. He had an urge, right now, to stop and do something totally unrelated. Something absorbing, like taking a short hike, sitting on a rock, and quietly sketching. Just to lose himself in the sketching – it didn't have to be a big or predatory subject, just something northern, hardy, elegantly adapted. Something unimportant and comical like a gopher. That's what he needed, a good laugh. But he didn't have time, and yet, if he took a moment, it might give him a handle on all this.

"Your crib?" Dr. Straun wasn't really asking a question, but delaying as he fingered two cards in his hand.

"Cut your luck," Jim replied in the usual, good-humoured banter of card games. His voice was energetic, but his face looked dog-tired. He was bandaged white from the earlobes up.

Tasker had come into Jim's hospital room in the middle of their game of cribbage and, after a few pleasantries, said he'd be glad to sit down until they finished. He had to move a woman's leather jacket and handbag he took for Kay's off the seat of the only chair available in the room.

"I should've snipped your card sense while I was in there," the doctor grumbled. "If I knew where it was." He placed the two cards face down on the hospital tray and cut the deck. Jim picked up a top card, a five of diamonds, and lay it face up beside the deck.

"Damn you!" the doctor swore gently. He stood up, took off his jacket and rolled up his shirt sleeves.

Jim let his head fall back on the stack of pillows and winked at Tasker. "I'm missing a great day outside, Warren. It's like the June day we found that pair of yellowthroats scolding in the riverwillows."

Tasker nodded, remembering too. Yellowthroats weren't more than a few grams of feather and hollow bone, Jim had pointed out, but this pair was staking out territory at least a hundred kilometres north of their normal summer range. Tasker tried to catch their cocky, scolding poses in a sketch later. Maybe, he thought, he could find that old piece and give it to Jim.

The doctor played a card from his hand. "How 'bout an eight of spades!"

"Eighteen." Jim stretched across his jack of diamonds.

"Twenty." Dr. Straun played a two of spades.

"Twenty-one for two." Jim dropped an ace and counted out the last two holes along the wooden board with his matchstick peg. He let his head fall back on the pillows again. "No more, I've had it." He smiled weakly at Tasker.

"OK. Time out for refreshments." The doctor stood up and carried his leather medical bag into the bathroom.

Jim's eyes followed after, past the framed print, "Autumn in a Maple Bush," on the green wall and down to the battleship-grey linoleum floor. He said to Tasker, "Glad you came."

Dr. Straun carried three paper Dixie cups from the bathroom. "This will help you sleep."

"I'm already drowsy." Jim took the cup and looked inside at the silky golden liquid. "My tongue feels thick."

"One shot won't hurt," Dr. Straun said, and passing the third cup to Tasker, downed his in a gulp. "It won't be long till the sergeant and I can take you fishing."

Tasker put his cup on the table and shook his head. "On duty. Thanks anyway." Dr. Straun looked surprised and shrugged his shoulders.

Jim sipped his whisky, while Dr. Straun downed Tasker's and then went back to the bathroom for a refill.

"You're going to have a bigger scar than if I'd had an operating room!" he called. "Like Flint's leg the time we sewed him up with fishing line, years ago. Remember the operating table was the one boulder we found on the whole sandbar?"

"I haven't seen my scar yet," Jim said. "I'm just glad to be around to peg you in your place."

The doctor sat down heavily and leaned back in his chair. "You're in good company – Pharaohs, Inca sun gods, neolithic European chiefs. One preserved proto-Peruvian cranium has seven holes – " he lingered over the names. "It's an old procedure and that tell-tale hole in the skull has been found around the world in noblemen's graves." His voice was especially resonant when he spoke on surgical history. "The medieval French called their instrument a 'trepan.' It looked like our brace and bit. In modern university hospitals with all their equipment, the procedure is now called 'trephination.'"

"Ever look into local Native – Athapaskan – medicine?" Tasker asked, trying to join the conversation.

"Witchcraft." Dr. Straun shook his head. "Soapberry roots, dried mushrooms, drums and animal tongues in dreambags."

There was a knock on the door and the nurse walked in. She looked at the cup in Jim's hand, glared at the doctor and marched out.

Taking advantage of the interruption, Tasker stepped over to the bedside and put a hand on Jim's shoulder. "You're not looking half-bad."

Jim touched Tasker's sleeve and quipped, "Your uniform is a little wrinkled-looking, but other than that . . ." Pointing to Dr. Straun, he continued, "I've still got enough left inside to skunk last year's cribbage champion!"

The doctor took another sip from his paper cup. "It's all superstition and fertility taboos." Dr. Straun was still onto Athapaskan medicine. "Lots of babies and then a high infant death rate. And now Northern Health is clamping down on the use of abortion as birth control . . . more paperwork." He shuffled to the bathroom for another refill.

Jim seemed glad to change the subject. "Any ideas what happened, Warren?"

"I'm working on it." Tasker grinned, still standing right beside Jim. "Remember anything?"

"No, nothing at all." Jim smiled and shook his head. "The biggest story of my life, and all I know is what everyone else tells me."

"You drove up to the magazine alone?"

"Yes."

The doctor returned from the bathroom and walked over to look out the small window. Tasker stepped forward so Dr. Straun wouldn't walk right into him. Kay, he thought, had probably walked out when Dr. Straun arrived – she'd have little time for him.

"When was the last time you went up with someone else?"

"Early Monday, with Peders."

"Anybody with him?"

"No."

"Peders used to take Larissa Stanley with him. Remember the last time she was up there?"

"Several weeks ago, maybe a month."

"What did she do with him?"

"She was interested, always got out of the van and looked around."

"Nosey?"

"No. I was just glad to see her show the interest. Such a change."

"From being a hooker!" the doctor spat out in distaste and walked back to sit down in his chair.

"More than that." Jim didn't leave it with Dr. Straun's remark. "Larissa's had a tough life."

"Peddling her ass, you mean," the doctor qualified.

"No." Jim sounded tired again. "I have this memory of Larissa at about twelve years old, sitting in the sunshine on the edge of the boardwalk in front of the hotel, her hair chopped off across her forehead almost hiding her eyes and cut short around her ears – she was wearing a crazy T-shirt that said, 'Get Stoned, Drink Wet Cement.'" Jim closed his eyes as he spoke. "She was happy, child-like, holding a big paintbrush. I guess she'd been helping with some local project, painting the church or something. I remember her arms; she had these scars on her arms; circles of white that were indented, sort of puckered down, and surrounded by red circles. They were symmetrical, not ragged. And behind her, that father, sitting in the sun too, his cowboy hat pulled down to shade his face, and chainsmoking." Jim opened his eyes and looked right at Tasker's. "I realized those scars – they were from that man's cigarettes. He butted his damned . . ." Jim's voice broke slightly. "And now she's a pretty young woman taking an interest in the world around her."

Dr. Straun cleared his throat. "The change wasn't all a miracle. I gave her some fatherly advice after Public Health sent her the fourth or fifth time. Her old man caused her all sorts of problems before he asphyxiated himself and his wife a number of winters back. Fell into a drunken sleep in his car with the engine on."

"What kind of help did she need?" Tasker asked, wanting to know, but not wanting to listen to Dr. Straun any more.

"Something doctors have provided since the dawn of time – putting the long-term well-being of the patient first." Dr. Straun spoke in his most reverberating voice. "And you're right; those were scars from the lit end of a cigarette. Larissa wasn't the only one. His wife had them too . . . By the way, Stanley was her mother's name. She hasn't gone by her father's name, Jenkins, for several years now."

Tasker broke in when Dr. Straun paused. "I can tell you're tired, Jim. Just two more questions – anybody asking about the magazine or the explosives recently?"

Jim shook his head.

"Hanging around a blasting site?"

Jim looked like he was having trouble keeping his eyes open. "We often have to chase Reggie and his friends away, but they're harmless."

"Any chance the records could be incorrect and no dynamite taken?"

"No, we used dynamite to clear the hopper Monday, so Joseph had a recent count. He's real careful." Jim was starting to slur his words with fatigue when Kay and the nurse walked in together.

"Visiting is over for now. That includes you, Freeman Straun, and your refreshments." Kay smiled, but stood her ground and cleared the room without another word being spoken.

Tasker walked into the hall – he hadn't got much information but that didn't matter. He knew Jim was going to make it, and that was enough for now.

Tasker checked his watch as he turned right off the blacktop and onto the Tsehki Junction road. After visiting with Jim so long, he'd miss the Friday-night ball game for sure. But maybe there wouldn't be a game tonight, he thought, out of respect. The sort of thing people in towns like Tsehki did without anyone ever organizing it. Then afterwards, they'd talk among themselves, proving a point, full of wonder at how they acted as one without ever planning it. Tasker knew he'd never hear of that sort of thing in Whitehorse.

Less than a kilometre down the gravel from the turn, Tasker

spotted a patch of blue denim against the bush – the jean jacket of a man hitching south. Steady stride, thumb out, a Corrections-issue duffle slung lightly over one shoulder. It had to be Howard Daniel, let out and heading home, Tasker thought. He took his foot off the gas and let the cruiser coast until he stopped just ahead of Howard, fully expecting him to refuse the offer of a ride. But Howard stepped up his pace to meet the cruiser, seeming eager for the lift. He climbed into the passenger seat, gave a nod to Tasker and started digging in his shirt pocket. Tasker smiled broadly and picked up speed on the gravel again. This was interesting company for the ride.

Howard pulled a new cigarette pack out of his pocket, Sportsman unfiltered. Probably the first thing he'd bought when he got out. The inmates get sick of rolling their own, Tasker once heard, and tailor-made becomes a symbol of freedom, even for those inside a short time. Funny rule, but fewer mattresses caught fire, the warden claimed.

Neither Tasker nor Howard had spoken since Howard climbed in, but Tasker felt comfortable. He didn't expect thanks for getting Howard off the hook; it was enough that Howard accepted the offer of a ride.

Howard opened his window a crack and said, "I'm ready to party."

"Worried you've missed any action?" Tasker asked. He could see that Jim and Blake weren't big in Howard's mind, but he'd let Howard get around to them in his own time. They had a two-hour ride ahead.

Howard didn't answer Tasker, but grinned happily and lit his cigarette instead.

Tasker ran through the local stations on his car radio and then backtracked to the sound of country music. He wasn't interested at all in the phone-in show or community message calendar. He gave it some gas and accelerated a little over the limit, looking for the right speed that let the cruiser skim over the washboard rather than thump through every bump on the gravel surface.

Howard stared ahead out the windshield in some kind of trance and didn't talk. The silence widened. Tasker kept glancing over at his passenger, waiting for him to say something, anything, until Howard's head loomed large in his mind even when he was looking forward at the road ahead. It got so Tasker figured he could map Howard's profile, like in one of those cabin games his mother loved, where, as a kid, Tasker got to look at something for a while, then it was removed and he was supposed to draw an accurate picture of what he'd seen. Without looking, Tasker could see Howard's thick black braid disappearing down his back, with a few wisps free around the ears; the small deep pits on his dark skin in the fleshy parts of his face above the eyebrows and in an arc over the top of his chin; the long black wires of his thin moustache; and the navy and white kerchief ringing his neck, with dirt and sweat stains showing from the inside. This looming head started to bother Tasker. Was Howard avoiding conversation or just off in some other space? Whose game was this anyway, Tasker thought. He had to work to keep his growing irritation from showing.

They were more than halfway to Tsehki before Tasker finally asked, "They tell you why they let you out?"

Howard nodded, still looking through the windshield. Then he said, "Big-time weekend coming up. Maybe we'll get somewhere in stopping the mine expansion this time." After another long silence he added, "Any sign of runners?"

Tasker said, "Not that I know of." The grease trail runners, Tasker thought; Blake had encouraged the revival of that old tradition. He sure wasn't getting any credit for it.

Tasker thought about the pile of burls that led to Howard's

release. "Did you finish what you were working on – the piece with no 'spiritual significance'?" he asked.

Howard laughed. "Oh that. I saw this picture in the paper of a Siberian bear hunter's mask – metal, one hundred years old. Sort of flat with spines sticking out to look like short porcupine quills. Bear won't fight a porcupine, you see. I got started, but it's tricky in wood."

After another silence, Howard asked, "What I hear about Jim?"

With that opener, Tasker recited the story of Jim's accident, Dr. Straun's operation, Tasker's following the path behind the magazine and finding the carving burls and the grizzly bear. He finished with a joke he'd been planning: "The grizzly was looking out for you – the Kakhteyi grizzly."

"The Crow people have a story that grizzly bear protects women. Women who pay proper respect to the bear." Howard was still looking straight ahead. "This girl in their story, she wasn't respectful, so the bear took her when she wandered off berry picking. He appeared to her as a man and she became his wife. When her brothers killed the bear, she and her children turned into bears and killed her brothers."

Tasker had heard that story before, but never with so little detail. It wasn't like Howard to shorten a good story. Maybe it wasn't his to tell. There were rules like that, ones Tasker didn't understand. He said, "Well, that bear led me to the pile of logs that freed you."

Howard looked steadily at Tasker but said no "thank-you's."

"Who else was at the big spruces the day Blake got it?"

"Jessica, the watchman, Larissa Stanley . . ." Howard drew out the names as he lit himself another cigarette.

"You saw Larissa?"

Howard paused and then said, "Yeah, I went to her tent when I circled to see what made the big noise."

"What big noise?"

"The roaring sound Jessica and I heard."

"And Larissa was in the tent?"

Howard stared at Tasker and nodded. "She was straightening things up. She was real mad."

"What do you mean, straightening things?"

Howard frowned, took a long drag of his cigarette and, as he exhaled, said through the smoke, "Well, she said Blake'd been in there with her and threw things around a bit."

"Did she say what happened?"

"I could see it was a mess."

"Did she see Blake often?"

"Sure, in town."

"Maybe she was surprised to see Blake out there."

"Could be."

"How long did you stay with Larissa?"

"Not long. She wasn't in any mood for company." Howard turned to look out the side window.

Tasker had something now. He remembered Larissa telling him and Jim, the day they found Blake's boots, that the only people she saw at the spruces were Howard and Jessica. Blake was not mentioned – she'd lied. No one else – she'd been explicit, he remembered that clearly. He'd told Sergeant Flint too. Tasker waited, the taste of excitement in his mouth, while Howard tapped the ash off his cigarette and rubbed it into his jeans, leaving a pale grey steak in the blue denim. Tasker said, "Go on . . ."

"Jess wasn't where I left her, but Blake was. He looked knocked out on the ground." Howard gestured with a lack of interest. "I guess he was in a bad way. He was lying, face up, holding the back of his head with one hand. I could swear he was coming to. I wanted to find Jessica – they'd obviously been fighting and I was worried about her – so I left him."

Tasker again waited, saying nothing.

Howard took another pull from his cigarette and then finished. "It took a long time to find Jessica. When I did, we sat down for a while. She talked about how much trouble she had with Blake. Then, when we walked back to get her stuff, Blake was gone."

"Did she say what had happened between them in the forest?"

"No, not really. Only that he surprised her and she pushed him and ran."

"See anyone else?"

"Come on. Leave this alone."

"I'm looking for help – OK?"

Howard frowned and then suddenly shoved his hand down into the inside of his boot and scratched his ankle roughly.

"Did you see Larissa on the way out?"

"Do I have to answer these questions?"

"No, but I'm asking you, did you see Larissa?"

Howard shook his head, sat up and stared out his side window again.

"Where'd you park?"

"At the end of the mine road past the mill."

"So you walked past the tent on your way out."

"Uh-huh." Howard nodded his head.

"You didn't know if she was in the tent?"

"I didn't look – I figured she was probably still there."

"Know what time that was?"

"Not really. We were back at the village bridge in the afternoon."

"So, who do you think could've wrapped Blake up in the net and sent him down the river?"

"Beats me."

"Any ideas?"

Howard shook his head. "It's not the kind of thing Native people would do."

"Peders? He likes Larissa too, I heard."

Howard jerked his thumbs outwards and shrugged, indicating he didn't have a clue.

Because this was all news to Tasker, he was starting to wonder how much Howard had told Sergeant Flint. How much Howard was questioned at all. Tasker had a lot of questions in his mind, like – Why was Blake messing up Larissa's stuff? Why had Larissa lied about not seeing Blake? Who would want to confuse Blake's cause of death? But he felt he'd be lucky to get one more answer, so he asked what had been niggling the most: "What d'you figure made that roaring noise?"

"Well – Blake trashing Larissa's stuff in the tent." Howard said it like it was so obvious. He bent forward and jabbed his cigarette butt into the ashtray, folding it over on itself and crushing it again and again. When he looked up, a grin had spread across his face so wide it closed his eyes into long slits. "You guys, you have so many fancy things that tell the time of death and blood types and all that, but sometimes you still know nothing. Why don't you just relax and let your insides talk." Howard laughed, more with his body shaking than with his voice, and then pulled out his cigarette pack again. This time he offered one to Tasker.

Accepting the smoke, Tasker said, "OK. But, why didn't you carry out your carving logs when you went to get Jessica's stuff?"

"That sure would've saved me a lot of trouble." He laughed out loud, settled into the back of the seat and stretched out his legs under the dash. "Jessica wanted all my attention." Then he said, "How about turning up the music. I like this one."

Tasker slipped the cigarette in his breast pocket. Howard

hadn't got around to offering him a light and that was just fine. He figured he'd got all that Howard was going to give, so he cranked up "We Got Married in a Fever" just short of being painful. Time to party was right – Tasker decided he'd call Ida when he got back to town.

Howard lay his head back, shut his eyes, stuck his chin up and nodded with the beat of the song and the rumble of the road.

11. REGINA. September 1991

Tasker dialled Ida's number as soon as they got around to installing the phone beside his hospital bed. Perfect timing – his senior officer had been in to tell him that no one wanted to see him at work for a month; he had to take the time off. They could survive without him. The staff sergeant went so far as to joke that Tasker wouldn't be injured if he hadn't been working so much overtime lately. Tasker didn't argue; he knew the staff sergeant was right. And he knew how he wanted to spend that month off.

Tasker hadn't phoned Ida three months earlier – Amanda's birthday – so he'd have to ride that one out . . .

He heard Ida's voice. "Hello?"

"Happy twelve-and-a-bit to Mandy! Sorry I'm late." His voice sounded flat. He picked it up. "How're you?"

"It's you – your call is half a year late."

"I know, no excuse. How're things?"

"As a matter of fact we're doing fine. Chip has plenty of work – there's more exploration this summer and lots of prospectors to fly in and out . . ."

"Enjoying the good life, then?"

"I made the choice I had to . . ."

Tasker let that remark bounce around. He'd risen to it long ago in letters and on the phone – he didn't have it in him to take another crack. As far as he was concerned, he'd had a right to make some choices too, but she didn't give him the chance. She never told him she was pregnant when they discussed his plan to leave the north. When she did tell him, after the transfer, she claimed she wasn't sure if he was the father or the pilot she'd met in Old Crow. But she made her choice, she decided Chip would make a steadier family man. She said Chip was in touch with himself more than Tasker – Tasker hid his feelings, ran away from them. But who was doing the running? he'd kept asking.

Of course, Chip was a big-enough guy, or fool, to marry her when she may not have been carrying his kid. But that was history now.

"Where are you calling from?" she was asking.

"Just Regina. Listen, Ida, tell me who got it from the Kakhteyi grizzly – in the newspaper. I read that an old doctor was killed with one swipe, his trunk split in half and the upper part of his body spun around facing opposite his legs."

"Oh! Is that why you called?"

He let that sit too.

"Dr. Straun," she said.

Tasker whistled softly.

"Yes, Freeman Straun." Her voiced warmed up. "Can you believe it?"

Even though Tasker had wondered, to hear her say so was weird. "What happened?" he rasped. "I'd like to know. It's struck a chord."

"Well, it seems he surprised a bear from upwind when they were both out fishing. They think the bear acted blindly and in self-defence. Got a grip on the doctor's shoulder. It was dreadful."

"God, shoulder." Tasker touched his own shoulder, trying to fathom how a bear could do more damage than a sawed-off semi-automatic. "It must've rocked the village."

"The band has demanded the Wildlife Service people *not* shoot the bear. Everyone agrees it wasn't manhunting. But some of the locals want protection for their families, particularly the children walking to and from school. The chief, you know Reg Daniel, is talking about calling in advisers from Alberta, and maybe Mohawk Warriors too. He keeps pointing out they've been meeting over twenty years, signing agreements, but the government isn't really listening. They want changes to their first agreement, more discussion. Some of the younger men took over the Grizzly Den and General Store for a night, but Reg separated himself from that and helped sort it out. Everyone expects another barricade to the mine . . ."

"So what d'you think is best?"

"Well, I have to agree with Reg, but it's too bad for the doctor. He served northern communities for half a century and now his death is all part of land claims, mixed up in this round of the media battle. You're not thinking he deserved it, are you?"

"Well – it feels good. Yes, I have to admit that." Tasker was starting to enjoy Ida's old directness, the way he could come straight to the point with her.

"You always had it in for doctors."

"Not true, it just looks that way." He didn't say he was in the hospital now and getting better fast because of fine medical care. He said, "Remember, Ida, remember our fight before we broke up years ago? About that girl we knew – you knew – with those scars on her stomach? I've been thinking about that part of the whole story."

"Yes, you always put a lot of importance in that. And it was a dreadful thing for him to operate without consent." Then her voice lowered. "I think we fought because we were young, we were idealistic, and neither of us could stand being wrong. Hospitals have ethics committees now . . ." Her voice trailed off.

"I've been remembering the night I called you in Old Crow, late – after Howard Daniel got out of jail and I drove him back to town. How you were able to put the case all together, instinctively, with what I told you that night. You know, about Jim being hit. I was thrashing around in details, losing sight of the bigger story. That's why Dr. Straun getting it from the grizzly . . . that's why I'm interested. An echo . . ." This time Tasker's voice trailed off.

Ida said nothing. Maybe she'd misinterpreted what he said. "No blame intended," Tasker broke the silence on the line. "I've been blaming myself for years so I know it's no good – just we were so close, hindsight is 20/20." Tasker figured he better change the subject, if only to prove to Ida that really, no blame was intended. "Seen anything of Jim or Kay?"

"No – but they look after each other better than any couple I know, any age. Listen, Warren, I've got to take the kids to a soccer match." Then she said quickly, "I hope you aren't just saying that. It's long past time – you should've stopped eating away at yourself . . . You were too young and didn't have the experience to know or anticipate, when you think of it now. The murder was craziness, revenge with a twist – a motive buried in sacred cows and taboos that no one talked about then. And the attempt to gloss over the underlying problem, people like you made it harder for things like that to ever happen again . . ."

"Maybe." Tasker forced a laugh. "I'll be getting leave in a couple of weeks – a month or so off. I thought I'd come up. Take Mandy on a fishing trip."

"That's a good idea. Should I tell her – are you really going to come this time?"

"Yes. I even got my ticket paid for."

"Warren" – Ida's voice was sort of strangled – "just a warning . . . You'll be surprised how much she looks like . . . Well, wait and see . . ."

On some level Tasker had known for a long time, from the

annual school pictures he was sent. But Ida almost saying it, and the fact that she didn't actually say it – that was something too. Still secrets, unspoken things about pregnancy and birth. They both needed to talk about what they were doing.

He said, "Better get to the soccer game." He found himself hoping his voice didn't show any emotion, but then wondered why that mattered any more. In fact it was part of his problem.

"OK. We'll look forward to seeing you."

Tasker hung up and let his hand dangle down to the shelf below the phone. He felt for the Glenfarclas in the little drawer. When he pulled it out, he stared for a long time at the label. He'd always liked the idea of single-malt Scotch as well as the taste. Each brand unblended, a distinct and hardy product from one northern valley – one source of soil, water and salt air – with one main ingredient fermenting on itself. The process was homestyle but refined, like sourdough. He pulled off the cap and the smell of lukewarm whisky prickled in his sinuses and turned his stomach. With the palm of his left hand, he slowly twisted the cap back on. The movement shot pain through his other, injured shoulder and down his arm.

Dammit, he thought, now he had the experience he didn't have back then, the confidence to work the levels of mean-ing . . . Better than a kid fresh out of school. Maybe he had it in him to really live life, move back north where he belonged. Was the story played out or was it beginning again? Or was he just coming to terms with it at last?

As he fell asleep, Tasker tried to picture what Ida might look like now. Was she still tiny and finely formed or had childbear-ing and the years gently widened her waist and softened her face so that those perfect almond eyes drooped a little, only tighten-ing when she smiled?

12. TSEHKI JUNCTION. June 1978

Tasker hit the alarm-off button and scrambled out of bed. This was no Saturday morning to sleep in with less than thirty-six hours before the cabinet minister arrived in town.

He grabbed a cup of coffee from the pot warming in the kitchen and carried it to the front office. Working up yesterday's report might help him focus on what mattered in the things he'd learned from Howard, Reggie, Eve, Jessica, Peders, Larissa, Chief Albert . . .

Sergeant Flint was already at his desk – probably a first, this early. He grunted, "Morning," bending over a list he was compiling, and without waiting for Tasker's reply, started on with orders. "Before supper, I've got two big jobs for you, and I want them done hard and quick, on top of accounting for those explosives." Then he looked up at Tasker, "Time's running out and things are heating up."

Tasker said, "Shoot," and grinned back, thinking this was the first time he'd heard those cop lines used on the job.

"Eve phoned last night." Sergeant Flint held up one finger. "She says Jessica wants to make a statement – to you, she said. I said you'd be over at 10:00 a.m. with the tape recorder."

"OK," Tasker said and laughed to himself. Good to her word. Once Howard was out, she'd said she'd talk. Should be an interesting session.

"And I want you to speak with Chief Albert and find out

what they got planned for tomorrow – in the way of trouble." Sergeant Flint counted off a second finger and held it up. "I'll be meeting the Whitehorse reinforcements for a security sweep of the forest late this afternoon. I don't want any surprises tomorrow. If he'll cooperate, tell him we'll give him some room. Tell him that."

"Got anything more on who hit Jim, the weapons mixup?" Tasker knew Sergeant Flint didn't.

"No, not yet." Sergeant Flint spat out the words, still standing stiffly with two fingers in the air.

"It's time, then, we brought in Larissa Stanley for a talk," Tasker said. "Find out what she knows, who uses that trail from the forest to the magazine. Howard says she was with Blake the morning he died."

He was at the door when Sergeant Flint called, "Yes, pick up the Stanley girl. Let's find out what she knows."

Tasker called out, "Got it," but didn't bother to look back – he knew he'd see three fingers wagging in the air.

[Excerpt from the statement made by Jessica Weiss on Saturday, June 18, 1978.]

"This is a true statement, as recorded by me, Jessica Weiss, for Corporal Tasker. June 10th of this year, as far as I remember.

"Yes, that's the last day I saw Blake. Everything about him I saw that day? . . .

"OK. I didn't see him at breakfast. Later, I heard a truck in the lane and stepped over to the window to look out. I'd been painting, trying an idea I liked, so I didn't hurry. I can't remember how long it was after breakfast. I lose time when I paint. It was before lunch.

"By the time I got to the window, Blake was out and collecting firewood at the back door. He was snapping up the wood with jerky grabs – I could tell he was mad. Just looking at the top of his head and the wood chips on his bush shirt started to take me away from the flower idea, so I turned back to my work.

"But I'd lost it. The stem looked round, I remember, but the colour of the flower seemed muddy now and the flower looked heavy . . . But you don't want to know all that.

"OK, sure. I remember ripping the picture off the pad and dropping it to the floor. I couldn't concentrate any more. Just seeing Blake did that.

"Then I heard his raised voice from the kitchen below – 'Yes, a few kilometres away, the protest is happening and I'm not part of it,' or something like that.

"Eve answered, but he kept on loudly, 'It was humiliating. Albert *excused* me from the protest. His way won't save anything. He just wants dishwashers and freezers full of fried potatoes.' I remember the fried potatoes part, Blake hated fried potatoes.

"It was quiet for a while and I went down to get a snack. I guess I could smell what Eve was cooking – stew, I think – and it made me hungry. She was talking to him when I got to the kitchen, saying, 'In a month we'll have fresh carrots. Radishes in a week. Why not take satisfaction in simple things?' Something like that.

"Eve offered me tea, so I sat down at the table near the stove. Carrie and Sheila were running around chasing the cat, barefoot, and Blake patted their heads or diapers each time they passed. Maybe that's the way Eve'll remember him. Not me, I won't remember him that way.

"Let me see. When Eve gave me my tea, she sank into the green chair. I could tell she wasn't in a good mood, so I picked up my mug and left for the hallway to go upstairs.

"I hadn't even got to the top step when I heard her say, 'I

need to talk to you. Something must've happened yesterday. It's not like Jessica to slap her cousins.'

"Of course, I stopped to listen.

" 'Maybe it's just adolescence, puberty,' Blake said. 'I'm going to use the telephone. I plan to stop the mine expansion.'

"With that, I figured Blake got out of it so I turned to go into my room, but Eve wasn't finished yet. 'Something must've set her off. She's never even shouted at the kids.'

"I heard the clank and thump of the poker jabbing the logs and then Eve's voice, 'Please talk to me. I'm upset. I'm having troubles with Jessica, but I never expected this.'

"I remember thinking Eve sounded like a social worker – so straight out with her feelings. I sat down on the landing, wondering what Blake would admit. And I didn't care really if they found me listening.

"Blake said, 'Dear, we found them – she found them. That's what matters. Youngsters wander off all the time.'

" 'But she said Carrie was knee deep in the creek!' Eve's voice was full of panic.

" 'Yes, and the creek's swift. But she found them. I didn't get the fence repaired and they never picked any berries.' Blake was good at getting the subject changed, he even said something like, 'I was wanting strawberry pie for dinner.'

" 'Maybe we're both overtired,' Eve said.

" 'Look, I'm in no mood for this,' Blake kept pushing. 'I have calls to make to Ottawa and Toronto about my park.'

" 'I think there's more than I've been told,' Eve was mumbling now, giving in.

" 'Surely it's perfectly natural for a fourteen-year-old girl to smack her cousin in anger just after the child, two children, run off and get lost. She wanted it to be their fault, not hers.' I could tell Blake was pacing around the kitchen – he did that when he lectured. He kept on and on, 'I should never have taken them upcountry to look for berries when there was fencing to do. Maybe she got daydreaming – that would be like her. Or one of the boys in the back of the pickup said something – they were horsing around. Maybe I said something, Eve!'

"At this point I almost marched right back into the kitchen. I was mad. Blake was so sarcastic – I wanted to tell what really happened. But then Eve was shouting, 'OK, OK. You're right. I give up.' That was so awful, to give up, it made me sick.

"'Goddammit!' Blake shouted, 'Why's it always my fault? No one ever listens to me. Jessica's a fool, like her vacant-headed mother.'

"'Forget it, Blake, it's just that . . . it hasn't been good with Jess.'

"'Look, I didn't pay attention. I was relieved we found them . . . I never talked to Jessica about her problems.'

"'I don't know what to do with Jess.' Eve kept talking, but in the voice she uses when she's talking to herself. 'She wants to go sketching with Howard to the big spruces tomorrow. Somehow she's persuaded him into giving her a lesson. Howard is eighteen and Jessica is – only fourteen, fifteen.' She never remembers my age. 'Maybe I'll just keep her home.'

"'Maybe she needs some time away from family, some independence. Going with Howard to the spruces is better than the fishing derby. I don't want any member of this family supporting that.'

"'Come on, it'll be fun.'

"'It's just a ploy by the mine PR department, the Toronto-fed boys, to show that pollution from their operation hasn't killed the lake yet. The bridge across the narrows will be plastered with their slogans.' Blake had this way of lecturing.

"'Blake, I need our old talks.' Eve's voice was whiny now;

that's how she was when he trampled all over her with lectures. 'Remember when we worked everything over, professor and student, when there were no kids?'

" 'Ah! Eve, not now. I have to stop this acid lake.' I could tell he was smiling. 'Environmentalists have never stopped a mine dead before, logging yes, but not a mine. I'll spend two or three hours phoning and planning – then after supper we can go to the village ballgame. Make an appearance in the community, just a diversion. Something for the body if not the mind?' Blake's voice was sick-sweet, but a putdown at the same time. He said something like, 'That's better. You look better when you smile. I'll have some of that fresh tea when it's ready.'

"It was over . . . the subject changed . . . Blake had done a great job of making it all my fault. Blake's a jerk, I was thinking, next time he bothers me I'll tell him to shove it.

"I decided there was no way I'd play baseball and then he wouldn't have that chance. Blake, all the guys are chauvinistic anyway. The whole field moves in when I get up to bat. They fumble the ball on purpose, and then laugh, thinking I don't notice. But you don't want to hear all about that . . .

"No, that's not the last time I saw him before baseball . . .

"What did I do? Upstairs, I went back to my sketchbook. I thought about moving out, about the new high school in Vancouver. The one that specializes in art, accepts students from all over B.C. and the Yukon. I decided to start a portfolio – later I burned it, you saw . . .

"OK. I got this idea of using no black or brown. Just red and yellow and . . . blue. I forgot about Blake and filled the whole page with just the centre of one lupine flower – no leaves, no edges, and no black.

"After a while, I heard a truck in the lane again. I thought, maybe he's leaving. I felt tired, my shoulders, my whole body was heavy, but I went over to the window to look. It was Jim leaning out of his cab. He doesn't usually come by in the daytime. I thought, maybe he'd give me a lift into town. I never get a chance to go into Tsehki Junk alone. I could sketch there.

"I ran down the stairs and out into the yard. Jim's telling Blake about the roadblock and I wanted to interrupt, ask, but Eve frowned, saying 'wait' with her eyes.

"Jim stopped talking and I asked.

"'Well, of course.' Jim smiled and, after he looked at Eve, he added, 'So long as Eve agrees.'

"I looked at Eve too. Her mouth was open and her eyes big.

"Blake put an arm around Eve's shoulder. He said, 'Why not? We can bring her home after baseball.'

"I ran inside to get my stuff before anyone could change their mind.

"Then I climbed into the truck. Jim laughed and said, 'Well, I guess it's time for me to get along.'

"Eve said, 'All right, but be at baseball by 8:00 tonight at the latest.'

"Blake moved round to my door. He put one hand through the open window and said, 'Don't go painting up your face, now.' It was his sick voice, the one he uses when he says, 'Do you miss your mother? I understand. I miss her too.' I picked up a bird book on the seat and looked at it until Blake finished running his finger along my bottom lip.

"That's the last time I saw the jerk until baseball . . .

"Howard? Yes, I spent most of the afternoon with Howard. We talked and stuff.

"Well, when Jim dropped me off at the Cultural Centre, Howard was sitting outside with his brother Reggie, carving. He said, 'Hey! I said tomorrow, not today. This place is for Native artists.'

"I couldn't tell if he was joking. There was no way I was going anyplace else. Sometimes I can't figure him out.

"Howard went into the building with Reggie for a while. I looked around for something to draw. Howard was gone, but his strong face hung in front of me like a mask, grinning. So I drew that . . .

"Yes, your cop car drove up about then. What did I think of that? I thought, what do the cops want? You know what happened . . .

"OK. I see. Well, you said, 'Jessica, remember me?'

"I remembered you. You went away to high school. I wondered why you ever came back.

"The sergeant said, 'If you see Howard, tell him we stopped by.'

"I watched you both drive off, and Howard comes around the building, carrying his carving and knife. He's grinning, walking tiptoe and pretending to be sneaky. 'What our peace officers want?' he says to me.

"I said, 'You.'

"Howard said, 'Ever notice when the sergeant takes off his hat, there's a mark where his hat's been – white scalp showing like fat along the top of a greying pork chop?'

"I laughed. He wasn't being mean, you know, just funny.

"He said, 'Did the chop talk?'

"I giggled, then I wished I hadn't. There was a long silence and I didn't know how to end it.

"Howard finally said, 'You're different. Most white girls, they talk and ask too many questions.'

"He bent over so he could see my sketchpad. I felt him breathing on my cheek. It was open at my sketch of his face.

"He hates it, I thought.

"Howard said, 'Why not try something better-looking next time?' Then he grinned.

"We sat on the step and talked most of the afternoon . . .

"Well, he told me a lot about his brother Gary. He said Gary was a better carver than he is – until Gary lost the use of his hands . . .

"Yes, he said how it happened. Gary got drunk one night and the cops found him passed out near the hotel bar. He never could hold his liquor – Gary was no drinker, Howard said. They dragged him by the legs down the boardwalk and up the steps of the station. The next day, Howard visited Gary, but Gary never moved. He'd peed his pants and lay in his own dirt. The cops said he was drunk. After dinner, he still looked like that and they called the doctor, and Dr. Straun said Gary's neck was broken because of a bar fight. But Howard knew it was because he was dragged by the heels, head and neck slamming along the board-walk and up those steps.

"Howard said you were with him when he visited the jail and he said you were a friend of Gary's and they never understood why you went off to cop school after that happened . . .

"No, as far as I know Eve had no idea what Blake did to me up fencing or anywhere, before he died, that is . . ."

[Excerpt from the statement made by Jessica Weiss regarding the events of June 11, 1978, as taken on June 18, 1978.]
". . .The big spruces, they were beautiful early in the morning. I remember watching a shaft of light strike the knot on the trunk in front of me. Circles within brown circles, like a pupil inside an eyeball, inside an eyelid, framed by an eyebrow. The eyes stared, wooden animal eyes, beaks, claws and teeth on the trunks of the huge trees where the low branches had broken off.

"Howard left me sketching on a log alone. He was off looking around for wood. He's fussy, you know, chooses only certain pieces.

"The trees, they're too watchful . . . I can't draw them, I thought, and I guess I said it out loud.

" 'When Gary and I first come here, Jessica' – Howard startled me from behind – 'we saw trout and bear and eagle and raven in the trunks and shadows. That's the power of Kakhteyi.' He dropped an armload of carving wood beside me. Thick pieces, as big as your arm, some with gnarled ends, burls he called them.

"I felt dampness soaking into my blue jeans. I remember I didn't want a wet spot on my pants so I shifted quickly onto a rock beside the log and said, 'Well, I'm going to paint this moss. See if I can get it looking wet.' It shone with moisture, with purple shadows.

"Howard sat down beside me. He shook a cigarette out of the pack. 'My brother carved a mask once after we camped out here. He carved a grizzly bear, with strong outlines of eyelids, teeth and claws – but the piece of wood still holds its own shape. Like these trunks.' He lit his cigarette and blew the smoke away.

" 'Why a grizzly?' I stared into the forest. 'Are there grizzly here?'

"Howard's eyes laughed but his lips didn't. 'They have their paths in the forest, but not right here. Grizzly walk the same trails, put each paw in the same track almost, year after year. If you're smart, like me, you stay away from them.' Now Howard laughed out loud and I did too. We both knew he was trying to make me feel safer and it was working. Then he got serious again, 'The grizzly I'm talking about, Gary's carving, it's from an old legend. The first people who lived in Kakhteyi offended the grizzly and were punished for it. Punished so hard, a man from the south had to bring that legend back and open our past to us.'

"When Howard told the story about Gary's accident, I wanted to draw, and I wanted to now too. I started to fill my whole page with the lines of the rock and a patch of moss.

"As he spoke, he bent closer to watch me. He put a hand on my left shoulder and I felt its warmth right through my sweater.

"'These lumps we're sitting on, we know they're the homes of our ancestors.' Howard moved the cigarette to his left hand and guided the pencil on my page. He can give width to a narrow line just with the twist of his hand.

"'Since our past is reopened to us, life has changed. People want to learn the old language, the old dances. Men and women who moved away and come back to visit, they find themselves wanting to stay.'

"'What about the one who told you of your past? Where is he?' I asked.

"'He came by each summer with many stories. Gary heard them all. He carried me too, when I was little, to hear. It was for him that Gary carved his mask. But then he stopped coming. Other people from the university helped us for a while . . .'

"I looked up at Howard, right into his black eyes. He was looking through me. I knew he was talking about Blake's work, that university stuff, but didn't say anything to him. 'Gary and I camped here in Kakhteyi many times alone. Our band, we kept the exact location of Kakhteyi a secret for a long time. Even after that other white man started coming to the tundra above the trees.' Howard paused and then his voice got harder. He said, 'Me and Gary, we checked over his helicopter and its square green numbers, but never realized that man was going to steal our land. We could have killed him right there before he found the copper. We thought he was looking at the old sheep drive, the one the university woman was so excited about – that's how stupid we were.'

"Suddenly Howard and I heard something rumbling through the forest. The sound went on and on. It must be large, I thought, like the bear. Howard thought the sound came from up the river and ran towards it. I waited there scared – it seemed like forever. Then I twisted to collect my pencils and pastels. There's a snap right beside me and I look up.

"It's Blake. His hand on my shoulders. I can smell his breath. I shove him hard and he falls back down towards Howard's carving wood. Then I run where Howard went. I run between all the staring brown tree eyes . . .

"Yes, I'm sure he fell on Howard's pile of carving wood. Backwards . . .

"No, I never saw him hit the ground. When I didn't find Howard at the river, I headed inland and got all turned around and lost. I was scared I'd be on one of those bear trails, you know, one that Howard talked about. Finally I sat down, I was too tired to worry. I waited a long time. A motor started and I panic, thinking Howard's left. But in a moment, there he was. We sat and talked. I thought I heard a motor again, far away. Only later did we go back and collect the pens and papers, our sweaters. Blake was gone . . .

"No, I have no idea how long – less than an hour, maybe?"

[Excerpt from the statement by Jessica Weiss, taken on June 18, 1978, regarding the events of June 16.]
". . . You want to know how much I told Eve about the fencing trip? Well, I tried to tell everything.

"It was the day after Blake's memorial, you know, service, and before Jim got hit, that same day. We'd all driven to town early. It was cool, kind of threatening rain, and I was minding the twins while Eve did business nearby. We started a small bonfire on the beach and were skipping stones . . .

"Right – the fencing trip was on the Thursday before . . . Yes, June 9 . . . but I didn't tell Eve until June 16. Yes, a week later. I told you what Blake told her about it before –

"Yes. When Eve finished in town – on the 16th – she walked out to join us. I watched her come, her feet sinking into the thick gravel along the shoreline. The twins squealed and toddled towards her, their pudgy fingers clamped around 'prettiest' stones. I poked the fire, moving the sticks apart, watching her walk up. She looked older, I thought. It had been peaceful with the smooth stones, the mist and the lapping shoreline, and I didn't want it to end . . . Is this what you want? . . .

"OK. But I don't think this helps Howard or anything.

"Let me see, Eve put an arm around my shoulder. 'You've been out here a long time,' she said. 'Let's go to the hotel for a hot chocolate and a piece of pie.'

"At that moment I loved Eve so much. Felt sorry for her – with Blake dead. 'I think I've won back Sheila's trust,' I said.

"'I'm glad.' Eve sat down in front of the dying fire and lifted Sheila onto her lap. 'That incident . . . It seems so long ago . . . ,' she said. Carrie stood poking the fire with a long stick.

"I decided then and there to tell Eve what happened fencing, putting in all the details. It seemed important to be honest and tell everything. But as soon as I got started, I just couldn't tell *everything*.

"'What happened fencing last week,' I said, 'was, Reggie had this bag of candy in the back of the pickup, and he kept passing mints around. The twins and I could see them sucking candies through the rear window. Then, when we stopped at the hole in the fence, the guys jumped out and carried the chainsaws into the bush.'

"Eve looked lost sitting there by the fire, but I kept talking, figuring she'd catch on. 'Blake told me where to find the best berry patch and then hurried off with the others. I thought Reggie had gone too, but suddenly he was jumping off the tail-gate with his bag of mints. He must have got one stuck when he landed because he grabbed his throat and stared at me, strangled-looking.'

" 'I never heard this before,' Eve said as she pulled Carrie backwards onto her lap beside Sheila.

" 'I was scared.' I kept on talking. 'Then I called for Blake and started thumping Reggie on the back. Blake didn't come right away, though I could see him. When he did come, he stood right in front of Reggie, bent over, and shouted, "Have you been greedy?" '

"When I was telling this to Eve, I didn't say that Reggie's mouth turned blue and it opened and shut like a fish's. 'Reggie nodded,' was what I said. 'And Blake said, "Promise never to be greedy again?" and Reggie nodded again.'

" 'You thought Blake was mean to –' Eve started.

" 'No,' I lied. 'I remember Reggie's shocked eyes. I was so scared. Blake squeezed Reggie's stomach from behind. Then Reggie vomited and everything was all right. They left me to go berry picking – just like that. I thought how Reggie must've felt when he couldn't breathe . . . and then, suddenly, the twins were gone.'

"Eve was stroking Carrie's hair. 'I see now,' she said.

" 'Blake wanted to teach Reggie not to hurt himself again . . . and he was mad at me for thumping – you're not supposed to thump.'

"The other part, just before Reggie choked . . . it had been only a moment. When I got to that part, I just couldn't tell Eve. It wouldn't come out.

"Reggie must've seen. Blake wouldn't come quickly when I called. Then he was hard on Reggie. That's why I shoved him away at the big spruces. That's why I pushed so hard . . .

"Eve just accepted what I told her there on the beach. She didn't seem to notice any holes. 'Then Blake was right. You found them and they were fine. And that's all that ever mattered.' She clapped her hands, 'Time for a treat, guys!'

"I remember that so well. I felt like a rat.

"We started to walk together along the beach towards the hotel. A cop car headed north with its flashers and siren going. I felt alone, even though Eve was so nice. I needed to keep talking, to smooth the story over. The part I'd left out had sharp edges, even if Eve hadn't noticed.

"'When I lost Carrie and Sheila, I ran around the berry patch looking for them,' I said. 'Then again. I felt panicked. I couldn't breathe. Then I heard the chainsaw and ran in that direction for help.'

"Eve and the twins stopped in the gravel listening, the twins on each side of her, staring at me.

"'Then I saw Sheila off to the side. She was giggling and ran away. She thought it was a game. I grabbed her and she laughed more. I screamed, "Where's Carrie?" but she just laughed. So I hit her, and when I turned around, the guys were watching. They took Sheila and went to get Blake. I found Carrie knee deep in the creek, laughing too. She tripped trying to run away from me. I saw her back arch, trying to lift her head up out of the water . . .'

"So that's all I told Eve, and it was nearly everything. When I finished, Eve turned away, cupped her face into her hands and she started sobbing. Her shirt and jeans, from the back, looked all soiled and crumpled like she wore them to bed.

"I walked over to her, put my arms around her and started crying too. We headed for the truck. We never did get to the hotel for a snack."

Tasker found Shorty smoking at the kitchen table in the barracks and drinking a late-morning coffee when he returned with the tapes from his interview with Jessica. Bloody, brown-red finger wipes smeared the bib and hips of the cook's white apron, and a warm, heavy smell of raw meat hung in the room.

"Done my part. Made two hundred patties for the women." Shorty stirred his coffee. "All they let me keep were a few bones. But it was a young male." He cleared his throat.

A large pot of bones, onions and carrots was coming to the boil on the stove. The rich warm smell of cooking moose would be around for a while. Tasker was tired, and with all the moisture in the air, he was tempted to relax and join Shorty for a coffee.

Tasker helped himself and sat beside Shorty at the table, stretching his heels far under it to enjoy the pull in the backs of his legs. He ran his fingers through his moustache, thinking it was getting long and better be trimmed. "Cough any better?" he asked Shorty.

"Some."

"I'm wiped and I've got so many crazy ideas in my head. Let me play out a scene for you. See if it makes any sense, if I'm getting any closer."

Shorty grinned and got up. "I'll grab the sandwiches." Then, from inside the walk-in fridge he called, "Has it to do with Dr. Straun's office, Jim or Blake?"

"Only Blake – so far. Well, maybe . . . I've put together some stuff Howard and Jessica Weiss told me. It's kind of interesting – but lots of pieces are still missing." Tasker set the scene while Shorty moved around the kitchen. "I'm back at the morning Blake was killed. At the spruces." Tasker pulled his feet back under the chair and let his shoulders and elbows circle the coffee mug. "It's dawn. Larissa's in her tent. Blake arrives about five hundred metres downriver to set his net, and Howard and Jessica drive out on the new road through the mine property, park and walk in. OK? We know all this."

Shorty slid a plate of sandwiches and napkins into the middle of the table and sat back down to his coffee.

"You think about it. These people are wide apart in a huge area, and it's something how they seem to find each other in all that space over the morning. Anyway, Blake takes a stroll around the forest after his net is out. It was a great morning for a walk, I guess, dry, clear, high pressure . . ." Tasker was enjoying this. "He finds Larissa in her tent. He stops there at least an hour – you know – and at the end of his visit, they fight. Blake dumps out her things, scrapes the furnishings around on the wooden platform –"

"Why?" Shorty interrupted.

"I don't know. I'll have to work on that too." Tasker ran one finger around the lip of his mug and then returned to his narrative. "Meanwhile, Jessica and Howard are doing their thing. They're inland some from the river, halfway from Blake's boat to Larissa's tent, but the three sites make a triangle. Jessica and Howard, they're together when they hear the loud rumble of the fight, Howard called it a roaring sound, and he runs to find out what's up. Blake storms from Larissa's tent and surprises Jessica as he charges through the bush back to his boat. He misses seeing Howard, who first ran to the river and then up to the tent. Jessica has been getting scared because she thinks the rumbling sounds of the distant row could've been a bear growling or something. Blake coming up behind her scares her more. She's had it with his bothering her, so she shoves Blake hard, with all the strength of her adrenalin pumping, and he falls on Howard's pile of collected burls in such a way that he knocks himself groggy. Jessica doesn't see him actually hit the ground because she takes off, terrified. She gets good and lost."

"A camp cot rubbin' along a plywood floor – it might sound like a bear over a distance," Shorty said and pushed back his chair to make a flat, scraping noise. "If the floor's off the ground, it'd be like a drum . . . but the moss out there'd soak up a lot of the sound."

"Yes, but it was a dry, high-pressure day, and sound would travel. Howard guessed it came from the tent and visits it himself. He doesn't see Blake, but he sees Larissa tidying up and they talk. Then he heads back to reassure Jessica. She's gone. Blake's there, lying on his back, but Howard doesn't figure he's dead. He doesn't look closely because he's getting concerned about Jessica now. He knows something about her problem with Blake and figures she's hurt somewhere else. When he does find Jessica, it takes time to calm her down. The exact location of that meeting place I haven't pinpointed, but it could've been a kilometre away. They walk back to collect their stuff and Blake is gone now. Jessica clings, so Howard leaves the burls he's collected for another time and walks Jessica back to the car. Hands full, so to speak. They pass Larissa's tent, but don't look in. Howard figures she's there, though."

"Three's a crowd." Shorty grinned. "If Blake were dead, you'd think Howard would sense that when he looked at him." He pushed the sandwich plate towards Tasker, but Tasker, concentrating on the details of his story, held up a hand, not ready yet.

"Let's say Ivan Peders has come to the spruces too. We don't know this, but I'm willing to bet on it. By the old road, not the new one Howard took. Those parking areas are a couple of kilometres apart at least, right? OK? Peders could arrive either before or after Jessica and Howard."

"You can't have another meetin' in all that country, come on!" Shorty drummed one hand on the lunch plate.

"He's looking for Larissa." Tasker paused a moment to choose a sandwich. He didn't want Shorty ticked off, and lose his audience, so he bit into a ham and processed cheese on floppy white.

With the rich smell of moose building in the kitchen, it was more tasteless than usual. The soup pot rattled at a full boil now, and let go a few drops of bubbly froth that dribbled down the side and sparked yellow and blue in the propane flame.

Tasker talked on as he chewed. "Let's say he knows about the fight between Blake and Larissa. Doesn't matter if he heard it or saw it – probably saw it since his hearing's no good. So he follows Blake, leaving his hiding spot near Larissa's tent. Peders has been wanting to expose Blake for some time – that grandstanding after the ballgame with his *Star* cartoon, the moose head thing, wisecracks he's made –"

"But it's over," Shorty interrupted. "Larissa hasn't been with Peders – in the bar, even – for months."

"Maybe for Larissa. Not for Peders. I've seen him with her at least once in his van. And he was trying to boss her around, but he'd lost it. I've seen him looking for her, on that old road, and I've watched him watch her in the bar – hurt glances, anger, that sort of stuff. OK. If Peders follows Blake, he may have seen Jessica shove him, maybe he finds him a little after; anyway, Peders finds Blake coming to and gives him another whack. He wraps the unconscious Blake up in the net and sends him floating downriver in the Zodiac. He even starts the engine and steers the boat into the current."

"Why?" Shorty blurted as the soup boiled right over in a big gush and splattered on the stovetop. Clouds of moose steam rolled around the kitchen, the smell so sweet it was almost sickening. Shorty jumped up and turned down the propane. When the pot had settled and he was wiping off the white porcelain around the element, Shorty asked again, "Why? What good's that do Peders?"

"He's jealous, furious with jealousy. He's trying to protect Larissa, and maybe Jessica too. Peders has a strong sense of right and wrong and a terrible temper – remember his outburst in the bar or the time he crashed his own van into the roadblock? That would account for the whack. Sending Blake downriver – that could've been an impulse, a chance to make a crazy kind of statement, like that moose head stuff was, remember? It exposes Blake as a poacher, makes it really dramatic. If he hit Blake out of anger and impulse, he might've figured Blake would come around. He puts the body in the Zodiac right side up, but the lake flips it somewhere along that shore near the dunes. Peders was as puzzled as anyone when we first noticed it at the derby."

"That it?" Shorty asked and shrugged. "Makes just as much sense as the case against Howard did – and no connection to Jim's assault. Maybe Blake headed downriver on his own steam after Jessica's push and got bopped by an overhangin' branch and was knocked out and maybe, maybe, maybe . . . Was Peders even there?"

"I know his tire marks were, but that could've been any time," Tasker admitted. "Could've been the next day, even. But Jessica heard two motors, one moments before Howard found her. It wasn't Howard's motor, obviously. Could've been the boat – then she heard another later. It would have to come from the old road for her to hear it. Whose was it? I'm guessing Peders's."

"How'd Peders move the body to the river? Was there enough time? He had to carry him, haul up the net, wrap it around a limp body – they don't cooperate, you know – and tease the boat into the current." Shorty pushed the sandwich plate and Tasker chose another. "Oh yes, and first he had to take off Blake's boots. Blake wouldn't have been wanderin' around the forest all mornin' wearin' no boots . . ."

"I haven't figured it all out. But there was enough time, probably. Both Jessica and Howard said they talked for quite a while." Tasker took a bite and thought for a moment. "Of course, if he got the body to the river before Howard and Jessica came back, he could be wrapping Blake up when they were collecting Jessica's stuff. They didn't walk right by the river. But that scenario, it doesn't account for the sound of the motors."

"I guess Peders could carry Blake – he's strong enough." Shorty zeroed in on another hole. "If Peders did it, what's this to do with Jim and the missin' explosives or the business at Dr. Straun's office? There's gotta be a tie-in with what happened to Jim, at least."

"OK." Tasker stood up to take off his jacket. The room was getting hot with the soup working on the stove. "I admit, it starts to thin there. The weapons used on Blake and Jim were from the same pile and both with Blake's blood on them. It's likely the stick Flint took for Blake's murder weapon actually wasn't, and the one that hit Jim also killed Blake. We'll know soon. Then it's either a wild coincidence or someone in the forest that morning hit Jim. The motive is different in the two crimes, maybe, but Larissa had something to do with both: she was in the forest for the first and she was in the explosives shed recently. I don't know why her, the extent of her involvement." Tasker sat back down. He looked inside his coffee mug to find it empty. He decided he didn't need another and pushed it away.

"Well, what do we know 'bout her?" Shorty was mulling this over. "She's been in the fight for Kakhteyi – she tented in the forest for a while. She was at the roadblock. She has a way with a lot of men round here, includin' Blake. So why'd she argue with Blake? We're back at that."

"Blake was the one mad. Howard says he trashed her tent."

"Well then" – Shorty was still tossing around ideas – "maybe she told him she was pregnant and wanted child care."

"Now that would be something – but she never got pregnant before."

"There was a time a girl wouldn't get a man here until she could show she'd have babies. Time's change." Shorty shook his head. "You seem to know all what happened, now it's time to fit the people in the right places. That shouldn't be too hard, Corporal." He laughed and stood up, stacking the mugs on the sandwich plate and carrying them to the sink. He turned on the tap too far and water splashed off the dishes and up over his apron. He stepped back from the sink as he started into one of his rolling coughs, eyes watering and sweat beading across his brow.

"Something happened in that tent that set Blake off. I'll see if I can find out from Larissa or Peders. I want to look at the soles of Larissa's shoes too." Tasker was feeling things were falling into place – but there were some wild cards. "Sergeant'll be back soon?"

Shorty stood there clearing his throat from the cough, then bent forward to turn off the tap.

Tasker waited for Shorty to say something, but when he didn't, Tasker picked up his jacket and said, "Thanks for listening. I think you're right, I'm not there yet, but I'm close."

As he stepped into the hall, Tasker was hit with the change to cool, dry air and buttoned on his jacket again. He remembered the old saying, "If you can't stand the heat, get out of the kitchen." It seemed funny, right now, really funny. He mouthed a coyote yelp. The kitchen door must have caught in the draught of cold air because it slammed behind him.

Tasker drove across the bridge over the river to the Cultural Centre. He wanted to get his required talk with the chief over with and, in the process, establish the whereabouts of Larissa. That might save searching all over Kakhteyi and the dunes.

He found Chief Albert standing on the steps, giving

instructions to a gang of kids, all shouldering rakes or leaning forward on them. A stack of speakers and amplifiers jammed open the front door behind. Between the road and steps, three carpenters were nailing one-by-fours onto a wooden frame to finish the boardwalk. It was fast work. One was measuring ahead with lengths of string and blue chalk marks while another cut the one-by-fours with a shrill, hand-held power saw. Towards the river two women wearing work gloves heaved scrap into the back of a pickup. The yard was beginning to look good.

Tasker leaned on the warm hood of his cruiser, out of the way in the sunshine, and waited for Albert to give him a moment. But, when the chief finished, he scowled at Tasker and then walked back into the Centre.

Tasker sprinted around the carpenters after the chief, and caught up as Albert stepped into an office.

"Give me a minute, Chief," he called, keeping his voice steady so as not to let any irritation show.

Albert stopped and circled slowly, as if winding up for something. But when full circle, facing Tasker, he said nothing. Tasker couldn't read the chief's face, but caught Albert's mood from the way his fists clenched where he crossed his arms high on his chest. The knees of Albert's jeans were muddy, and his green bush shirt was sprayed with sawdust.

"I'd like to go over the plans for tomorrow," Tasker said easily. "We'd like warning of any protest. We'll be glad to give you a hand if you cooperate."

"We're doing nothing of concern to RCMP."

"We'll be moving in on anything unexpected, even if it looks innocent. Security's going to be tight. With cooperation though, we can facilitate matters, work in the best interest . . ."

"Who says RCMP ever looked out for our best interests as defined by Native people?"

"Look, let's cut the − "

"Look, it happens every day, big things, little things. For example, my nephew was refused emergency care." The chief hurled out each word. "And RCMP does nothing, doesn't make Dr. Straun deliver, just works on his cover-up − "

"Straun was shaken from a robbery, in no condition − " Tasker raised his voice too, surprised, thinking they'd already gone over this days ago. Tasker hadn't put together it was the chief's nephew, though.

"We hold RCMP responsible for what happened to the boy." The chief was shaking a fist. "If there are any after-effects − "

"Sergeant Flint had him in Whitehorse fast. He got better care than − Dr. Straun couldn't keep his hands from shaking. His clinic was − " Tasker was going to say "trashed" but stopped at the word. His unfinished sentence hung in the air. There was no point saying the boy had recovered well and was up to mischief setting off cherry bombs. Tasker didn't like covering for Sergeant Flint or Straun either. He stood there while his energy drained out.

His gaze wandered up the wall to Gary's carving of the grizzly dancing. It had a quality he hadn't noticed before. An unpleasant expression around the nose and mouth, like it was disgusted with its viewer, or maybe with its partner. Repelled, but seducing with its body . . . The way Gary had used the wood grains and knots to show all that was something.

The chief turned, strode into his office and leaned against his desk, his arms folded across his chest again. Tasker moved into the doorway.

"If he'd been white, you and I know Dr. Straun would've found the strength." Albert's tone was measured, but more resigned than angry. Then he changed the subject. "The environment minister is our guest and will be treated with that respect. We'll tell him what we want formally. We plan no demonstration tomorrow."

"So the minister goes from the mine to the forest – what's happening there?" Tasker wanted to get it clear.

"We'll hold a ceremony in honour of the runners," the chief answered in his slow way, looking past Tasker and out the door of his office. "We'll receive their gift from the coast. There will be words from all important visitors and elders. Then we return here with the grease to serve traditional food. All will be done with dignity, in the traditional way."

Tasker was thinking that access to the forest would be monitored and all trucks and cars checked. That sure wouldn't fit with the spirit of the ceremonies. He said to the chief, "Unless we find the missing explosives, our security will be tight – we'll have to be everywhere."

"Our young people collect at Kakhteyi tonight. There will be a vigil." The chief started to escort Tasker out of his office into the foyer. "If you want to keep away trouble, talk to creeps like Peders. He's out there too often with no good business."

"Is Larissa Stanley there now?"

"I hope so. Everyone else is busy in town still, that was our deal."

Tasker was being dismissed by the chief, but he stalled to look at Gary's carving again, trying to figure it out. From the corner of one eye, he saw Shorty disappear into an office down the hall. Funny, he thought, he'd never seen Shorty involved with the band before. Then he remembered the moose meat patties.

Driving north out of town, Tasker spotted Jessica and Eve by the roadside hammering in stakes at either end of a fabric sign. Although the sign was facing the other way, he read "Listen to

Us" in the daylight shining through the cotton lettering on its background of dark green dye. Tasker gave his siren one whoop as he passed and both faces jolted up.

Embarrassed, Tasker saluted with a couple of turns of his cherry flasher.

He decided to take the new mine road into Kakhteyi. The one time he'd seen Larissa walk in by herself, she'd come that way. It was the road Jim avoided when he could, where the mine piled waste rock and where they'd cut some of the big trees.

As he passed the cut, Tasker wondered how management would explain those stumps to the cabinet minister. The message was pretty obvious.

The mine road then crossed where the old slide had bottomed out. But the rockfall was tamed with brush and lichen, some trees among the boulders at the bottom. Blake was right, the slide happened long ago.

Where the road ended, there was a widening for cars to park, but it was empty now except for Tasker.

Looking around, he noticed the bright sky seemed to deepen the rich, rubbery greens at forest edge. On the ground, at trail-head, several tiny saxifrage blooms glistened with their own liquor despite being shaded from the sun. He started down the trail – a neat depression along the forest floor marked the trail bed, yet not so worn the moss had lost its spring. A trail used for years, but infrequently. The rush of the river grew louder.

He was going over what he knew about Larissa. It seemed she was close to what was going on – was she protecting someone? Why hadn't she mentioned Blake visited her the morning of his death? Why was her print left on the door jamb of the explosives magazine? Most of all, what was Larissa's and Blake's fight about? He ran through reasons why you'd "trash" someone's tent. Frustration? Disgust or anger? Maybe that's what happened at Dr.

Straun's clinic. Whoever trashed it could've been frustrated and not looking for anything. But frustrated about what?

Tasker had seen Blake's temper at the ballgame. But he'd just shouted. His anger at the bar and at the moose heads had been contained as well. What would make him so angry he'd throw around stuff in a tent?

Tasker entered the gloom of the mature forest. His nostrils prickled with the smell of fresh spruce, registering that something had passed by recently, snapping twigs.

Tasker stretched his memory to think what the watchman's tent had in it the day he looked in – after he and Jim had found Blake's boots. What was there to throw around? He remembered the cot, with bedding on it, and the leather swatch and beading lying on the pillow. There'd been a table with camp stove and fixings for tea. Yes, and in the corner, he pictured that pile of junk . . . a coil of wire – not extension cord but wire – batteries, a radio . . .

Now, it dawned on Tasker – Larissa had the makings of an electrical fuse in her tent. Did she know it? Did Blake?

He stopped short and inhaled deeply. His sinuses rushed with the pungent mint smell of freshly crushed young spruce. The tingling sensation in his cheeks and forehead only added to the shock of his question. Why? Who was into explosives? Was that why she had this thing with Peders, to learn how to use explosives? Or was someone using her?

Tasker picked up his pace, felt for his gun. As his right arm swung back past his hip, he let his finger and thumb trip the safety.

He walked quietly up to the watchman's tent. There was no sound, no movement. The canvas flap was down and tied from the outside.

Tasker called out. No reply. He pulled the tape to untie the knot and threw up the flap. Inside – the cot, the cooking table and a dirty ashtray. And those electrical units or parts were all attached, forming a circle on the floor. It crossed his mind they were for practice – for practice making electrical circuits.

Tasker turned around and took in the view from the tent. In the distance and up a hill partially obscured by the trees, the flash of denim blue meeting white caught his eye. The colours didn't move.

The sound of the river filled the forest, but Tasker felt intensely alone. He couldn't imagine what those colours were ahead. They weren't natural to the forest. It could be a trick of the eye – depth of field, or something.

He strode down a shallow ravine and lost sight of the colours altogether. It was a longer walk down and up than he'd thought, cross-country, no trail bed under his feet. The deep sponginess of the forest floor muffled his footsteps, and his own silence was unnerving.

When he got near the top of the rise, he made out a man's figure ahead in the clearing – standing there with arms held up high, elbows bent but hands up. Frozen in gesture, pelvis slung forward.

Tasker pulled out his gun and started to run. The man wore overalls and a gaily embroidered white cowboy shirt.

"Shit," Tasker swore out loud. It was Blake's clothes, stuffed and formed into an effigy. There was even a beige-coloured head with a makeshift ponytail hanging down back. The figure was guy-wired into pose with rope running high up the trees.

Tasker ran into the clearing where the form hung, feet resting on a knob of ground and facing away from him. He was thinking he'd forgotten the boxes of Blake's clothes when he realized the gesture was crude, the way the hips were jutting forward.

Tasker took a wide circle to face the figure. He didn't see, right away, that another form lay on the moss in front of it. A human form. A man's body face down in the moss.

The body was in tatters. Tasker ran towards it. A heavy, blond-haired man – it was Ivan Peders. The back of his head, the flesh on his neck and shoulders, along with his coveralls, had been shredded with knives. Sliced. Ligaments, tendons, brains, bones exposed. Dry, cracked brown blood everywhere. Tasker sucked in his breath. The smell . . . Tasker startled violently at the sound of an animal groan, and then realized the sound came from his own throat.

Then Tasker heard, far away, from back at the parking area, horns honking and people shouting.

He swivelled and looked up into the face of the giant sculpture, up into the nylon-stocking formless face, then down the overalls to the open fly and a nylon-stocking penis jabbing out.

On the ground beside the sculpture sat the clothing boxes, newspapers, piles of women's pantyhose and coils of rope.

"Christ! What was Peders doing?" he said aloud. It was obvious, though. He'd been working on another crazed, public message – this time for the environment minister.

Peders lay face down, hands under his chest and his right leg oddly pulled up by his side, gone slack in mid-crawl. The sound of voices persisted, and doors slammed. Tasker knelt down, gun in his right hand, and ran his left palm up Peders's pantleg from the workboot. The skin was clammy cold.

The voices were nearer. Tasker crouched over the body, shivering, his mind blank. Waiting.

Finally, Tasker made out figures moving between the trees, then Reggie and Howard broke into the clearing. He stood up and screamed, "Howard!" his voice panicked and shrill. Tasker held up his left hand to stop them and called, "Howard, I need you. Alone." His voice wavered, but he was more in control this time.

Howard didn't hesitate. He ran forward, staring at the figure of Blake, but stopped short at Peders.

"Man," Howard murmured, and looked up at the effigy again.

From behind, Reggie added, "We just saw a sow and two cubs cross the road – where she often does."

"He's dead?" Howard's voice faded away.

Tasker nodded.

Reggie stood behind Howard on tiptoe to get a better view of the body. He looked up at the effigy and, pointing at it, shouted recklessly, "Now that's some kinda' pole."

"Peders was . . . But this . . ." Howard couldn't finish. There were no words left, not even for Reggie.

Tasker picked up the plastic tube with two ping-pong balls inside and blew in hard. The balls rose partway up the tube. They wouldn't let him out of the hospital until his breath could push those balls another two centimetres.

The head nurse said the more he walked and the more he exercised with this gizmo, the sooner he'd get back his puff.

Well, he'd take a walk. Tasker pushed away the food tray, swung his legs over the edge of the hospital bed and let himself slide down the edge until his feet hit the cold linoleum floor. Battleship-grey linoleum – like in the Whitehorse hospital years ago. This end of Regina General's men's ward could use a renovation.

He stood up and took a deep breath – it jerked shallow. Then he shuffled over to get his slippers and dressing gown. Still huffing.

He'd walk down the ward to the sitting lounge and back a couple of times.

Tasker never did know how Dr. Straun and Sergeant Flint got on the trail of that female grizzly so fast. No way Howard or Reggie told them, he knew that.

Tasker himself was still at the police station dealing with Peders's effects and remains when Sergeant Flint came in flushed with success.

Tasker had never asked for the details, maybe because giving Sergeant Flint a chance to tell the story condoned it. Anyway, Tasker could imagine very well just what they did.

The sergeant hears about the mauling over his car radio on his way back from Whitehorse. He drops in on his pal, the local doctor, who needs a little adventure to lighten up his day. The sergeant and the doctor are so set on their mission, they even forget to tell Tasker, or anyone, that Straun's nurse, in running through the doctor's files, has found Larissa Stanley's is missing. Not the sort of thing that seems important when there's killer bear to shoot . . .

They grab the biggest rifles, the high-power sights, one each, and the big RCMP eight-wheel-drive police truck with all-terrain tires. They drive up the mine road, across the mountainside, park at the top of the slide scar and strike off uphill, above treeline.

On the tundra, ripping up the sod and sifting the earth for grubs or lemmings with their fifteen-centimetre claws, the bears are easy to spot.

The doctor, for a change, keeps his grumbling, self-important voice quiet. He likely pants with the exertion of walking up the old slide.

They'd been able to get into such a good position, Tasker overheard Sergeant Flint boast to Shorty, that they only needed three shots. Two from the sergeant's gun and one from Dr. Straun's. They each killed one bear – the fatal shots entered the left lung, pierced the heart and then likely got as far as the second lung. Three shots, two dead. Quick and neat. And they'd left the carcasses on the mountainside. The sergeant told Shorty to get his Native friends to pick up the meat. One juvenile got away, but it likely wouldn't survive, anyway.

A pretty, black-haired young nurse took Tasker's arm as he stood staring out the window of the patients' lounge. She was wearing a touch of perfume. One of those new harsh scents with a name like "Vicious" or "Narcotic."

"Come, Steven" – Tasker had never corrected what the hospital staff took as his familiar name from "Steven Warren Tasker" – "you have to work on taking longer breaths. Let's walk the hall again before your supper."

Tasker sighed and said, "Fine."

When the same nurse brought in his meal later, Tasker only picked at it. He wasn't getting Sergeant Flint out of his mind. He remembered an old conversation with Kay. Yes, he did remember when: Kay pulled him aside, in the hospital corridor after one of those many visits to Jim, and she'd said, "Don't let Sergeant Flint get under your skin, Warren. He's burnt out at the end of a long career and is marking time until he retires. In ten months and a day he can take up full-time fishing, and that is all he ever thinks about. The quickest way for him to get there is to control everything and everybody. Don't take it personally – just let it go. It's him, not you."

The trouble for Tasker was that just letting someone like Sergeant Flint go thirteen years later took a lot of energy. Maybe part of the problem was that Flint hadn't been absolutely wrong, and Tasker hadn't been entirely right. It would have been easier if Flint had been corrupt. As it was, all sort of grey, Tasker was still giving in to Sergeant Flint.

14. TSEHKI JUNCTION. June 1978

Past midnight, Tasker was cruising Tsehki and looking for Larissa. She'd been missing all day. Albert said she'd be at Kakhteyi for the afternoon, but she wasn't there when Tasker found Peders. She hadn't been seen at the forest vigil, and Tasker couldn't find her at the dunes, or here in town either.

It was hard to see anything now. Twilight had finally become night, but it wasn't dark enough, or the right kind of dark, for headlights or homelights or even stars to penetrate. It was a brown dark.

Town dogs yipped and howled, restless in the strange light. On early summer nights like this, kids were usually restless too. Most homes had flat black curtain liners on their windows to fake real night. The older kids would normally roam the town in packs or hang out at the beach, stoking bonfires to keep warm; but tonight the streets were empty with all the action in Kakhteyi forest.

It had been a long day for Tasker. Ever since he'd finished with Peders, he'd been tired and shaken, running on empty.

Tasker and Howard had stretched the body out on the cot, no mattress though, from the watchman's tent, and carried it to the road. There'd been no talk. Reggie flanked their procession, noiselessly skirting trunks and hopping deadfalls. From there, they'd transferred the body to the back of a camper truck and driven to Tsehki hospital. Tasker emptied Peders's pockets when they laid him out in the basement morgue for Dr. Straun. He kept the van keys.

Then Tasker went back out to the forest clearing, taped off the mauling site and dismantled the effigy. Reggie broke the silence by suggesting there might be a bomb in Blake's pants, but Tasker didn't have the time or inclination to consider the possibility. He just wanted the thing out of there before the security squad did their sweep of the forest.

Next, Tasker went to examine Peders's van, parked, no surprise, at the washout on the old road where Jim and Tasker had seen tire tracks a week before. Tasker went over the van carefully.

He was interested by the way the inside was fixed up. The driver's seat had plush cushioning and a special curved back. To the right of the steering wheel, a small writing stand had been rigged to the dashboard so the driver could take notes on the move. It was just below shoulder level with enough length to give support to the whole arm. On the stand, closed, lay Peders's logbook. Tasker flipped it open.

Only the first quarter or so was written in, in the neat, thin spidery hand Tasker had noticed when he flipped through it in the Grizzly Den Bar. The entries went back a couple of months, and were all pretty well made with the same pen. Most days had a short entry, including date, location, milepost number, a reference to job, a notation of time, expenses, materials used. Often there was a word or two about road conditions or weather, or game sightings. Didn't seem much use at first glance though.

Tasker flipped along to the first day he ever saw Peders, the time they both were driving down the Tsehki road. The entry read:

June 10 4:35 a.m. Left Whitehorse. Clear.

6:00 a.m. Milepost 62. Coyote across road, something limp dangling from its mouth. Mangy female.

6:30 a.m. Reach Tsehki mine road.

7:30 a.m. Job delayed to Monday. L. at road-block, making a fool of herself.

There were no more notes for that day, and the rest of the log looked just as barren for his purposes. Tasker closed it and carried it back to his cruiser. He drove to the Chevron station and arranged for Hank, the mechanic, to tow the van out of the bush. It was then, when he got back to the police station, that Sergeant Flint and Dr. Straun blew in, talking about how they'd shot the grizzly. After Sergeant Flint left to drive Dr. Straun over to the morgue and then on to the security sweep of the forest, Tasker got to reading the rest of the log.

As he'd expected, it was mostly work-related. Except for an entry on the previous Monday that read:

June 13 7:00 a.m. To mine magazine. L. on the road wanting to come. I tell her no, not to work any more, ever. She says, OK, never again means it's over for good. I say fine.

A number of entries through the week indicated trips to Kakhteyi, and the last entry read:

June 18 9:00 a.m. To the forest again.

Tasker thumbed through the unused pages of the log to be sure there were no other notes. Satisfied, he closed it. All it told him was that he'd better question Larissa. She knew something and he had to get it from her.

And he'd been out looking ever since. He knew he'd earned the night off – a beer too many could take him away from all this.

Tasker nosed slowly down Main Street with his window open, looking between the stores and listening for footsteps on the boardwalk. There was a dim light shining in the General Store. Tasker coasted past to see that the proprietor had set out souvenirs in a display in the front window. The panes were so stained it was a wonder she bothered. Tasker made out some souvenir gold pans with local scenery painted on the bottom and the name "Tsehki Junction, Yukon Territory" around the sides. He wondered where the usual window-dressing was stashed – wilted lettuces and carrots, bruised apples and bananas. Visitors from the bigger towns coming down tomorrow for the minister's announcement would have no interest in her standard Tsehki produce. The regular bestsellers – tins of Spam, corned beef, sliced peaches and evaporated milk – they'd likely remain where they always were, on shelves behind the cash register. Those tinned goods were what Larissa would eat, he guessed dully, and probably why her backpack was so heavy. They were the foods the owner sold on credit until the welfare and government cheques came in. Then, when they'd evened up, locals would buy her spotty produce, thinking it was something special.

Villagers went to Flo's General Store because there was no other choice short of a drive to Whitehorse. Tourists, however, searched out the historic store with its dark, smoke-stained walls, high ceiling and one narrow aisle – food on the left, dry goods on the right, hardware along the back, penny candy at the cash.

Guidebooks talked about the old forty-five-gallon drum turned on its side and converted to a wood stove – "witness to the ingenuity of frontiersmen and -women." The only fresh paint the place ever saw was the sign outside over the door: Flo's General Store. She had basic marketing sense.

The one winter's day last year when Tasker had brought Ida to Tsehki, she'd found the store worth taking a picture of. Somehow it was just too familiar for Tasker to get excited about, especially the musty smell inside that reminded him of the plain fare coming up whenever his mother resorted to picking up supplies there. Ida had bought one of those souvenir gold pans, but the lake and mountain scene rusted out in only a few months.

Down the boardwalk the door to the Grizzly Den opened, but it was only the bartender sweeping out. He kept brushing in the doorway so that all the dust dropped through the slats in the boardwalk outside. Tasker remembered that, as a kid, it had been worth getting a rake once a week and pulling that dust out on the chance of finding a few coins. There were stories from gold rush times of bartenders who used to collect the sweepings in a pan and let the swish of water separate out the gold dust. When Tasker was a kid, sifting through dust for seven cents a week was worth it for the twenty-one blackballs he could buy next door. He wondered if seven cents was worth anything for a kid in 1978. Then he wondered why he was thinking about all this.

Tasker drew right up beside the boardwalk and asked the bartender, in a low voice, "Seen Larissa Stanley tonight?"

"A slow night," the bartender said as he shook his head.

Tasker smiled wryly to himself. It was a slow night all right, in more ways than one. There was no way Larissa could be interested in dynamite for herself, he thought, but she was involved in all the recent incidents – fight with Blake, thumbprint on the magazine door, possible detonators in her tent, interest in Peders's blasting business, now her medical file missing from the vandalized clinic. But why? She probably didn't know about Peders. No one had seen her.

Tasker turned left to drive down Peders's street. Hank, the mechanic at the Chevron station, had told Tasker in the afternoon that Ivan Peders had a pump organ in his cabin. He'd helped assemble the inner workings while Peders did all the cabinetwork. Recently, Hank said, Peders had ordered the parts for a harpsichord, and they'd discussed the setting of the quill points just last week. Seemed an odd hobby up here, Hank admitted, but Peders was a good craftsman so it had been fun working with him. Peders meant to give one of the instruments to the Catholics when he finished both. Tasker listened to Hank, thinking here was Peders's eulogy. Not many people knew Peders well enough to mourn his death.

Tasker got out of his cruiser and walked around Peders's cabin. The back step was covered in trays of empty 7Up cans, but no Larissa. The street sat silent – Jim's cabin empty at one end and Peders's at the other.

Tasker noticed lights a couple of streets over and drove there. It turned out to be the Anglican Church Hall. When he poked his head in the door he saw a number of aproned women setting up long rows of tables. Eve was there too. Rose Daniel, Howard's mother, looked up first, and Tasker asked if Larissa had been around.

"Not tonight." She smiled. "If you see her, tell her we could use the help," and she pointed to the stacks of boxes in the small kitchen. "She usually picks flowers for us at least."

Tasker crossed the bridge to the Native village to check the new Cultural Centre, but all was quiet. He started thinking it was on a brown night like this that he'd met Ida a number of years ago. In Scott Lake. He'd been in town with the night off from his summer job at a nearby cattle ranch. Ida was working at the nursing station, her first placement with Northern Health. He'd come to town by freighter canoe and they'd met in the coffee shop. They were sitting on the steps of the station trailer, eating Kit Kat chocolate bars in the brown light, when a woman drove up and asked Ida for help. A friend lay in the back seat, bruised on the face with skin broken around her lips and nose. But despite the blood and swelling, Tasker remembered the softness of the woman's expression.

Tasker had waited all night on the steps of the nursing station trailer while Ida and another nursing sister tended the woman inside. He heard a moaning now and then, that was all. When the helicopter finally came from Whitehorse at dawn, Ida asked Tasker to help again, this time to carry one end of the stretcher. He remembered the difference between the woman's impassive face and the grim tension in Ida's, although their features were similar in Tasker's eyes.

Ida left with the helicopter and, later, told Tasker the baby was born while they were airborne. It died before they landed, three months premature. The Whitehorse hospital kept the woman for six weeks before they let her return to Scott Lake, the bruises and cuts on her body were that bad.

What Tasker remembered most about that night was Ida's face, the resolve in it, as she climbed into the chopper. The same expression crossed her face again when she told him the outcome of that story. Tasker liked the gutsy strength in Ida. After she told Tasker about the baby's death, she took his hand in the same matter-of-fact way, and marched him down to the flats along the riverbank. There she coiled her legs around his body and slipped her tongue into his mouth. She was always able to do that – able to let go of other people's problems when she couldn't help any more and take care of her own needs.

Tasker laughed softly to himself. He was so exhausted, he couldn't imagine having the energy for Ida right now.

He coasted along the front of the Tsehki hospital. The lights were all out. Dr. Straun had finished with Peders's body.

Tasker took a left and eased past the clapboard house. His eyes drifted over Dr. Straun's car, a late-model, blue Buick. There, standing in the shadows, was Larissa Stanley.

"I think you'd better get in with me," Tasker said quietly, and he stepped out of the cruiser.

Larissa jerked left and right; saw she was trapped in the blind alley between clinic, hospital and house; and then let her eyes slowly rest back on Tasker. She stuffed an object into the back pocket of her jeans, crossed her arms, leaving the long fringe of her jacket swaying, and strode towards the police car.

Tasker opened the back door and held out his hand. "I'll take a look at what's in your jeans pocket there."

Larissa slipped her left hand down into the pocket, slapped a wide roll of plastic tape into Tasker's hand and sat down in the back seat of the cruiser. Tasker pocketed the tape, walked around to the driver's seat and took his notebook out of his breast pocket. The cigarette Howard had given him the day before flipped out on his lap and Tasker caught it and offered it to Larissa. "I can give you a smoke if you've got a light."

She nodded and took the cigarette. She pulled a wooden match from the front pocket of her jeans and lit up.

Tasker said, "I've got a number of questions for you, so what I'm going to do is drive back to the police station and we can sit beside my desk and have our talk."

Larissa nodded through her smoke and Tasker started up the

car. It was about a two-minute drive and he watched her the whole way through the rear-view mirror. She wasn't jumpy at all. She had her arms crossed, with her hands resting on her elbows, and occasionally lifted her cigarette the short distance from her elbow to her mouth while she looked off to the side out the front passenger window.

At the police station, when she sat down again under the harsh lights of the office, he saw her hands were dirty – not just dust, there was grease or something on them ground into her knuckles and her nails – and the elbows of her fringed jacket and the knees of her jeans were scuffed. Under her jacket, Tasker could see part of a necklace that looked like it was made from animal teeth strung on a leather thong. She still hadn't said a word since he'd spotted her in the shadows near the clinic.

Tasker rolled a sheet of paper into the typewriter while he thought where to start. He noticed a note on the blotter that said "Phone Ida." He looked at his watch. Three a.m. Too late.

"There've been some things going on in town that you've had a hand in. You're going to tell me about them." Larissa slouched down into her chair and crossed her arms. There was nothing knowing or controlling about her at all. She was like a cornered animal, vulnerable, exhausted, frightened and frightening at the same time. Tasker couldn't help speaking gently. "You're going to start by telling me about you and Blake the morning he died," then after a minute, "You let on to me some time ago you never saw him that morning. But you did, didn't you?"

She nodded almost imperceptibly.

"Blake trashed your tent. Why'd he do that?"

Tasker put his notebook on the desk and waited for Larissa to start her answer. She stared back at him, but said nothing. She shifted her hips so that one shoulder sat lower than the other, her arms and legs still crossed.

"Why'd he trash the tent?" Tasker repeated, his voice still soft.

Larissa shrugged and said, "I don't remember."

"Was it because of what he saw in there?"

She widened her eyes but said nothing.

"Like the makings of an electrical detonator?"

Larissa's eyes widened more and she sank deeper into her slouch. Her eyes closed slightly. Tasker was losing some of his sympathy.

"Tell me why you wanted dynamite. You don't need an electrical fuse for that."

Larissa stared back at Tasker through her eye slits, but kept silent. Time to stop fishing and get to the point, Tasker thought. He had her off balance a bit, though, he was sure.

"You heard what happened to the person who taught you to use explosives?"

She shrugged and a little smile crossed her face.

Remembering that she might not know, Tasker was careful. "Ivan Peders is dead. Did you know that?"

She sat up straight and said, "Don't bullshit me."

"I'm not. Here's his log, his personal effects." He pulled the two plastic bags of stuff from Peders's van out from behind his desk.

"What happened?" she whispered.

"Grizzly bear. Near your tent." Tasker's voice grew husky as the image of Peders's shredded body returned.

"Shit," she said and slouched back, digging in her breast pocket and pulling out a cigarette. She looked at her fingers, turning the cigarette over and over. Several long minutes passed. He noticed it was extra long with a mottled brown filter, a Dunhill. She likely bummed that one too, he thought. Then he remembered all the brands of cigarettes butted into the moss above the explosives magazine. Suddenly that crazy assortment made sense. It wasn't from many smokers; it was from one smoker who bummed. Another connection to Larissa, and still no motive.

"Why're you into dynamite?" Tasker asked again.

She put the cigarette back in her pocket and looked at Tasker defiantly. "I don't have anything to say."

Tasker looked at her feet, her sneakers, and he saw they left a trail of prints with those little circles all across the burgundy linoleum up to his desk. The same tread as on the paper in Dr. Straun's examining room.

Suddenly Tasker realized Larissa wasn't a witness, she was a suspect. Why hadn't he twigged before? She was implicated from so many angles. Had he blown his chance for getting a conviction? His hands fumbled forward to pick up his field hat. His fingers searched the inside for the pocket where he kept his "rights" card. He had to read the suspect her rights now, and make no mistakes doing it.

"You're under arrest." Tasker started reading the familiar text. ". . . You are entitled to the advice of counsel . . ." Although he looked at the card, he recited the words from memory. There was comfort in repeating the prescribed text for Tasker, like saying prayers in church. But, like memorized prayer, the comfort was time-sensitive, ending with a quick check of the watch. He wrote the time down in his notebook.

Larissa responded with a defiant "I've nothing to hide."

Tasker was relieved. Even if she wasn't guilty, at least he'd squared away the rights business. He could always un-arrest her. No one ever expected to be un-arrested, but what else did you do with someone who, for a moment, you thought was a suspect and then clearly wasn't? There was nothing permanent about an arrest . . .

"If you've nothing to hide, I've got all night." Tasker realized he sounded almost apologetic, not threatening at all, though his words were. "You're not leaving here until I'm satisfied, and if your story is like I think it's going to be, you may not be leaving here even then."

"You've got nothing on me."

"You cooperate, we'll see where we can go. You don't, you sit in the cell on a vandalism charge. Vandalism of Dr. Straun's clinic and office. I got you on that. Same footprints." He pointed to the floor. It was a matter of fact.

"I've got nothing to say." There was something final about that remark.

"Maybe you better think about that inside." Tasker stood up and walked over to stand above Larissa. "Let's go."

Tasker put his hand under Larissa's elbow and inadvertently brushed her breast.

"Don't touch me," she cried and jumped up.

"Steady," Tasker said and led Larissa past the desks to the door on the side of the room, holding her right arm above the elbow but pulled away from her body.

She looked up at his face and bent her head forward. Then she jerked up her elbow and bit Tasker's left thumb hard.

Tasker swung in front of her and clamped his other hand across her forehead, pushing up until she let go her bite. Then he pulled her elbow up behind her back, swearing, "Damn you!" and marched her down the hall to the holding cell, his thumb squirting blood all along the wall beside them.

Tasker tried to grab a couple of hours' sleep after he typed up his report for Sergeant Flint, but his mind only simmered on the edge of sleep, going over and over the points he'd made.

First of all, no dynamite found yet and no definite idea why it was missing. Second, no certain lead on who assaulted Jim. There was no confirmation for his idea that Peders killed Blake then wrapped the body up in the net either. But they did have a firm connection between Larissa and Dr. Straun's break-in – her missing medical file and the pattern from her sneakers on the examining-room paper. This, added to her thumbprint in the shed where Jim was hit, the butts, her lie about not seeing Blake the morning he died, her living right next to that pile of "clubs," and her confirmed fascination with explosives.

But why? Tasker kept asking himself. It made no sense. Last night, she'd seemed the victim type. Other times, she'd been more sure of herself. He kept getting this picture of her over and over in his sleep, eyes staring at him, dark and knowing and then changing into wild eyes, terrified and, at the same time, threatening. And when she had the wild look, she'd start lunging at him, and her big hands and fingers were claws streaking for Tasker's face, but he couldn't defend himself because he couldn't get away from the hold of her eyes.

Shorty came into Tasker's bedroom in the middle of one of these replays, with two cups of coffee and a message: Sergeant

Flint wanted him to hustle down to the Chevron station. Tasker reared up from his pillow on one elbow, groggy, and shook his head to wake up, get rid of that terrifying image of Larissa. His legs felt too heavy and flabby to move, let alone hold him up.

Shorty kept at him. "Sergeant Flint says the missin' dynamite's been found. He'll join you down there."

Tasker put his feet on the cold floor and scratched his hair and bristly throat. "Chevron station?" he repeated. The rubbing hurt his thumb and he looked at it – two deep toothmarks in the flesh on the front, three rips under his nail on the back. The wounds felt dry and pulling.

"Yeah, taped under the bumper of Dr. Straun's car."

"Shit." Tasker sat right up. "Anyone hurt?"

Shorty shook his head, and held up his hands, jiggling the coffee. "I heard no blast – and I bin up for a while."

"I'm out of here," Tasker said, grabbing his trousers. Suddenly he stopped, pulled the roll of wide tape out of his pocket and said, "Christ, I picked up Larissa right beside Straun's car last night – with this in her hands." Tasker froze for a long moment, too stunned to think, then slipped the roll of tape back into his pocket and smiled, slowly drawing up his pants and letting his fingers mechanically work to close the button. "Christ." He shivered and punched his arms into his shirt.

Shorty backed against the door, still holding both cups of coffee, and started one of his rolling coughs. Tasker swept past him, tucking in and grabbing a coffee as he went. He heard Shorty gasping, "Watch out. That girl, when she sets her mind to somethin', she can up-end . . ." The coughing finished his thought.

But by the time he reached the north end of town, Tasker had settled down some from the thrill of connecting Larissa finally and firmly with the case. He was glad he'd read her her rights, but still felt he was one step behind whatever was going on. The reality was that he was only reacting to events. Sergeant Flint, he knew, would like the way things sat – they had the dynamite, they had a suspect, and now he could relax for the Minister's visit. Meanwhile, Tasker had less of an idea what was going on than ever. Why would Larissa want to blow up Dr. Straun? What did Straun have to do with anything so far – with Blake's death, Jim's injury?

The Chevron station came into view on Tasker's right. Across the highway from it, and looking back towards the station, stood Dr. Straun and Hank, the garage mechanic. Dr. Straun was dressed in fishing gear, with yellow and red feather flies stuck into his khaki hat. Tasker stopped behind them, turned off his cruiser and jumped out. "Where is it?" he asked.

Dr. Straun, his hands pushing down his pants pockets and his eyes shaded behind dark glasses, lifted his chin to point towards the gas station across the road, crowded in by scrubby bush, picked-over wrecks and rusting forty-five-gallon drums. Up next to the one wall sat the shattered, windowless Toyota a local priest had been driving when he'd hit a moose broadside on the highway. There, inside the building and up on the hoist in the bay, was the doctor's Buick.

The place was deserted on this dry, sunny day, but the jingle of a radio drifted across from inside somewhere, making the scene feel like the set of a cheap western.

"Dr. Straun, here, smelled something burning under his car as he was leaving to go fishing," Hank explained, "so he came in here for me to take a look. I put her up and see this bunch of wooden matches taped around the muffler and a black cord coming out from them and also taped all along the tailpipe. I see the plastic tape's melting and smoking. I follow the cord, and at the end of it, there are what have to be sticks of dynamite under the bumper. That's when we cleared out." He widened his eyes at Tasker, then hawked and spat on the ground. "Good thing we turned the engine off."

"Cool yet?" Tasker asked.

Hank nodded. "By now."

The three men stared across at the blue Buick. Tasker was looking to see if he could make out any dynamite or tape from where he stood. At the same time he was thinking how close a call it must have been. A voice, from the radio across the road, chattered through their silence.

"Gotta knife?" Tasker knew it was his job to go in there and cut out the explosives. He might as well get started.

Dr. Straun unclipped a fishing knife from his belt and handed it over. Tasker ran his good thumb along the blade and found it sharp, just right for cutting that wide tape Larissa had. He thought of the way she pinched up her big, dirty hands to pull the tape out of her jeans pocket. Tasker nodded his thanks at Dr. Straun's sunglasses; he couldn't see the doctor's eyes shaded behind them. The sun wasn't high enough to create any glare yet.

"Keep back. Same for anyone who comes along. Well back." It was an obvious thing to say. Tasker walked across the road to the hoist. He remembered Peders had offered to do this job for him once – he could use Peders now.

A phone was ringing inside by the cash register, but Tasker ignored it. He walked under the hoist and looked up. Wedged in the small space between bumper and body of the Buick were three dynamite sticks taped together. Tarry, black primer cord was jabbed through the thick brown covering of one of the sticks. With the bone-handle end of Dr. Straun's knife, Tasker flicked the cord out of the stick and, with his other hand, ripped down hard on the cord to get it well away from the bumper.

He took a deep breath and nodded briefly at the men across

the road. Hank started towards him, but Tasker held up a hand to say stop. The damn phone hadn't stopped ringing. Tasker's head was full of the smell of dust and grease and oil mixed – that distinctive smell he'd only ever noticed in places where all the roads were gravel. If this station went up, he thought, it would make some crater. Somehow, though, he wasn't concerned right now – he couldn't be.

He shuffled the few steps deeper into the bay until he was standing at the other end of the cord, looking up at the muffler. There was the bunch of wooden matches. The plastic tape had melted all around them so the tips were coated and useless. That's why they hadn't lit yet. An amateur job – the tape had been placed neatly but without thought to the plastic in it melting with the heat of the exhaust and smothering the ignition point. Kind of pathetic, in a funny way. He slit the few threads of tape still holding the bunch of plastic-congealed matches to the muffler and caught them as they fell. They were cold. He dropped the mass into his breast pocket.

So, Tasker thought, Larissa is behind this. He pulled back that mental picture of her standing beside Dr. Straun's car in the dark, looking for an escape and jamming the roll of tape into her jeans. What could she have against Dr. Straun? Slowly, as if coming to, Tasker remembered it was Larissa's medical file missing from the mess on the floor of Dr. Straun's clinic. Tasker would like to take a look at that file. Yes, there may be something in there that would explain. And she might have it stashed wherever she was camping these days.

Tasker scanned the floor of the garage, his eyes searching for a cardboard box. Any box. At the door, with easy access to the air pressure pump outside, he noticed a barrel of water and the tire rimmer. No box. On a shelf behind were all the patches and plugs for fixing flats, and one of those calendars with a picture of a half-naked blonde. This one was all in pink and fondling the spout of an oil can. Gas stations and welding shops – Tasker smiled to himself – they always have calendars like that. Funny what he noticed while he had dynamite to defuse.

He needed a box. His eyes tracked across the rest of the wall to the back, past rows of tires and above, lines of fan belts hanging on nails. At the back, where the light was poor, Tasker spotted crates of antifreeze and Castrol motor oil. That's what he was looking for.

He dumped out a box of Chevron brand heavy-duty motor oil and carried it back to the hoist. After carefully slicing the tape where it held the dynamite in place, he pulled the bundle down from inside the bumper. Once in his hand, he slit through the tape binding the sticks together and lay them out singly in the bottom of the box. He was aware of a Credence Clearwater Revival song, "Proud Mary," on the radio. The phone had stopped ringing.

Shorty had said something once about Larissa and medical problems, Tasker remembered, his mind restlessly jumping all over the place – there was another thread to pick up. Yes, when Shorty knew her at the Detention Centre, she'd had medical problems. He'd better ask, see what Shorty had to say about that.

Tasker picked up the box and started out of the garage. Sergeant Flint was pulling up in the RCMP wagon, so he strode over and handed the box to him. Tasker found himself crowing, "A present for you."

Tasker stuffed his hands in his pockets. He realized he was jiggly all over, not just in his head – his pulse had obviously been racing for a while, he was shuffling his feet around and kicking pieces of gravel. "It didn't ignite because the plastic tape melted and coated all over the matches on the muffler." He pulled the matches from his pocket, figuring the others wanted to hear the details. "But, it was only a matter of time."

"If all's in order then," Dr. Straun said. "Let down my car and I'll get on with some fishing."

"Hey, hey, hey." Sergeant Flint stopped that idea in a chuckling way. "Not until we've dusted that bumper for prints."

"And got a few answers," Tasker blurted, not believing this turn in the discussion.

"Just forget it," the doctor said.

Tasker looked at Dr. Straun in his baggy khaki fishing suit and his sunglasses, his small hat jabbed with yellow and red feathers. The guy would be hilarious if it weren't so serious.

"Who'd want to kill you?" Sergeant Flint said good-humouredly. "Last week you get robbed; today you get dynamite rigged up to your muffler."

"And Larissa Stanley." Tasker was still racing, his head pounding. "What's she got against you? I picked her up last night loitering beside your car with tape in her hands and all dirty like she'd been wriggling around in the dirt, probably under your car."

"Come on." Dr. Straun's voice rolled with authority again. "You're dealing with some stupid little fool. I haven't any idea what's on her mind . . ." He pulled his hands out of his pockets and crossed his arms. "And no little whore or terrorist's going to stop me fishing."

"Look, this dynamite is why Jim got hit. There's something premeditated here, even if it doesn't make sense yet." Tasker let loose a quick laugh. "There are obvious angles to check out. Maybe Jim will remember more."

"Jim will remember nothing," Dr. Straun corrected. "That's the nature of his injury." Tasker could see his own round face reflected back in Dr. Straun's sunglasses. His face – he snapped shut his gaping mouth not wanting to look like he was losing this.

"Tell you what, Freeman. Get in my car and we'll talk, see

what we come up with." Sergeant Flint was still good-humoured. "I have to keep moving and you need some protection." Sergeant Flint handed the box of dynamite sticks to the doctor. "Carry this – you've got the guts." He laughed. "And we'll drop it off at the station. Tasker here, he'll dust for prints and move your car to the pound. Then, we'll take a minute and decide what to do with Larissa."

Tasker and Hank looked at each other. Tasker shrugged and grinned, letting himself enjoy the craziness of defusing a bomb and finding it a nothing. He slapped Hank on the back. "Well," he said, "we got our orders."

But, when Sergeant Flint was driving off, Tasker's satisfaction lost its edge. He wondered, what will Sergeant Flint get from Dr. Straun that's any use? This was why the investigation was stumbling along – Tasker kept handing Flint strong stuff and then watched it get watered down. And if they botched up this case, it was going to hang around his neck a lot longer than Sergeant Flint's.

Tasker followed behind Hank's truck as it towed the Buick to the pound. They wouldn't need to store the car for long because Tasker had good prints off the chrome on the bumper. In fact, they'd stood out nicely, already dusted from the road.

A beat-up old pickup approached, driving north. The driver slowed down and dangled a loose arm for Tasker to stop. It was Howard, with Jessica sitting beside him in the front seat.

Tasker asked, "How's the kid who got the rod in his knee? All better?"

Howard didn't smile and his eyes were serious, but his face looked relaxed. "He's going to be OK. Already up to his old tricks."

Tasker nodded and looked across at Jessica. Her red-brown hair was combed down her back and she was wearing clean jeans and a loose, hand-embroidered blouse that gathered loosely around her neck. He found himself once again noticing the real natural beauty of this girl-woman.

"Didn't keep him and Reggie away from the dump for long," Howard said, his hand still dangling down outside his driver's door. He asked, "What you got Larissa Stanley in there for?"

"Stealing dynamite, attempted murder. Someone tried to blow up the good doctor's car, and we think it was her. Don't know why, though."

Jessica let out a sound that was a mixture of a groan and a whistle. Howard's body started shaking slightly, like he was laughing.

"I'm serious," Tasker said. "I wish I wasn't."

"You got some job." Howard shook his head. "I wouldn't want your job for nothing." Jessica stared out the windshield.

Howard asked, "Coming to Kakhteyi forest today?"

"No, I'm stuck here in town."

"It's going to be a good time."

"Yes," and Tasker brushed off feeling sorry for himself. It was his turn for a good time.

"And you got no idea why she's out to blow people up?" Howard went back to talking about Larissa.

"No," Tasker said.

Howard lifted his hand back up into the cab and dropped it onto the steering wheel. "She's one crazy, mixed-up kid," he said. Then he laughed, looking at Jessica. "We're all a little crazy at times, I guess."

"Yeah." Tasker smiled back, wishing he could find it funny too.

Jessica cut in, "It's the doctor who's got a thing or two to learn." Tasker felt the sharpness in her voice, like when she told him she had nothing to say until Howard was out of jail.

"Well, we'll be going." Howard nodded to Tasker and started to coast forward, heading north out of town.

Despite the good feeling coming back with Howard, Tasker was more than uneasy. All this about Dr. Straun and Larissa – what was at the bottom of it?

Tasker entered the barracks kitchen from the back to find Shorty and Straun sitting at the table, going over the story of Dr. Straun's car. The room was warm with the smell of brewing coffee.

"I'm 'police protection' now." Shorty grinned. He pulled a cigarette off his lower lip, and lifted his cup in a mock salute.

The doctor smiled back, relaxed in Shorty's company. He was still wearing sunglasses.

"Things a little bright in here?" Tasker asked. Dr. Straun grunted.

"Sergeant Flint's inside. Girl says she has somethin' to say that'll get her out," Shorty said to Tasker. "He wants you to go in, but not till after you understan' she knows nothin' about the doctor bein' safe here."

Tasker nodded and slipped out of the kitchen and on down the hall into the main office. The room faced north, and this early in the morning everything felt gloomy, although it was bright outside. Larissa was slouched in a wooden office chair with her arms crossed so high she hugged herself. Her hair was tangled and standing up at the back, her jacket off. Tasker could see all of her thong necklace now, strung with animal teeth and claws, hanging down her greying T-shirt.

Sergeant Flint jerked his thumb towards the tape recorder on the desk facing Larissa. Tasker got the message and took his place behind it, sitting square in Larissa's line of vision. His chair felt cold and he shivered up the back.

"I'm due at the forest in less than an hour, so it's time to get on with it." Sergeant Flint took his jacket off and leaned on the edge of a desk beside Larissa, looking at her profile, with his arms braced behind him on the desktop. His pose would make Larissa good and uncomfortable, Tasker knew, just within her range of side vision and blocking the main window in the room. Sergeant Flint nodded to Tasker, "She says she can talk her way outta here, make it worth our while forgetting what happened at Dr. Straun's office. Go ahead."

Tasker understood he was to run the interview. He pushed the "Eject" button on the tape recorder, took out the cassette and put it back in – all to kill a few seconds so he could form his approach. He pushed 'Record,' and with the mike close to his lips entered the date, location and names of all present into the machine. Formalities over, he pushed "Pause," still considering his first question. But there wasn't much choice about where to start; it might as well be where she was prepared to cooperate.

Tasker pushed "Record" again and said, "What do you want to tell us?"

Larissa took a deep breath. "Ivan Peders was the one who killed Blake." That was it; she stopped, and an awkward silence dropped over the room.

"How do you know that?" Tasker started it up again.

"Ivan walked up while Blake and I had our argument. After it's over and I'm standing there, Ivan says, 'Don't worry, I'll see he doesn't bother you again.'" Another long silence. Tasker remembered Larissa had been cool in the forest when she had said she saw no one except Howard the morning Blake died. She could be a cool liar.

"Go on," Sergeant Flint snapped again, moving his hands to

his hips. "No way you're outta here with that."

"He came back to the tent later and says I don't have to worry about Blake for a long time."

A thump from the kitchen startled Larissa and she stood upright and looked around frowning. It occurred to Tasker she was expecting to hear the explosion and he followed her eyes. But she dropped right back down to her slouch, eyes nearly shut and shanks of dark hair falling forward.

Tasker said, "Blake died by drowning."

"I know. But Ivan was out to do something, and I'm sure he did."

"For all we know, Peders and Blake fought, Peders knocked Blake unconscious and then Peders got scared and sent Blake downriver in the boat so he wouldn't be implicated. And chance made the boat flip and Blake drown."

Larissa looked puzzled and then shook her head slowly. There was a delay between each shake, and her straight hair, catching up, mesmerized Tasker the way the fringe on her jacket had done days before. That was the same time he'd wondered if the slowness of her moves was covering a lie. Larissa repeated, "Ivan was out to do something. He made a big thing about me spending time with Blake. He didn't understand when I said I had different friends teach me different things."

"Teach? He was jealous?" Tasker said. "All right. What did you and Blake McIntyre do?"

Larissa let her hands go loose on her lap, her big, scuffed knuckles sticking up. "He'd come and visit me sometimes, with a pack of cigarettes. Sometimes chocolate, he knew I like chocolate bars."

"Cut the shit. What you really do is fuck him!" Sergeant Flint growled. Larissa immediately crossed her arms again, and hid her hands under them.

Tasker broke in gently. "What did you and Blake do this time?" Sergeant Flint could take that as criticism if he wanted, Tasker didn't care.

There was a long pause while Larissa examined her hands before she decided to answer. "We sat and talked for a while." There was dignity in her voice. "We went out walking. He was interested in tracking where the grease trails crossed the forest – he knew where they entered and where they left it, but he wanted to see if there was any evidence of a trail bed within the forest itself. He thought by walking in bare feet, he might find where the subsoil was packed from years of traffic. Then we went back to the tent and talked more."

"That's why his boots were off!" Tasker almost shouted. He brought himself back to Larissa's story with renewed interest. "Did he find the trail he was looking for?"

Larissa shook her head.

"What did you do when you got back into the tent?"

"We talked about the forest and me being sort of watchman and him wanting the forest for a park. He loved stories of the forest. He knew history."

"You learned history from Blake?"

"Yes, I always like the man to teach me something."

"What did Peders teach you?"

"Science – how a light bulb works, stuff he does at work."

Now, Tasker thought, she'd loosened two threads he could tug – the fight with Blake and her interest in explosives through Peders. He decided he'd work on the Blake thread first because that's where she wanted to cooperate. Tasker realized he had all the makings of a noose and was pleased. So long as he could keep Sergeant Flint with him. He asked, "You and Blake had a fight that morning he died. Why was that?"

"That was stupid, he got so mad." Larissa was opening up. She unlocked her arms again and looked down at her hands.

"What was he mad about?"

"I showed him the little moccasins I was making. I was sewing the beads I'd made on the tongue piece like a little toy truck." Larissa sat a little more upright. "And I told him they were for our baby, the baby we were going to have. I said I knew it would be a boy."

"That made him mad?" There was a dreamy note coming into Larissa's voice that didn't sound right to Tasker.

"He says, 'What baby?'" Larissa lifted her shoulders: she seemed in wonder at Blake's comment all over again. "And I say, 'Our baby.'"

"So, he wasn't expecting you to get pregnant?"

"No. He says I'd never have babies. So I told him I already had lots."

Tasker looked at Sergeant Flint to see if he took in that remark. But Flint wasn't looking puzzled, just bored, like it was a waste of his time.

Tasker asked, "Lots?"

Larissa widened her eyes and whispered, "Lots."

She's insane, Tasker thought. He said, "What got him throwing things around in your tent?"

Larissa looked surprised. "I told him he had to tell Eve we were going to have a baby boy and if he didn't I would."

"And then he started throwing things around?"

"No, I told him if I told Eve, I'd also tell her about how he stepped out of line with Jessica. That's when he grabbed at my beading, but I wouldn't let him have it." Larissa was sitting up straight now, lifting her arms as if she was fighting Blake off. "So he grabbed at my shirt and started pulling at it and pulling at my jeans and yelling about my belly, the scars on my belly. But I wouldn't let him keep hauling off my clothes and hurt my skin or our chance of having a baby, so he started throwing around all my stuff. He shook the cot I was sitting on back and forth. Then I screamed at him and screamed at him to stop, yelling for help, and he finally left." Larissa was suddenly quiet, slumped back into her chair.

"And it was Peders's turn next?" It was Sergeant Flint again.

"I wasn't expecting Ivan. He just showed up. He must've seen the mess Blake had made to the stuff I'd been working on. He told me not to cry, he'd look after Blake so he wouldn't bother me any more."

"OK." Tasker left no time for Sergeant Flint to interrupt. "Try to remember his exact words."

"I told you already."

"Why didn't you report him?"

"Because Ivan was my friend then, my teacher." She emphasized the "then."

"You didn't care if Howard took the blame?"

"Howard didn't do it. I knew he'd get off . . . The club that hit Blake was found beside Jim in the munitions shed, right? That was after Howard was in jail, right? Same weapon." Larissa's voice dropped, almost with deliberate mystery, and her body curled back into her chair.

Tasker shivered with interest. How was she going to explain this knowledge? His intuition told him to leave it for a minute. So he said, "You never actually saw Peders do anything to Blake? You think he deliberately acted to kill Blake based on what he said to you?"

Larissa didn't answer. It was like her mind was far away.

"Did Peders ever describe exactly how he hit Blake or wrapped him up in the net?"

Larissa sighed impatiently and started crossing her arms tighter. It looked like she wasn't going to cooperate any more. It occurred to Tasker he hadn't been hearing what she was telling them. He had to listen beyond words, beyond the facts and details.

"This stinks." The sergeant slammed his palm on the desk. "How do you expect us to believe this? Peders can't defend himself now, that's why you're stringing us along. I bet you did it, Larissa. You killed Blake! You were the one who was angry."

"No!"

"You're lying!" Sergeant Flint started to pace up and down between Larissa and Tasker. "What you're telling us isn't going to get you out. It's locking you up tighter."

"No!" Larissa shouted back, twisting her head to follow Sergeant Flint. "Ivan even brought the club with blood on it back to my tent."

Sergeant Flint stopped his pacing and faced Tasker.

"What did you do with it?" Tasker asked softly. His gentleness and Flint's harshness, mixed – they were getting results.

"I hid it out back after Ivan left." She sounded bored now, maybe resigned.

She'd made another dangerous admission – did she know, Tasker wondered? Something told him to keep backing off, make her feel safe and feed her more rope . . . "So you're saying you know Peders killed Blake because you saw him with the weapon."

Larissa nodded.

"When did you see Peders after that?"

"He come out next day and took me to the village for cherry pie at the hotel."

"Did you talk about what he did to Blake?"

"I told him I didn't want him to do what he did. He made like I owed him."

"How did he take that?"

"He said he thought he'd done me a favour. I won't owe anyone, I told him."

"So then what happened?"

"I said, I want to go back to the forest."

"You broke off with him?"

"Partly. When I tried to go with him on his work the next day, he said he wouldn't take me. So I decided we were off forever."

"You liked going to work with him?"

Larissa didn't answer.

"What was there about his work that most interested you, Larissa?"

She shrugged and said, "I was just interested."

"And when he wouldn't teach you about his work any more, you broke up with him?"

Larissa stared back at Tasker but said nothing. Tasker was getting this feeling that something wasn't adding up.

"Is that why you had to go and steal dynamite from the munitions shed?" Sergeant Flint struck out. Tasker watched Larissa closely to see how she reacted to Flint, to see where to go next.

When she ignored the question, Sergeant Flint kept on. "Peders stopped taking you along on jobs, didn't he, and there was no hope you could slip any dynamite from him. But you knew where to get it, you'd been there before. And you took the club along, didn't you? That's why both Blake's and Jim's blood is on it."

Tasker saw that Larissa heard. She sat there biting and working away on her lower lip. Her eyes were slits again, or what you could see through her contracted eyelids. He thought she murmured, "I don't want to . . ."

Sergeant Flint was shouting, "Girl, there's someone in the

other room I'm going to bring in. You got a lot of explaining to do." Sergeant Flint stood down from the desk and strode over to the door into the kitchen. He called, "Come on in, both of you."

When Dr. Straun appeared at the door, Larissa snapped her head to look away, her face contorted, her lips pulled thin, teeth bared. The doctor stopped still, Shorty behind him. Tasker could hear Larissa's shallow breathing.

Sergeant Flint was still shouting. "His car didn't blow up, because you didn't lay the charge right. So tell us, why'd you try to kill this man?"

The feeling was so strong in the room, Tasker flashed this sudden, vivid image that Larissa would lunge for Dr. Straun's throat, that she'd try to shake him like a dog or a wolf, and Straun would be flat on his back before he or Sergeant Flint could finally straddle them and grab at her hair and forehead. Dr. Straun would make horrible, high-pitched sounds, and the chairs and tables and lamps would scrape and bang and tip. When they finally could pull her off, Larissa's face would be red and there'd be blood in her mouth. She would scream and sob. Sob what? Tasker asked himself. What did she have against Dr. Straun?

But Larissa did nothing. She stared down the office towards the door to the holding cells, her eyes nearly shut.

"This girl has the right to counsel," Dr. Straun said smoothly, and walked forward to stand directly in front of Larissa. He took off his sunglasses. "There has to be some mistake. What possible reason could she have to kill me?"

"You killed all my babies." The words came from deep in Larissa's throat.

There was a long silence. No one moved and the room pulsed with emotion.

Dr. Straun said, "I told you, one more time . . ." It was a threat.

"I had no choices." Larissa was barely audible.

"You couldn't keep that kind of birth control," Dr. Straun answered. "I told you that." He crossed the arms of his sunglasses and put them in the vest pocket of his fishing jacket. Then he mumbled, "The vandalism, it was little help, I bet."

Larissa turned to Tasker. "I would like to go back inside. Now." She stood up tall.

Tasker stood too, and involuntarily took her arm. He said gently, "Before we walk down the hall . . . What happened to Blake and Jim, Larissa? Tell me again."

Larissa sighed, looked at the floor and started in a flat, matter-of-fact way. "After Blake left, I got so mad thinking he knew why I couldn't get pregnant. I kept thinking, why should Blake know when I didn't? So I followed to ask him." Larissa looked at the doctor wearily and shook her head. "It only takes a medical dictionary to translate into something anyone can understand."

She turned away from the doctor. Tasker gently said, "Go on."

"I found Blake walking around funny, complaining and wiping a cut on the back of his head." Larissa's voice was quiet and passionless. "He didn't answer my questions, just told me to ask Dr. Straun. I pleaded, 'Tell me what you know,' and he said, 'All you girls are whores, anyway, filthy whores.' And he started to walk away, just walk away from me when I wanted to know. I got so mad, I picked up a stick and hit him hard on the head. He fell, and then suddenly Ivan was there. He said he'd fix Blake up. He said to go back to the tent."

Larissa seemed to have finished and was pulling gently on Tasker's arm, indicating she wanted to walk down to the cell. Tasker asked, "When did you next see Peders?"

"I told you, he came back with the stick. I didn't want it so I left it out back."

"So, finish the story," Flint said irritably. "You said yourself that stick was used again on Jim."

Larissa didn't answer at first. Tasker was thinking he'd have to step in with something to soften Flint's remark, but he wasn't coming up with anything. It was like his mind was locked and silence didn't matter anyway.

Larissa inhaled slowly, lifting her shoulders, and as her shoulders dropped, she started to speak quickly. "When I saw the medical file, I wanted to blow Dr. Straun to pieces. Just like rocks in a hopper." The doctor's name came out with disgust. "I decided to break into the munitions shed and get whatever I could. I'd take the stick and leave it there. A little lesson next time Ivan went inside, show him I didn't need his help any more." Larissa's voice became flat and matter-of-fact. "But Jim drove up when I was inside. I wasn't expecting Jim. And when he saw I was carrying the stick like the one that hit Blake . . ."

She started to pull Tasker down the hall to the cells. He was looking into the side of her head, into her black hair. "I'm sure Ivan had it in for Blake," she said. "And I'm sorry about Jim. That was a mistake."

He felt cold from her story, drained of response. He was aware of the smell of sweat — sour — and he didn't know if it was his own or hers.

Sergeant Flint's voice followed them down the hall. "Fine. Take her back. We'll get the rest of this later." His voice was quick with good humour and energy.

Larissa was pulling Tasker beside her now, not looking back at Dr. Straun or Sergeant Flint or anyone, but sort of drunken across her black eyes. Her hair was all matted to the back of her head and her beads hung askew off one shoulder.

Tasker heard Sergeant Flint laughing behind him. "She thought she could talk her way out, but instead she talked herself in." Larissa may have heard too, but Tasker didn't think she was listening. She was moving quickly into the cell – all she seemed to want was to lie down on her bed and close her eyes. Tasker looked at her small, tired face and wondered what it was that he just didn't get.

When Tasker walked back into the office, Shorty was questioning Dr. Straun. "How old was she?"

"Nine, eleven, twelve, fourteen, some string like that." Dr. Straun had his hat off. "They start early."

Sergeant Flint walked over to put his arm across Dr. Straun's shoulder. "Well, let's go. We got your little terrorist locked up."

"And what did you do about the men doin' that to her?" Shorty persisted, his voice accusing.

"It was just one man, her father." Dr. Straun and Sergeant Flint were walking to the door. Flint's head snapped left to stare at Dr. Straun and at the same time let his arm drop from the doctor's shoulder.

"What you do about him?" Shorty's voice was distant now, more wondering.

"There was nothing I could do," Dr. Straun said and looked back at Shorty with surprise.

Shorty whipped around and disappeared into the kitchen, his body shaking with a rolling cough.

Sergeant Flint looked back at the papers for a moment and then called, "Tasker, nice work." Then came the orders, with his fingers numbering them off: "Type up the report. Call White-horse and see if they found any fibres or hair on the club that hit Jim and Blake we can match with her – you can tie this all up by tonight."

Sergeant Flint then held the door open for Dr. Straun,

formally, at the same time asking, "Will you go fishing or to the forest?"

Tasker dropped down into his desk chair. He fingered the tape recorder on his right and rolled the paper into his typewriter again. An empty gesture. The message "Phone Ida" on the blotter caught his eye.

He thought, "It's Sunday morning in Old Crow too," and impulsively dialled direct.

The phone was picked up and a sleepy voice said, "Just a minute," and then there was a long wait for Ida. Shorty slipped past carrying a tray of food down to Larissa's cell.

Ida's voice was crisp when she got on the line. "Hello there." Her alertness made Tasker realize how spent he was this early in the day.

"Ida, got your message . . ." He liked hearing her voice; it sounded straight up, the way it usually was.

"Warren! How's Jim? I've just heard about Dr. Straun and the heroic measures he used." Ida was in her professional mode.

"He's coming along. It'll take a while," Tasker said.

"Well, I had a crazy thought about what's behind things down there. It may not help – but I've been worrying about it, so I thought I'd share it with you. You'll have to be discreet though, because it breaks a professional confidence."

Shorty was coming back from the cell empty-handed, heading for the kitchen and scowling at the floor. "You're going to break a confidence?" Tasker couldn't help himself.

There was silence on the other end of the line.

Tasker hated saying he was sorry. "Look. We got Larissa Stanley in here and it's got me uneasy. I found her last night just after she taped explosives under Dr. Straun's car. It looks like she slugged Jim because he got in the way when she wanted to steal dynamite to blow up Dr. Straun in his car. She also trashed Straun's office and stole her own medical file. But Ivan Peders, who she claims put Blake in the boat and sent it downriver, was just killed by a grizzly. So we can't verify anything with him. And there was crazy talk of abortions between Larissa and Straun when they confronted her. Abortion – murder for abortion? Does that make sense?"

"What I know will help, but you won't be able to quote me even if it does. You'll have to find another way, but that won't be hard, from what you've said."

Tasker said, "Shoot. I need all the help I can get."

"Remember the story – the girl I thought was sterilized without her consent?" Ida paused and then said, "That girl was Larissa Stanley and her doctor was Dr. Straun."

"Sterilized?" Tasker echoed. "OK. Larissa and Dr. Straun talked about abortions," Tasker said, thinking out loud.

"Doctors can put their patients under when they do abortions, and while Larissa was out, a surgeon could presumably carry out the other procedure."

"Dr. Straun sterilized Larissa as a young girl without her knowing, never told her? Just left scars?"

"I'm pretty sure. Larissa said Dr. Straun had been her regular doctor. It makes sense, given what we know of him. He has the reputation of taking things into his own hands. You need courage to be a good surgeon, and he is courageous – but he goes too far."

"Would Straun report in her medical file that he sterilized her?" Tasker knew he was repeating himself, but he was trying to get around the implications of this.

"In some way. It was a couple of years ago when she and I had our discussion, but it has always bothered me. I never came out and told her she was sterilized – but I asked her where she got those scars on her stomach and told her they were likely from a special operation. She should talk to her doctor. Mostly she denied she'd had any special operation, but she was angry. She pointed to a number of scars on her arms and said they looked the same as the ones I'd pointed out on her stomach. She said she didn't believe me. There was something threatening about how she dared me to be right – it's bothered me since that I never told her what I suspected."

"What you're saying is starting to explain things."

"You can take it from here."

"Larissa has said most of this on tape. I just didn't know what it all meant. Am I a dolt?"

"Yes," and Ida laughed. "You told me I should get the police involved in such a case when we talked a couple of weeks ago. You know, I've been thinking, what was my responsibility? I'd been wondering, if some doctor did that to me, whether I wouldn't look for . . ."

"Revenge?"

"Yes, I was going to say compensation. But the point is, here is a young woman robbed of ever having a family, and left to find out about her loss on her own. The drive to have children can be strong. And some men won't marry unless they know the woman is fertile. Once you start thinking about it . . ."

Tasker shifted uneasily in his chair, conscious of his own sex. Somewhere deep down he knew he wanted to have children, but not for a while, and it wasn't something he thought about. The idea of some doctor tinkering with his privates when he was supposed to be doing something else – that made him squirm again.

Tasker wasn't coming up with much to say – too much was sinking in. The door opened from the kitchen, and Shorty, still scowling at the floor, headed back down to Larissa's cell. Tasker said to Ida, "When I think how I jumped on your story a couple of weeks ago – I want to say I'm sorry. I'm not very good at that!"

Ida laughed. "There's always a first time."

"After this is over, Ida, I'd like to pull together some cash and come visit you up there."

Ida took in her breath. She said, "Um, I don't know about that . . . I think I've . . . well I've started seeing someone . . . maybe, give me some time . . ."

From down the hall, Tasker heard Shorty shouting, "Hey! Hey!"

"Ida, there's a problem here. I'll have to call back." Tasker dropped the phone and ran to Larissa's cell.

Shorty was still hollering when he came into Tasker's view, bellowing and wrestling hands with Larissa over a dinner spoon.

Larissa's food was untouched. It looked like she'd been using her spoon to shred all the fringes off her leather jacket. Shorty was trying to take it back from her.

When Tasker nipped the spoon from their writhing fists, Larissa started to shake and Shorty whisked up the food tray – the milk and fruit cocktail spilling all over the sandwiches – and backed out of the cell.

Larissa glared at Tasker. "Take it easy," he said. "Settle down. We'll get a lawyer in here. I'll get one down here first thing tomorrow."

Larissa flung herself onto the cot at the side of her cell, keeping up her glare and working her mouth, strings of her hair caught between her lips. As Tasker pulled the door of her cell shut, she let fly a mouthful of spit at him.

Tasker sat down in front of his report. All was quiet from the cell now. Dr. Straun and Sergeant Flint showed their colours in different ways, Tasker was thinking, but it amounted to the same thing. They looked out for each other and their own kind. The coolness of it all, given their power, made Tasker's skin crawl.

He was getting no pleasure in wrapping up this case; it was clear the real victim was the one behind bars. But then, he thought, maybe he was losing his stomach for the hard-nosed stuff. Larissa was charged with serious crimes. There was no way Tasker wanted to accept he was part of what failed her. He didn't like being one of the bad guys. Just about every man in her life so far had mistreated her – except Peders. Funny she didn't seem to appreciate his efforts to protect her. Maybe she hadn't known enough kindness to recognize it when it was offered. Right now, though, Tasker didn't like admiring the girl's spunk, her attempts to educate herself, to take control of the events of her own life. He didn't like not having put it together earlier. What could Tasker salvage from this mess for himself? "What?" he mumbled out loud.

Eve walked into the office, her arms making wide sweeps along beside her, and before the door shut, started into Tasker. "Warren, it's all over town that Larissa Stanley is in here and you brought her in. You got to do something about that – you guys can't keep making mistakes like this." There was accusation in Eve's voice and it rankled with Tasker. It was one damn thing after another, he thought, but, then, he owed Eve an explanation.

"Sit down." Tasker pointed to the chair Larissa had been in not long before. "I'll give you a bit of the story. Unfortunately it affects you too." His own voice might even convince himself, Tasker thought wryly. Placating, cold, smooth. One of them. He'd tell the truth, straight out.

He leaned forward in his seat, and with his left palm up, numbered off what they had against the Larissa: "Fingerprints found inside the doorframe of the munitions shed after Jim was assaulted, found loitering beside Dr. Straun's car with a roll of tape in her pocket matching the tape that secured the dynamite under it, fingerprints on the car bumper superficially match hers – that's to be verified – her sneaker footprints all over Dr. Straun's vandalized office, her medical files the only thing taken . . ." Now he was coming to the hard part for Eve; even so he ploughed on, but quieter, more slowly. "And now she tells us, in a voluntary statement, that she spent part of the morning Blake died with him in the watchman's tent. They argued; he trashed up her stuff and stormed away. She followed in a rage, gave him the skull fracture and left him for Ivan Peders to send down the river. Peders brought back the club to her tent – the weapon she took to the munitions shed and used to hit Jim." Tasker glanced up at Eve. "I'm sorry."

Tasker had been intent on listing the evidence; now he inhaled deeply, steeling himself for Eve's reaction. He watched her sitting there, her head bowed and her arms flopped beside her body. He found himself apologizing to the pink scalp down the part in her hair. "And we have no proof otherwise because Peders is dead and Jessica and Howard didn't see . . . We're getting a real sophisticated analysis of that weapon to see if it killed Blake and hit Jim too, if it was swung by Peders and Larissa or just Larissa . . ."

Eve looked up at Tasker and said, "It may sound bad for Larissa, but everything you say could be interpreted differently. I don't know what the answer is, but scapegoating Larissa isn't it." Her voice cracked with emotion and she took a deep breath, concentrating on a spot on the desktop, and said, "Peders was jealous of Blake. I knew that. Ever since Blake started to visit Larissa." Eve's green eyes shot up at Tasker. "Yes, I knew. In fact it started right in my house. They took to each other right away – sort of kindred spirits." Then her eyes fell back to the spot on the desk. "I felt betrayed, not by the sex as much as by the denial of our intimacy, Blake's and mine. It was as if the affair never happened, as if I was crazy to be talking about what I so clearly saw."

Tasker searched for some comfort for Eve. "Maybe because Peders is dead, maybe not much will have to be said."

"Shit, Warren," Eve cried out, lifting her arms up in the air, "not you too! It's got to come up in Larissa's defence if her lawyer is any good!" Eve braced her hands on the edge of his desk and her eyes swept across the top. Then she sank back in her chair, and said, exhaustion colouring her voice, "Let me tell you something about Larissa. From the time I moved up here until I got too pregnant with the twins, I used to go to White-horse and give music lessons at the Detention Centre. She was one of my pupils, the only girl. It was a lonely life for a girl in that place. I guess she began taking lessons when she was about twelve. It was voluntary, so she wanted to take piano, and she's good. She had health problems when she was fifteen, sixteen, and missed a lot. Real problems going to sleep. I was getting big with the twins when she got back and she was fascinated with my pregnancy. She had many questions, little ones that she'd worry over week to week, like how do you know there are two babies? and how will they get out of there? I realized she had no understanding of basic biology, still didn't understand most of the cause-and-effect stuff – even though she was in there for promiscuity, among other things, and was a fully developed woman. Maybe it was because of her screwed-up childhood. So I gave her books to read and let her touch my stomach to feel the twins kicking. And I invited her down to visit when they were born, because she would be out then. That's when she met Blake. I knew she was living a loose kind of life in Whitehorse, but when she came down and lived with Ivan Peders for a while, I had her over now and then too. She liked to play the piano for the babies. Eventually she stopped coming when she and Blake got going regularly and Blake was denying it. But while she still visited, anyone could tell she loved kids. She adored them. She talked about wanting to be a mother and having her own. I figured that her loose ways were her just trying to get pregnant herself. But she never did get pregnant." Eve sighed and then carried on. "Once she asked, and I'll never forget it because it was so odd and it was the last day she came to our place as my guest, she asked if it was possible a man could burn a woman's belly skin so deep with his cigarette so that it couldn't stretch and grow to hold babies. I said I didn't think so. She said, 'Good, because if he could, he should pay big time.'"

Eve stopped and looked back up at Tasker. Her green eyes were stony and cold. "I can figure what she has against Dr. Straun. You better be sure of what you're doing because, if Larissa goes to court, I'm going to see she has the best lawyer in the north. I'll want to see the courtroom floor wiped with Sergeant Flint, Dr. Straun and you."

Tasker felt good and mad. "Look Eve, we're doing all we can . . ." He stopped, unable to find any more words in his frustration.

"There are rumours that more than one girl has been sterilized by that doctor when he had them under for something else. I would never take Jessica there voluntarily."

Tasker stared back, thinking that, if she suspected, why the hell didn't she do something about it before now?

Eve took his silence as a chance to leave, stood up, drew in her breath and said, "It's time for me to start living again."

Tasker stared woodenly as Eve swung out of the office and disappeared down the outside steps.

Tasker kept staring at the door long after Eve was gone. He was so angry he felt winded. Eve had cut deep. If he was sensible, he told himself, he'd push that all aside and get on with it. "Damn this case. Damn Larissa Stanley," he swore out loud.

One thing, Eve had widened up everything, he thought; she'd given him a case against Dr. Straun – at least for a complaint to the medical society, maybe more. By rights, Tasker had to report to Sergeant Flint, and then Flint would look into it and take it to the Crown in Whitehorse, if there was enough to go on. But what was the hope of that? He could go around Sergeant Flint, saying he was on loan or because things were dancing down here today, but that might just get the investigation bogged down. Unless Larissa's counsel was walking down the same track. Tasker wondered if that wasn't the way to go – someone had to start working on Larissa's behalf. There were going to be odd wrinkles, like where to hold her, anyway. She'd not likely make bail and there was no woman's lockup in the Yukon . . .

Tasker strode down to the cells. He'd get Larissa to decide on a lawyer and get her to call. If she had no ideas of her own, maybe a Brotherhood lawyer like Howard's, good and adversarial, rather than one from that firm that did the government work. Those guys – Tasker shook his head – they spent their lives jockeying to buy summer property on Quiet Lake or Judas Creek. Not much in fees from a scrappy girl who needed a lot of work . . .

Tasker found Larissa lying on the cot. She had bundled up her jacket for a pillow and seemed to be sleeping on her side. She does sleep, he thought. Her one hand was buried under the jacket and the other hung in a fist over the edge of the cot. Her dark hair nearly covered her face – maybe she wasn't asleep, just wanting to be alone. An innocent kid or what? Tasker wasn't even going to wonder now; he'd let her be.

He walked back to finish the report and typescript of her "statement" so far. When he finished he looked at his watch. Things would be in full swing at Kakhteyi now.

Shorty would have left supper trays, so Tasker went into the kitchen for those and carried Larissa's down to the cell section.

He knew before he fully entered the room that something was wrong. It smelled wrong, urine maybe. And Larissa's head hung forward at a funny angle, her hips and legs had no body to them even though she was standing.

Tasker jerked forward tentatively, puzzling over her posture. There was no way she could hang herself in here, he thought, but that's sure what it looked like. Sliding the tray to the floor and working for the keys in his belt, he looked up into Larissa's face – she had colour, pink dots above and below the eyes. She must be alive.

She was hanging by the neck with a cord made from her thong necklace and those small pieces of fringe from her jacket tied together. Small, infinitely patient work. The cord was anchored around the door bar at the top and front of the cell. No way she could have broken her neck; there was no fall. Her feet were twisted and her ankles touched the ground and her soles faced each other – maybe the leather stretched, he thought, but it still didn't make sense.

The door rattled as he turned the key – he had to open it easy in case the cord caught and tightened more. Once inside, he grabbed Larissa by the hips and lifted the weight of her body from her neck. Her head flopped backwards, her chin up, exposing a blue-red bruise line across her throat where the leather cord had been.

Tasker had no knife, but when he held her body with his left arm, bracing himself with his legs wide apart and his back arched, he could pull the leather and release her neck from the noose. Her body was limp and moist and sour. He was holding Larissa so low down that she fell with some force when he tried to put her on the cot. Her head wobbled, but the neck wasn't broken; it had strength to it, he told himself. He was sure she was still alive.

Tasker put his ear to her chest. No heartbeat. The narrow bruise was high around her throat like she had been strangled. She was not cold, she was flushed. He lifted Larissa to the floor.

Alone, no time to search for an assistant, Tasker locked himself into the rhythm of cardio-pulmonary resuscitation – thrusting down with his splayed palms on her rib cage and then swinging over to breathe for her, his lips sealing her mouth, and then back thrusting down from his shoulders on her chest again. His instructor had said not to worry about breaking ribs, the big thing was to start the heart pumping. Funny, he thought, the dummy he learned CPR on gave the same way; each time he jolted down on her chest, Larissa's head lifted, her upturned hands rocked and her body wobbled at the hips. Once, when he locked on her mouth, he thought of rubber. There was and there wasn't any closeness between them. Sometimes it felt like an exercise; sometimes it felt personal.

His eyes caught Larissa's each time he worked from her chest to her mouth. Black eyes, no sight. A piece of the cord she'd knotted lay on the floor where he gazed each time he shifted back from her mouth to her chest. The knots were pulled so tight they looked hard, determined, like ball bearings. The skin around her lips started to grow colder – maybe from his saliva, he thought. His own lips were getting tender and swollen.

How could she have knotted the leather so hard, his mind asked, the question set to the rhythm of his movements. The pieces of fringe were hardly longer than a finger's length each. And then he knew what had happened. She'd strangled herself by mistake. She'd passed out trying to hang herself, and the weight of her head falling forward tightened the knots and finished the job. He broke his rhythm and looked down into her face. Every other mechanical move she'd tried had been ineffectual – prying open the munitions-shed door, taping the matches to the muffler of Dr. Straun's Buick. This one better have failed too. He put his ear back to her chest but heard no beat. He thought, she did it this time, she's dead.

"No, no, no," he shouted – he had to bring her back. There was something so alive about her. There was still colour in her face, brightness in her eyes. But, as he worked, her skin grew colder and colder, and the pinkness looked more like purply blue.

His shoulders and back tired, but he kept on, it must have been for an hour. When he finally gave up, empty of all strength, he sat back on his heels and looked at the rumpled young woman. Her skin was cold and blue. Her stomach lay bare, her jeans sagged down her hips. There, for anyone to see, were the twin sterilization scars low on her pale moon stomach. Tattooed around them were fine black lines that turned the scars into eyes, eyes on an animal's face looking past the belly-button nose up towards her neck. He grabbed one hand and lifted it up, the elbow still on the floor, but when he felt the hand's angular coldness, he dropped it like a dead weight.

Tasker pushed his face into her stomach and started to cry. He sobbed until he had no more crying left, it had all drained from him, and he was empty-chested and muscle-exhausted.

Tasker lay on his hospital bed remembering the despair, but his eyes stayed dry. He felt completely spent, as if he'd been crying for a long time, for years. Long ago he'd tried to bury memories of that Tsehki case, and now that he looked through them again, he was struck by how much life was in them. Warm pain and not despair . . . Real people in a screwed-up place and time.

His mind had drained clear, and Tasker found himself trudging along through the aftermath, the events of the next months and years that brought him to now.

At first, his life seemed to move in slow motion. There was nothing to it – no texture, no distractions – just the successive jolts of the playout of Larissa's story.

All he remembered, for instance, of leaving Tsehki was Sergeant Flint's fury that this had to happen in his territory, that he could expect a pack of social workers breathing down his back now. Tasker suggested they look into the charge that Dr. Straun sterilized women without consent, but Sergeant Flint rolled his eyes and told Tasker he could get ready to head on north.

Back in Whitehorse, Tasker spoke to the superior officer about Dr. Straun and was assured it would be looked into. Several days later the inspector invited Tasker into his office and said there wasn't enough evidence to go bothering Dr. Straun – no medical records. The tape recording of Larissa's so-called statement was either missing or taped over, Sergeant Flint and

Shorty didn't remember much of what Dr. Straun and Larissa had said, and besides, if the police could establish a sterilization had been performed by Dr. Straun, they couldn't now likely establish, beyond a reasonable doubt, that it was done without consent. The inspector commended Tasker on his rescue attempt and suggested he take a well-earned leave for a week or so. The inspector seemed genuine enough, and Tasker left his office completely frustrated.

Sergeant Flint did get into trouble with the press. In fact, he got publicly roasted until the day he retired. The town, the whole Yukon community, shuddered with the horror of Larissa's death. Shock waves and aftershocks. For a while an orthopaedic surgeon in Vancouver got into the act, a specialist who saw Gary Daniel now and then. She was quoted in the papers on the subject of shoddy police cover-ups in Tsehki. Dr. Straun's nurse quit, but stonily insisted it was for personal reasons, that serving the doctor had been the most important thing she'd ever done in her life. Eventually public opinion passed on to another cause, and Larissa was slowly forgotten.

While the community was still beating its breast about poor Larissa, but in fact doing nothing about it, the cabinet minister's visit was largely ignored. All he did was make what Albert called a spineless non-announcement about studies and impact state-ments. It was one of those frustrating, insidious things that five years later, and fresh after an election, resulted in a partially expanded operation and a small acid lake. Tasker read about that in the Regina paper.

The media anguish over Larissa, the plight of young delin-quents, the lack of resources for women in the north, inadequate police training – little of it stuck to Dr. Straun. Tasker tried to stir up trouble with visits to the Brotherhood and the newspaper editor, letters to the surgeon in Vancouver; he even persuaded

Ida and Eve to talk to the inspector. Nothing. He went and talked to Shorty, who told him to mind his own business.

Then Tasker's personal life fell apart. Ida said she couldn't choose between Tasker and the bush pilot she'd met in Old Crow, but she seemed to spend all her time with the pilot. Tasker's mother moved to Vancouver to live with her sister, but once she got there, she refused to unpack, hang up her favourite pictures or place her personal belongings around her room. Tasker's aunt kept writing urgent letters asking what to do. Tasker got that palm injury in the child-abuse case, was off work for a while, and started spending evenings drinking Seagram's 83 at home, waiting for Ida.

Finally, the inspector called Tasker back into his office and slapped his wrists hard for undermining his fellow officers, in particular Sergeant Flint. The inspector said he himself had to claim some responsibility for Tasker's being sent to a job in Tsehki at all. Most officers had trouble in their own home towns, and the RCMP normally didn't assign men back home if they could help it. Because of that, the inspector was prepared to manoeuvre a little on Tasker's behalf. He could take a transfer to an opening outside – and there was one in Saskatchewan now – or be offered no promotion for at least two years where he was. Then he advised Tasker to buckle down and stop taking things to heart – there were lots of people who chose to live screwed-up lives, and the police were not personally responsible for their choices.

Tasker took the transfer. Ida said that he was running away, and married her pilot. Tasker ended up in Regina, where he was given the pitifully small job of drug surveillance.

However, over the years, the drug scene started to heat up in the Midwest and Tasker was able, finally, to make his mark in the force.

He couldn't point to the time when he stopped actively blaming himself for what happened in Tsehki. But now that he had pried off the scab, he really didn't feel shocked by the reality underneath any more. At least he could look at it now.

Lying there in the antiseptic ward, he began believing that real living meant going back to that old sore, those old feelings, rather than killing time where he was now. Was he up to moving north again?

Two weeks later, Tasker drove southeast out of Regina. He passed the carwash where, less than a month ago, he'd taken that shot in his shoulder. He had a crazy urge to honk the horn like he might have done years ago. He thought, Why not? A couple of passing drivers stared at him, and a young carwash attendant jerked up. Tasker honked lightly twice more. Anyone would think he was nuts – especially if they checked out his passenger seat, for seat-belted beside him was a huge, stuffed blue bear. He'd seen it last night at a mall and bought it impulsively for Mandy. He worried for a moment that a twelve-year-old girl wouldn't think much of a stuffed toy, but then he figured she had to have a sense of humour.

After all those times he'd promised himself he'd go back, this time he really was. Ida had phoned earlier in the day to be sure he was really coming and said there were going to be one or two faces from the past at the airport to meet him. He guessed one would be Jessica Weiss's because she'd sent him an invitation to the opening of her Whitehorse art gallery. The invitation had a handwritten note about coming into the gallery any time, she'd like to see a number of his field sketches and there'd be a sip of champagne. Tasker preferred single malt, but one flute would be all right, as long as it was the real stuff. He smiled to himself

– for little Jessica Weiss's success, he'd even sip Okanagan bubbles.

Ida said it was all arranged; he and Mandy were going fishing with Howard and were expected to stay several nights with Jim and Kay. Howard was a partner in an outfitting business that had its ups and downs, but he wanted to show Tasker his new spots on Natasahin Lake, and the lodge and cabins he and his brother had built.

Although this pilgrimage back north had begun with Dr. Straun being killed by the grizzly, the doctor didn't have much to do with it now. Somehow that was all behind Tasker. Eve's words the day Larissa died, about getting on with life, they were what was taking him back.

Anyway, he'd brooded over Larissa long enough – and over how Dr. Straun had never even got a slap on the wrist.

Tasker remembered driving his cruiser up that long climb out of the Tsehki valley years ago, his ears plugging and the engine straining with the altitude. He swore, at the time, it'd be forever before he drove back down into that valley again. Sergeant Flint had so enraged him then – but the sergeant's reaction to the suicide just seemed that of a tired old man now.

Tasker parked his car at the long-term lot outside the airport and, tucking the huge blue bear under his arm, grabbed his suitcase and portfolio from the trunk. When he got back north everything wouldn't be right, he knew that. There'd be something – a new hitch in the long-festering land claims, problems with the acid lake, eulogies for the great doctor, getting elbowed by Shorty in a bar one night, sour words from a derelict Sergeant Flint – but it would be alive and human and home.

Maybe the Whitehorse official memory of his career there would have faded and the detachment would be open to a transfer back. Maybe not. Maybe he wouldn't want it once he got there. He'd take it as it came.

Tasker felt the side pouch of his carry-on to be sure his old chessmen were there. There was no way he'd win against Jim, but a game would be fun anyway. He wondered if, once he got off the plane, he wouldn't start reliving the old story once again. Maybe he'd never understand it. Was it possible to relive a story at all? Can you ever start over? Maybe you only start new stories – it was like there never were complete stories, only the beginnings layered on top of each other. The despair of this one had eased with the retelling, but the pain was still there. Maybe stories don't end, he thought, but only deepen.

What if the most significant part of this whole story was the acid lake or Jessica's new business or Reggie becoming chief? No, Tasker thought, for him right now the most significant thing was showing his ticket to the stewardess and sitting down in his window seat. With luck, it wouldn't be over the wing.

ACKNOWLEDGEMENTS

The author gratefully acknowledges help in the process of writing, and in surviving the process, from many people, including: Fran and Will Barnett, Judy and Ian Barnett, Kathleen Barnett, Neil Beatty, Donna Bennett, Jack Brickenden, Matt Dewar, Jane Drake, Beverley Endersby, Ricky Englander, Harry Fishbach, Barbara Greenwood, Julie Hunt-Correa, Valerie Hussey, Sue Leppington, Gage and Betty Love, David, Melanie, Jennifer and Adrian Love, Betty Macpherson, Carol McDougall, Mimi McEvenue, Kevin Pal, Rhonda Polisuk, Steve Pugh, Esther and Mike Robson, Debbie Rogosin, Paul Sochaczewski, Vern Sparks, Greg Taylor, Paul Wachtel, Laurie Wark, Barbara Wehrspann and Val Wyatt.

The following people provided vital help of a specialized nature with regard to medicine and surgery, policing, social work and art: Henry Barnett, Ed Bartram, Bob Brown, Jim Drake, John Kaufmann, Mary Ann Lewis, Kathy Parrish and Rob Tuckerman.

The shaping of *Grizzly Dance* was influenced by stories and snippets of stories shared over the years by many people, among whom are Ted Abbott, Marion Blake, Peter Brimacombe, Sandy and Greg Bryce, Kathy and Bob Clay, Ray Clennett, Judy Currelly, Ross Dawson, Jackie and George Dewhurst, Ruth and Charlie Drake, Ray Fletcher, John Frame, Craig Freeman, Millie Gourlay, Sister Halder, Mryka and Bart Hall-Beyer, Ted Harrison, Hilda Hellaby, Spence (Barb) Hill, Dorothy Hopcott, Johnny Johns, Dave Kallas, Gerri Keddy, Dan Kemble, Bill Laceby, Charlie Lenz, Bill Leslie, Mary-Ann and Rob Lewis, Helen Lucas, Brian Marshall, Carolyn and Scott Marshall, Andrew McDonald, Don McLellan, Harlan Moën, Tony Penikett, Michael Perley, Chris Peters, Lucy and Sam Peters, Dave Rankin, Jim Reid, Yvonne and Jack Sellers, Ulrich Schroeder, Virginia Smith, Aldine and Ken Snider, Margery and John Snowden, Ed Stenson, Ruth and Walt Stewart, Dennis Stitt, Jan Storer, Kip and Ron Veale, Doris and Len Vickers, Flo Whyard, Margery Wiig, Henry Wilkinson, Lorraine Young. These people are in no way responsible for the story of *Grizzly Dance*, which was made up by the author.

Thank you to Anna Porter, Susan Renouf and all the people at Key Porter Books. I am especially grateful to my editor, Jonathan Webb, for his care, encouragement and insight.